A PLACE
TO CALL HOME

A PLACE TO CALL HOME

AN AMISH ROMANCE

STEPPING STONES
BOOK TWO

LINDA BYLER

Good Books

New York, New York

A PLACE TO CALL HOME

10 9 8 7 6 5 4 3 2 1

Library of Congress Cataloging-in-Publication Data is available on file.

Print ISBN: 978-1-68099-949-5
eBook ISBN: 978-1-68099-955-6

Cover design by Godfredson Design

Printed in the United States of America

CHAPTER 1

Traffic crept on country roads, drivers peering anxiously over steering wheels clutched in fingers stiff with tension. The snow was piling up at an alarming rate, driven in by the force of a New England nor'easter predicted to scour the eastern coast from Canada to the Carolinas. Lancaster County was a few hundred miles inland, but the fury of this January storm was unabated. Horses and buggies clipped along in the blinding snow, the drivers confident in the grip of the well-shod horses' hooves, the weight of the steel-clad buggy wheels cutting through the snow with remarkable efficiency.

Mary Glick was upstairs in her Aunt Lizzie's home, a cozy throw wrapped around her legs on the footrest of the recliner, a battery lamp casting a white light on the book she was reading. She had no idea what the subject of this chapter was all about, as her mind was busy replaying scenes of her past. *It must be the storm creating a restless vibe*, she mused, though really, she knew it was far more than that.

She laid her book on the small table beside her chair, flung the throw on the loveseat, and got to her feet. She shivered and pushed her feet into silky furred Uggs, a gift from one of her customers at the bakery.

Going to the window, she hoisted the pleated blind, taking in the whitened countryside, the picturesque houses and barns, the whirling white snow and wind as far as she could see. It was beautiful, but nothing could compare with her home in Pinedale, New York, the home of her father, stepmother, and ten siblings, all married, their homes dotting the beautiful mountainous area.

In her twenties, she'd had her share of life knocking her around. Unmarried, without prospects, she felt a deep sense of restlessness, despite owning a successful bakery in the city of Lancaster and having every material thing she could possibly want.

She propped her arms on the windowsill and watched the clattering snowplow slice a curtain of snow from the road, an oncoming horse rearing its head before mincing past in terrified steps, the driver yanking his window open to gain control. Sighing, she turned from the window and made her way downstairs. Lizzie was at a quilting somewhere in the neighborhood, which in Mary's opinion was unwise. She hoped those fur-topped overshoes, as she called her boots, would bring her efficiently through the ever deepening snow.

She put the kettle on for a cup of tea and searched the cupboard shelves for honey. As she unwrapped the Twinings chai tea bag, her mind went back to the evening with Paul Beiler, the amputee.

Why couldn't she have just appreciated his strengths, his ability to relax and enjoy a game of Scrabble, a challenge they both loved? He was a super nice guy, his parents like family, but all she could feel was an ever deepening sense of insecurity, as if she had slipped the anchor of a boat and realized she had lost the oars.

It wasn't that absent arm, was it? She had never thought herself shallow, but who knew the secrets and sins of their own heart? God knew she did not want to live a single life, but maybe that was her destiny. Three times she'd dated, three times she'd been in love, and three times she'd lost them.

There had always been a spark, that familiar thrill of being in a suitor's presence, knowing he was attractive and found her attractive as well. A little flame of recognition.

With Paul, they'd been together like comfortable siblings, devoid of the tiniest bit of romance. She poured boiling water into the white mug and upended the honey jar, shaking her head at the memory of his yawning, the casual handclasp as he told her goodbye.

And nothing, absolutely nothing since.

She sipped the scalding tea, thought of the coconut macaroons in the white box in the pantry, but reminded herself of the need to reduce her wide, soft girth. The numbers on the scales had caused her to frown repeatedly until she'd finally sworn off sugar and white flour.

Her weight was a constant concern. She knew she was turning to food to complete her, to comfort her when life gave her a battering. Running a bakery didn't make it easy to avoid eating sweets. But the bakery was her passion, her heart and mind occupied with perfecting the everyday menu, scouring cookbooks for new recipes to astound. She reveled in the praise from appreciative customers who stopped every morning for breakfast sandwiches, pastries, fresh doughnuts, carrot muffins, and cookies. And she was always there, nibbling, grazing. A freshly glazed doughnut hole here, half a chocolate chip muffin still warm from the oven there, a sip of coffee laced heavily with French vanilla creamer. The calories added up. She tried to restrain her reach for fresh bits of warm sugar-laden food, but was never very successful, justifying the delicious bites by her constant moving about the bakery. All the walking between the oven and the counters, rolling out the pie crusts, kneading bread, wiping down the tables—it all burned calories, she reasoned.

She winced at the tight fabric stretched across her chest, hooked a finger in the belt of her bib apron, and tugged. Tight. Everything was tight. Ugh. What, exactly, was one to do in the middle of winter? Live on limp salads with tasteless, low-calorie dressing?

But she couldn't help wondering if her size was the reason for Paul's lack of interest. He'd never tried to contact her since, and she'd never really wanted him to. But still, she couldn't help wondering about his sudden and lasting silence.

She had closed the bakery for the duration of the storm. She should have opened her sewing machine, cut out a dress or a few bib aprons, but she found herself in a state of lethargy. She was stuck in a tired, restless funk, her bones reduced to a wet sponge, her mind the only active thing remaining. Afraid of burnout, of finally cracking under the pressure of running the bakery, she paced, then settled into Aunt Lizzie's recliner and reached for the book sitting open.

Now what was she reading?

Another God book. Seriously, was that the only type of book she ever read? Surely she knew every single thing there was to know about God. Her eyes scanned the pages, but she felt no need to go into deep spiritual learning.

Her father had always warned her to stay away from anything explaining the Bible from an English man or a woman's point of view. It was all misleading, and no daughter of his would ever be caught up in that dangerous rubbish. The book, like countless things in her life, was viewed through the stern eyes of her father, an ultra-conservative man caught up in the *ordnung* (rules) of the Old Order Amish faith.

He adhered to the law of the forefathers to the letter, teaching his children well, the ten married ones following his admonitions wholeheartedly, living lives in the approving light of their father.

Their mother had suffered and died, buried beneath sighing fir trees, a plain granite stone to mark where she lay in her wooden casket. Her father had remarried in the allotted time, to a single maiden lady by the name of Jemima Peachey from Belleville, Pennsylvania.

That was when Mary returned to Lancaster, to Aunt Lizzie and a more liberal lifestyle. She visited family infrequently, well aware of carrying the questionable label of the black sheep. Her father lamented her state of worldly living, wrote long, tear-filled letters containing every judgment against her, the chance of her entering Heaven constantly becoming slimmer.

His voice was in all her decisions, unless she took a great deal of effort to block his threats, to mentally align her own conscience with God's will for her life. The bakery was his greatest concern now. The money, the traveling in cars along city streets . . . it was all a deadly slide into worldliness. So far, she'd successfully batted his warnings aside, but she could never be completely free of the weight his words placed on her.

Mary sighed, closed her eyes, the slow hum of crawling traffic creating a drowsiness. The tea in her mug turned cold as she fell asleep in the middle of the day.

BACK AT WORK the following day business was slow, so Mary's four employees were put to work cleaning the refrigerator, the supply closets, and the floor. Careful to keep the inspector's rules, they kept cleaning fluids and buckets away from the food.

The girls were young, vibrant, ambitious, and energetic. They chatted happily amongst themselves as they worked. Most of their conversation was about boys, clothes, or weekend plans, exactly in that order. Confident, secure in their upbringing in homes with loving parents, they were often the delight of Mary's own life.

Whistling, singing snatches of songs, checking their phones behind her back, they were interesting and pretty young women whom she truly loved. And they were skilled, able to follow instructions and forge ahead with all manner of different foods, humble enough to accept correction where it was necessary.

This morning, the conversation centered on Karen, the short, blond-haired girl who had just turned seventeen. Mary's ears perked up.

"Yeah, Karen, you're going to have to decide," Marianne quipped, stopping to drape an arm around her shoulder.

"Hush. Just hush. He said he'll give me time."

"Who?" Ruthie asked, pausing between her swipes across shelves.

"What? Who asked you?" LeAnna asked, getting up from the floor and smoothing her skirt.

Karen waved a hand, her eyes shining.

"It's Christian Beiler. You know him," Marianne said in her competitive tone.

A collective gasp, squeals of congratulation.

"Oh man, Karen!"

"Seriously, girl!"

"Dude!"

Mary smiled to herself but stayed out of the fray. Once, she had been seventeen and had felt the thrill of being attractive. But she lived a much more cloistered way of life, a lifestyle preserving the old ways, where young men wore hats and homemade black coats, drove roofless courting buggies, and kept all romance top secret. Where dating was done only on Sunday evening, surreptitiously sneaking into a dimly lit kitchen, drinking coffee, and talking in low undertones. Where faces turned red at the mention of having had someone bring them home from the singing.

No, she had never wanted any of these obedient, God-fearing young men, had found their conversation childish, their square cut hair and pimply faces disgusting. She had gone through stages of feeling abnormal, as if she needed an adjustment, but could no more help herself than she could change the amount of flaming, copper-colored hair on her head.

"I don't know. It was between Christian and Kevin. I don't know if Christian is going to cut it. Kevin is . . . Mm!"

Karen curled her fingers into fists and shoved them under her chin, her eyes rolling to the ceiling.

"He's so-o cute!"

"Christian is better looking," Ruthie piped up.

"Oh, come on, Ruthie," LeAnna groaned.

"Looks aren't everything," Mary said quietly.

"You sound like my mom," Karen said, rolling her blue eyes.

"It's true, though," Marianne said soberly, her eyes going to Mary's. "Customer."

Mary hurried to the register, putting on her business smile, offering a bright good morning, how are you? They ordered and she rang up the chai latte and a black coffee with two bacon and egg sandwiches on whole wheat toast.

These customers were thin women, dressed to the nines. The bacon surprised Mary. Usually, it was an egg white and spinach wrap for this type. Whatever was wrong with eating an egg yolk, really?

She took the order to the grill, and Marianne stepped up, peeled on plastic gloves, popped the bread into the toaster, then poured a splash of oil on the grill.

Mary turned away, knowing Marianne would have the order done in record time. She was good with her hands, very swift, her movement all efficiency and management. She was grateful for all her workers, but could only smile and shake her head at the differences in what was normal for this young woman compared to what was "normal" for the rest of Mary's family in Pinedale Valley.

But who was she to judge? Who was she to compare the dress code of her upbringing with that of these liberal girls who lived by the rules their own parents set for them. How could both be labeled Amish when they were so very different from each other? She mentally shook away the voice of her father, the dire premonitions of his judgment, the way of perdition for the *ungehorsam* (disobedient). She had wrestled internally with his strict views for years, the turmoil of it all causing the beginning of an acidic stomach that would drive her to the Prilosec, the Maalox, anything to settle the pain and discomfort.

For years, she'd shuttled back and forth, her mind deciding on one thing, then another, a restless hovering ghost never quite leaving her alone. "Respect your elders." "Children, obey thy parents, so the time may be long and blessed in the land you live." She'd pondered it. If she strayed off the narrow path, did it mean God would send metaphorical fire and brimstone on her life now, and actual hellfire and eternal misery in the life to come?

Sometimes she could stuff these fears into the backseat of her conscience, other times they were all-consuming. She could never be quite sure she was saved, that grace was sufficient. She longed to move on earth with complete assurance of God's love for her, but that sort of confidence eluded her.

She listened to heartfelt sermons in the same German language she heard as a child, and always felt the load of guilt. Somehow, at the end of every church service, the peace she longed for was out of reach. She had learned to live with it, to blame herself for the roiling doubts, and to go ahead with her life as best she could.

"His car is in the garage, he said," Karen was saying, waving an impatient hand. "It's always somewhere."

"Well, he can't help that."

"I know, but you should see Kevin's new ride. Oh my word. It's, like, unbelievably cool. A Mustang."

Mary listened half-heartedly, feeling old and pinched and bitter.

Shake it off, she told herself.

"Customer."

She hurried out. "Yes. Good morning. How may I help you?"

"Good morning to you."

The man was in his early thirties, maybe late twenties. Hair cut neatly. He wore a navy blue winter coat. No hat, a round pleasant face.

Not someone who would stand out from a dozen others.

She smiled, made eye contact.

He smiled back. "Are you Mary?"

He didn't wait for an answer, but turned his back to point to the sign hanging from the sturdy wrought iron arm above the large window.

"I am."

He turned. "You've been quite successful. I'm impressed. God has blessed you abundantly, has He not?"

She stammered some ordinary reply, lowered her eyelids.

"Well, at any rate, this little bakery is the talk of the town. Literally."

His eyes went to the menus.

"Are you eating in?" she asked.

"I would like to."

"Then you may be seated wherever you choose, feel free to take a menu. Would you like coffee?"

"Certainly."

He turned away, and Mary took up the signature heavy white mug and brought it to him. He looked up at her and asked if she had time for a short interview. His name was Chester and he was writing an article for the church paper, the *Glorious Messenger.*

Instantly, Mary's warning flag was waving, a red splotch of burning conscience. What had her father said? To own a business in the city would thrust her into every temptation imaginable, the worst among them the wolves in sheep's clothing, the wiley ravenous marauders who would present God in misleading ways. She tried to swat the voice aside, but found her breath coming in gasps, little fish like puffs of air that caused her to go hot all over.

She shook her head. "No, I can't. I'm sorry."

"That's alright, I understand. I won't pressure you."

She took his order, her mouth compressed, her heart beating wildly. Pancakes with bacon and scrambled eggs.

"That sounds perfect on a snowy morning," he said.

Mary smiled, nodded, jotted the order, and left.

The bell tinkled, admitting more customers. Ruthie came out, a bright, happy smile on her elfin face.

"Oh, Chester. Hi there. Good to see you," she said, as she passed the man's table.

"Hey, Ruthie. How's it going?"

"Great."

When she had a moment, Mary asked her how she knew him.

"Chester? That's Chester Nolt. He goes to my sister's church. They left the Amish a few years ago and go to this Mennonite church. Not sure what they're called. The women wear those little watchamacallits."

She circled a finger along the back of her head.

Mary nodded.

The following week, Chester was back. He was actually standing outside waiting till opening time, hurrying through the door after Mary opened the lock and stepped aside to allow him entry.

"Brr, is it freezing or what?" he boomed, laughing.

Mary couldn't help smiling in spite of herself.

"Seat yourself."

"I will. I've been dreaming of your pancakes all week. Plus, I'll take a dozen doughnuts to my workers. Cold morning, warm hearts."

The seating area was filling up rapidly, with others standing in front of the showcase, bent double to study the array of homemade doughnuts. The scent of coffee was rich and earthy, the sun streamed through the large plate glass window, illuminating the fresh white paint and the gleaming antiques hung tastefully on the wall. She'd bought fresh flowers to put in small glass pitchers for every table, which added a bright, natural touch.

She loved this part of her day, when adrenaline was coupled with real energy, when she felt the challenge of keeping up with everything and knew she was up to the task. She had a great crew, respectful girls who did a wonderful job. She was thankful and felt the stirring of a song in her heart.

Chester came over to the showcase, asked which doughnut was best.

Mary told him for a mixed crowd it was best to stay with the plain glazed or the filled and powdered. He nodded in agreement.

After he paid, he leaned forward only slightly and asked if she'd changed her mind about the interview.

"Not really. I'm sorry. I suppose I'm a bit old school, but . . ." She shrugged.

He caught the anxiety in her eyes, the raised eyebrows and worried lines across her forehead. He noticed the way she caught her lower lip in her teeth, the swallowing and blinking.

"Mary, it's okay. No worries."

His gaze was so patient and kind, she responded with visible relief.

"Thank you," she murmured.

"Your convictions are respected, Mary."

He took his box of doughnuts and left without another word, leaving Mary mulling over the word "conviction."

Was she really convicted? Did she personally believe relaying her story to a Christian man to be printed in a church paper was wrong?

Not really. But what if the joy and gratitude she had felt only moments before was based on a lie? Could she experience blessing at all while blatantly disobeying her father?

It was impossible to know whether running the bakery was right or wrong, but there was no sense drawing attention to herself through an interview. She didn't need to add pridefulness or vanity to her list of potential sins.

She tried to enjoy the remainder of her morning, putting aside any thoughts of right or wrong. She listened to the girls on break; obviously, Karen had decided to hold out for Kevin.

"I mean, Karen and Kevin? How cute is that?" she trilled.

Mary smiled to herself. With those looks and that sweet personality, there would be more Kevins and Christians, no doubt. She loved it, though. Loved to listen to the lives of these energetic young girls, and she genuinely wished them well.

She made a salad for herself, drew a Diet Pepsi, then gave in and used up the leftover bacon in a thick BLT with potato chips. She sat at a corner booth and pored over a Restaurant Store catalog. Lost in the wonders of available items, she finished her lunch and felt the need for something sweet, just a few bites of chocolate.

Her chocolate croissants were new and one of the best things she'd ever made. Just a few bites. She grabbed one from the showcase and returned to her table, trying to stabilize her guilt, as always.

Before she knew it, the croissant was gone. She crumpled the square of waxed paper, sighed deeply, and told herself she wouldn't eat supper. She would tell Aunt Lizzie she wasn't hungry. It would all balance out.

Besides, that croissant was worth the guilt.

But by evening, she was ravenous. She caught the scent of hot tomato sauce as soon as she stepped through the door and figured Lizzie had made lasagna or spaghetti, her favorite pasta. She groaned.

Aunt Lizzie welcomed her warmly, set a plate of perfect lasagna in front of her, the cheese browned and melted, the rich sauce like ambrosia.

Aunt Lizzie told her of the quilting, the neighborhood news.

There was a new baby at Jesse Riehl's, a daughter named Rachel Jane.

"Why they would name a girl Rachel Riehl is beyond me," she finished, dabbing at her nose and mouth with the napkin she kept by the side of her plate. She always used a napkin, saying old folks with dentures were sloppy eaters, that was simply a fact of life.

"Rachel Riehl. It has a certain ring to it," Mary answered, happily halfway through the wonders of her lasagna.

"And, get this. Chonny Esha ihr Jonasa left the church. Imagine. They're in their forties, have married children. I tell you, the world is coming to an end. It can't be far away. They say she doesn't even have her head covered. Oh, it's terrible."

Mary nodded, reaching for another slice of garlic toast.

"But judge not lest ye be judged, right? *Ach*, we are all sinners. But still, we can pray to remain steadfast to our promise we made to God and man."

Mary wanted to ask, "What? What did we promise?" but decided to hold her peace. Sometimes joining the church in Pinedale Valley seemed like one big question. She had not understood much at sixteen, only knew she'd obeyed her parents and was expected to live a godly life, help build the church, and always dress according to the rules.

"Oh, and Mary, there's a letter, from your father, looks like."

She felt the familiar thud of her heart slowing with a thud, then speeding up with an erratic rhythm. Suddenly, the lasagna went cold and congealed, leaving her without appetite.

She left the table, found the rectangular white envelope with the round post office seal from New York, bit her lip to steady it, and went to her room. She took a few deep breaths before she allowed her shaking hands to open the seal.

What was it this time? What act of immorality, what gross overreaching sin had she managed to carry out? And how much had she grieved her father with her disobedience?

CHAPTER 2

To my daughter Mary,

   Greeting you in *Namen Jesu*.

   I am hoping this finds you well in body and spirit. I don't know
how that can be possible, given the way you define obedience, but
I continue to pray.

   Jemima has been down with the flu, so the house is filled with
the smell of her onion plasters. I have learned what it takes to peel
an onion. She seems to have it in her chest, but won't see a doctor
in spite of my urging.

   We missed you at Christmas. I hope you know your place of
business is now your idol, which you choose to worship instead of
the true God.

Mary imagined herself prostrated in front of the bakery, praying to
the sign.

You must repent, Mary, for the day draweth nigh. Daily, I see you
in that color red, with the white apron, walking the way of the
heathen. Daily, I pray for your repentance while you are still here
on earth. My old heart is getting weaker. I am hastened to an early
death on your account. Please come back, Mary. Come back to the
blessed land of your family, take back the faith of Abraham, Isaac,

and Moses. You have been scattered by every wind of untruth,
have clung to the fables, and are not ashamed by it.

She folded the letter and stared vacantly into space until her heartbeat slowed to a more reasonable pace. Reopening it, she read on, her
molars grinding unknowingly.

Dannie and Salome welcomed their ninth son. They named him
Amos. A good Amish name, and only one. These middle names
should not be tolerated, and the high-minded mothers who want
them should be brought to task.
    Salome is the salt of the earth, submissive to Dannie in all her
ways, her price above rubies, as Proverbs tells us.

Mary imagined Salome as a pillar of salt, like Lot's wife, her head
piled with rubies. Homely, skinny Salome, her nose like a beaker, grateful to have a husband, especially one as tall as her.

If only you could realize the peace and happiness you forego,
living in the hub of liberals, enjoying the lusts of the eyes, the
jewels the world has to offer. My sister Lizzie must answer for this
someday.

Every paragraph was marinated, skewered, and grilled in bitterness.
His wounded pride ate big chunks out of his love and happiness, his
goodwill and forgiveness toward her and every person who lived without his idea of righteousness.
    He had enjoyed the status of good parenting, every one of his chil-
dren walking uprightly in the sight of God, and Mary had brought him
low. She knew this, had always known it.
    He ended his letter with another plea for her to come to the light so
her deeds could be made manifest. Jemima had written a sheet in her
small, cramped style, but there was only her health, her work, and the
weather. Housebound, coughing, she was looking forward to spring.

And Mary experienced an unexpected longing for spring in New York. After the long winter, when snow crystals clung in white heaps like frosting, dotting the thick layer of rotting brown leaves, a brave green shoot of dandelion emerged from beneath, questioning the bit of warmth from the sun. When the creeks ran full, ice and snow sliding down sharp ravines, melting into waterways until they doubled in size, the earthy tang of flood waters would fill her nostrils and inflate her spirit. The whole earth expanded and breathed as the sun smiled down on winter-weary souls finally digging into warmed soil.

There was a certain longing, a faint sadness at no longer experiencing this. Perhaps, she never would, no matter where she lived. Perhaps you only felt the thrill of spring in your youth.

After she'd read the letter, she folded it slowly, put it back in the envelope, and laid it on the end table. She threw herself back on the cushions of her loveseat, crossed her arms, and pouted.

She was angry. Her whole being protested. She put a foot on the coffee table, sent it sliding across the floor. She curled her fists, ran her knuckles down the side of her face. She wanted to sleep and sleep and sleep, anything to escape the roaring of her mind.

How could he judge her in this harsh light? How could anyone judge another person at all? A thousand questions tumbled and spun.

Would she ever get away from him, or would his words follow her to her grave? She shivered.

She must pray. She pressed the palms of her hands together, closed her eyes, and thought her prayer to God. She begged Him to show her the way, to send her encouragement or to warn her if her father might be speaking the truth. Her faith was not strong enough to wave away her father's voice. Smothered, belittled, she felt too weary to resume her struggle, so she settled into a no-man's-land, in a way, where there was nothing, no faith of hope or love, no doubts or fears of destruction. There was just nothing at all.

She considered the changes he required, which included selling the bakery. Could she find it in her heart to do this?

Without being aware of it, she was doing what she always did, taking each sentence apart, examining the contents and putting them in specialized compartments for agonizing over in the coming months.

There was only darkness now, a cold unforgiving void she had to endure. She got up, went to the window, and watched the lines of cars rushing by, the stars barely visible in the manufactured lighting from below.

And her heart broke into streams of tears from her eyes. She stood and allowed them to flow without restraint. The night blurred in a watery mass of headlights, stars, snow, and night sky.

She pictured the sharp contrast of mountain and night sky in New York where only the clear, white stars were visible. Closer, and so beautiful. She loved it most when a crescent moon hung low in the sky, and all the earth was soft and still.

But when the sun rose on reality, there was torn linoleum in filthy houses, babies born in rapid succession, overflowing diaper pails, and runny-nosed children in torn Tingley boots, an exhausted mother cooking yet another pot of bean soup to save on grocery dollars, a husband smelling to high heaven of cow manure and sour milk slopped onto his cheap black polyester trousers, his hair unwashed, his appetite for his wife never flagging.

She could not live like that.

CHESTER NOLT BECAME a regular, and before she knew what was happening, she began to look forward to seeing his wide, friendly face. He was always the same, filled with a strange, bubbling happiness, a love of life and everyone around him. He always talked to Mary, but never mentioned the interview again, and for that, she was grateful.

One morning, however, he came up to the register and asked if she'd like to come to their spring recital at church.

"You mean, go with you and your wife?"

"No, I don't have a wife. Just you. Go with me."

Her eyes narrowed. "Wouldn't that be strange?"

"Why would it be strange? We're only friends. We're both a bit older. I respect you being Amish. What's wrong with it? I just think you would really enjoy it. You seem like the kind of person who would enjoy the poetry, the worship of God in spring."

She felt flattered that he thought she might enjoy poetry. Did she seem a bit of an intellectual? She certainly wasn't simple and had always thought it might be the reason she couldn't live like her siblings.

"Let me think about it."

She told the girls, who smirked and nodded, said they'd seen it coming. A guy didn't come in three or four times a week without some motive other than doughnuts.

"No, it's not like that. I'm Amish. He's not. Nothing can come of it."

"It could," Karen said quickly.

Marianna nodded. "People leave for different reasons."

"It's only to enjoy the recital. He said so himself."

Karen rolled her eyes. "Yeah, and the moon is made of green cheese. But you know, it could work. He's not bad. Not bad at all. And neither are you. If you wore some foundation, a bit of powder, and darken your lashes with mascara, you could be a knockout."

Mary stopped in her tracks.

"Now Karen, I know where to draw the line. I am not, as you put it, a 'knockout.'"

Karen lifted her face and laughed, a flowing, uninhibited sound of glee that made Mary wish she could laugh like that more often.

SHE DRESSED IN a light spring green, sans the makeup, combed her hair with a careful eye, and sprayed a liberal amount of hairspray. She felt pretty. The evening was warm and mellow and beckoning. She told Lizzie she was going out with friends, and she nodded halfheartedly from her chair as she went out the door.

He drove a huge, cream-colored SUV, a vehicle unlike anything she'd ever ridden in. Who was this man? Withdrawn now, she sat as far away from him as possible and spoke only when he asked her a question.

She kept glancing surreptitiously in the half light from the dashboard and thought his profile rather neat, but of course, told herself it made no difference.

"You're being unusually quiet this evening."

"Well, your vehicle is scary."

"What?" He turned to look at her. "Are you kidding me?"

"No. I know I'm Amish, but I know a 60,000-dollar vehicle when I see it. I don't belong here."

For a time, he said nothing, then he spoke quietly.

"See, Mary. I knew there was something different about you. Do you know how many girls would never be honest like that, but pretend to be someone they are not? Do you know how truly classy you are?"

She instinctively shook her head, denied the praise the way she'd always been brought up. Praise made people proud.

"At any rate, Mary, it's refreshing. And since we're not romantically involved, we can say whatever we want, right?"

"Right."

The church was a sprawling red brick building with a lighted sign on a brick base with Hope Mennonite Church in black letters. The gravel parking lot was almost full, with families and young people standing around, waiting till it was time to enter the church.

He parked at the far side, turned off the engine, and waited.

"I'll be the only Amish girl."

"I doubt it. Lots of friends show up for this recital. It's quite good."

He watched her face, but she seemed to be scowling at some inner thought. He noticed she drew her purse to her lap and rummaged in it, then seemed to have found the necessary item.

"I cry easily, so I needed to check my Kleenex supply."

"That's alright. I think tears are a sign of a soft heart."

"Huh."

"What?"

"You don't know me at all."

"Why?"

"You just don't."

"Well, that's true—this is the first time I've seen you outside of your bakery, so of course I don't really know you yet. But we're only friends, so I'm not worried about it. No rush, no pressure. Right?"

"That's right."

"And there's no reason we can't enjoy each other's company at a church recital."

"Right."

When they noticed groups drifting toward the opened door of the church, he opened his door and came around to hers. He extended a hand, and she took it, stepping down easily. Immediately, he let go, and she was grateful.

She was greeted warmly, handed a program of the evening, then ushered into the church.

He told her they normally sat men on one side, women on the other, but at recitals or plays, they sat as a group. She nodded agreement to the back row, where they would not be noticed. Both knew tongues would wag, that everyone would assume they were dating.

A burst of joyous hymn opened up the recital, with a group of teenagers dressed in spring colors coming together in rapid succession, before facing the audience and continuing their praise. It was heart-stoppingly beautiful, and Mary felt her throat tighten. She blinked in desperation to stop the flow of tears, but knew it was futile. As quietly as possible she drew tissues from her purse and held them to her nose. He never turned his head.

When they launched into the old favorite, "Up from the Grave He Arose," she was drawing ragged little breaths and shaking inwardly. The sheer beauty of it lifted her to new heights of she knew not what. She honestly didn't know. She only knew her soul was stirred like never before.

When she wiped her eyes and dabbed at her nose, he did look over, but she didn't realize.

He saw the trembling of her chin, her whole face revealing the inward stirring of emotion. After the singing, when a pretty young girl recited a poem she had written, Mary was leaning forward, her face rapt with wonder, her lips parted as she breathed in the words of the poem.

The hour came to an end too quickly. Mary felt a sense of loss, knowing she would never recapture this amazing spirit lifting again. She would have to contain it somehow, perhaps ask Chester how it could be accomplished.

But that might be too personal.

"They are serving cake and ice cream in the basement, Mary."

She shook her head. "People will talk. Could we just get a cup of coffee somewhere?"

"Of course. Good idea."

Again, he put her in the passenger seat, then went around to the driver's side. She clicked the seat belt in place, sat back, and breathed deeply.

He backed the vehicle out before asking if she enjoyed the show. Mary told him she'd honestly never experienced anything like it.

"I've only attended German hymn singings in my life, which are beautiful in their own way, but common everyday singing. This music transcended my spirit, something I don't understand. I think maybe the closest thing to this was standing on the mountain in Pinedale, New York, in spring, when the beauty around you is almost too much."

"Is that your vacation spot?"

"You mean . . . New York? No. I was born and raised there."

"An Amish settlement?"

"Mm-hm."

"So what brought you here?"

"It's complicated."

He sensed her discomfort and changed the subject for the time being.

"Where would you like to get a cup of coffee?"

"Doesn't matter. I'm not well acquainted with eating places."

"Well, here's Denny's, but the clientele this time of the evening is questionable. Let's try this little place called Jane's."

They both ordered coffee with cream, then sat together in a green upholstered booth. He seemed larger sitting across from her, and she saw how the cowlick in his hair created the absence of bangs.

He looked at her in the dim single shaded cone of light and thought he'd never seen hair quite that color. He wondered what it would look like, undone. But he was a man, and that kind of thinking was dangerous territory.

"So tell me, Mary, what brought you to Lancaster?" He tried again, gently.

"Um, my aunt needed surgery, so I was sent to help her."

"That doesn't sound complicated."

"It wasn't. Not that part."

She took a sip of her coffee, then began pleating and unpleating her napkin, her eyes downcast, her brow furrowed.

"Well, you've clearly done well for yourself."

"Yes. It appears so."

An awkward silence ensued. He waited. Her hands were lightly sprinkled with freckles, the restless fingers worrying the napkin.

Suddenly, she looked at him and blurted, "My family in New York is ultra-conservative, and I am a child of disobedience unless I repent."

Incredulous, he gaped at her. "What are you talking about?"

"That."

She toyed with a napkin, drank coffee, pushed her mug around as if it would help to alter her tumbling thoughts.

She told him her story. Chester was a good listener, attentive, encouraging, so she talked on, holding a clean tissue to her nose or eyes, her closeted emotions bursting through the lock.

"You see, I am living a life that disappoints my father. And he says no blessing will ever rest on my soul. So I kick all that aside, like troublesome garbage, and forge ahead doing what I love most, which is the bakery. But always, his threats are there, unsettling, vicious, like chained dogs lunging at their ties."

For a long time, Chester was silent. So long, in fact, Mary thought she might have angered him.

"You know, Mary, there's this idea among many Christians that the Amish aren't saved, which I have never believed personally. But no matter, your father reminds me of many people in all walks of life. What so many lack is the knowledge that every man's conscience has different levels, different ways of directing the person."

Mary looked troubled, perplexed.

"That confuses you, right?"

She nodded, her brow knitted with worry.

"Okay, is it truly wrong in your own conscience to own a bakery and live in Lancaster?"

"No. Well, yes. I don't know."

She was biting her lower lip now, twisting the napkin in restless fingers, her coffee forgotten.

"You don't know, with your father's words so deeply ingrained."

"Yes. I mean, I'm never free. I am always chained to his voice. His letters."

"He writes?"

She nodded. "As do my sisters and brothers."

"So, you're considered an outcast?"

"Of sorts. I'm not excommunicated, not in the way people are when they choose alternative churches. It's just . . . well, I'm disobedient."

He leaned back, watched her as one expression then another flickered over her face. The waitress brought the coffee pot, but they shook their heads.

Mary glanced at the round white clock above the door. Past ten.

She had an urge to leave, to get away from this man she really didn't know, and who was firing uncomfortable questions. He had no right.

He watched the discomfort on her face, the way she kept glancing at the clock.

He sighed. "Well, Mary, it's getting late. You have church tomorrow?"

She nodded, her eyes downcast.

"Then we'll get you home."

They did not speak on the return trip. As they neared her home, she became self-conscious, afraid she had said or done something wrong.

"Thank you for going with me. I appreciate it, and I enjoyed your company. I'll be around at the bakery. It's addictive."

Mary smiled in the dim interior of the car. So she hadn't really made a mistake, or was he only being polite?

"Thank you. I was thrilled to hear the singing. I have never heard anything quite like it."

As he turned in the driveway, Mary felt a hot rush of shame. How stilted she was, how old-fashioned and formal. And all the painful aspects of her embarrassing life in New York. How had he managed to siphon them out of her?

She put her hand on the door latch, suddenly eager to be away from him, to gulp fresh air and have her feet on solid ground.

Her father's words rang in her ears, the dire threats of being misled, the old familiar bile rising in her throat.

He came around to her side of the vehicle. Her stomach churning, she told him a hasty goodbye in a strangled voice, sounding strange to her own ears. She pushed past him and walked away.

In the safety of the kitchen, she realized she would be sick and rushed to the bathroom, the nausea overtaking her.

After wiping her mouth, she flushed the commode, then made her way to the sink, reaching for the Listerine. A tap on the door, Aunt Lizzie calling softly, "Mary?"

"I'm alright."

"Can I come in?"

When there was no answer, she heard her aunt move away. Peering at her white face, Mary felt disgust—her red splotched cheeks, the unruly red hair, her whole life nothing but a huge mistake made up of bad choices.

Aunt Lizzie put the kettle on for a cup of tea, waiting till Mary appeared, shamefaced, the guilt wracking her features in the dreaded gripping anxiety she had come to fear. Questioning would do no good, so she turned her back to fiddle with the tea bags.

A sigh, a soft defeated sound as she lowered herself into a chair.

Lizzie stayed silent. Another sigh.

"You can go to bed," Mary said hoarsely, clearing her throat. She coughed, blew her nose. The kettle began its high whistle.

Lizzie brought two cups of chamomile tea, placed one in front of Mary, then sat down opposite.

"Tell me, are you ill, Mary?"

It was the kindness in her voice smashing her defenses that made her lower her face and catch her lip as she struggled for control.

She shook her head, the emotion in her throat choking her voice.

Taking up her spoon, she worried the tea bag, not seeing or caring about the tea or the fact her aunt had provided it. For a long moment, there was only silence, the clock on the wall ticking steadily, the tea kettle pinging as it cooled.

Finally, Mary exhaled, a long whoosh of soft breath, before grabbing the mug with both hands and shaking her head.

"I don't know," she said hoarsely.

Lizzie gave her a penetrating look, but kept her peace.

"I just don't know. I don't know anything about anything."

Lizzie shot her an anxious look. What had occurred during the night that caused this meltdown? Fear gripped her mind.

CHAPTER 3

"STUFFY IN HERE."

Lizzie got up and went to the window to open it slightly. The sweet night air wafted through, a hint of lilac and the pure scent of budding peace roses. Lizzie caught the scent, the night reminding her of youth and past love, of Leroy and all the beauty of their relationship.

When she returned to her chair, Mary looked at the opened window as if the soothing scent would give her courage, then finally met Lizzie's gaze, her own eyes wide with troubled thoughts.

"I just don't know," she repeated.

"Mary. Tell me."

Mary sighed again, her hands reaching for a napkin, the twisting and folding already starting.

"Lizzie, what am I to do? Tonight, I went to a recital at a Mennonite church. A rather liberal one, I suppose you'd say. The singing was unreal. The youth were singing, the girls in beautiful dresses, their hair so styled, so pretty. The young men with their hair cut and . . . well, it was quite a picture. When the singing began, it touched a place in my soul. The experience was unreal. I was covered in goosebumps, the tears welled up before I could do anything about it. It was like a glimpse of Heaven. It was as if I was starving and I could eat delicious food. All of it, everything I wanted."

She stopped, confused.

"Then why is that wrong? Why can I be touched like that if it's wrong? How do we know it is?"

"Who told you it was?" Aunt Lizzie asked quietly.

"My father. My whole life's teaching. My upbringing. Everything I have ever been told. Stay away from the wolves in sheep's clothing. And, Lizzie, I was transported, carried away by the sheer power of their voices, until I heard this voice along the edge of my conscience, and I literally saw a snarling wolf dressed in a sheep's clothing."

Aunt Lizzie realized the thin ice she would navigate, the depth of Mary's turmoil. She placed a hand on Mary's anxious, restless ones, and said nothing.

"I'm so sick of my father's voice in my head. I'm sick of living in constant guilt. I long to be free. When I was angry, when I came back and ran with the really wild youth, it was almost easier. The anger and rebellion overrode the guilt. I was strong. Now, I'm back to square one."

"Mary, believe me, the Mennonite church and the singing wasn't wrong. You felt the power of the Spirit, and that's a good thing."

"But how do you know? How do we discern spirits? My father says anybody who is out of the *ordnung* does not have the blessing of our Lord. He said that. He says it still. And I think I may not have the blessing, the way I dress, the way I own my own bakery with electricity, serving the English people in a fancy dining area. And now, because I am so far out of the *ordnung*, the devil has a hold on my life, and I'll just slowly be led into perdition without being aware of it. Like Chester, he's . . ."

Aunt Lizzie broke in. "Who's Chester?"

"A friend. A man who comes for breakfast. It's not like you think. We're friends, nothing else. He wanted to interview me for a paper, but I said no."

She lifted her tea mug, and Lizzie saw the shaking of her hands.

"Every single thing I do is wrecked by my father's voice. Everything. And yet, I go against it. It fades into the distance, and I think peace will be attainable, and it all comes back full force eventually. Sometimes I'm afraid I'll lose my mind."

"Oh, don't say that, Mary."

"I threw up when I got home. My body reacts to my crazy out-of-control thoughts. Isn't there something I can take, some pill, that will help me?"

"Ach. Mary."

In truth, Aunt Lizzie wasn't sure. What was wrong and what was right for Mary? Who was she? A maverick, a nonconformist.

She opened her mouth, began tentatively.

"No, Mary, it wasn't wrong. Not the church or the singing. Probably not your being there, either. I'm so glad you got to experience that. But you must know, in your conscience, what is right and what is wrong. If you felt guilty for being there with Chester, then likely it would be a good idea to let it be the only time."

"We're not romantically involved."

"I know."

Weren't they? Hadn't she felt the stirring of attraction at his profile in the light of the dashboard? Had she not been thrilled to ride in the expensive vehicle?

"But, Lizzie, I want a boyfriend. Someday I hope to have a husband. I don't want to travel through life alone. Three times I did enjoy a relationship with a fine young man, and three times it ended."

Her face took on a hard look, her eyes turned into dark orbs.

"It was my father. And the last time Jemima was as bad. I hate them both."

"No, no, Mary. Please. We can't go around saying such things. Unforgiveness is a cancer. It will bring you nothing but slow death, if left unchecked."

"So now you're on their side?"

"I didn't say that."

"Yes, you did."

"Mary, you're not thinking straight. It's getting late. We have church tomorrow."

"I'm not going."

"That's your choice. But I believe we have visiting ministers from Ohio, so you may want to go. Perhaps there will be an answer in their message, just for you."

"I doubt it. Every sermon is the same, and I don't get much out of all that German."

Lizzie's eyes opened wide. Her eyebrows shot straight up.

"Are you serious? And when did this start?"

Mary shrugged her shoulders, the trace of a pout on her lower lip.

"I don't know. I just know I'm confused. To be painfully honest, can you imagine me with anyone here in Lancaster? Who would ever ask me out? You know I thoroughly ruined my reputation when . . . things got really bad." She thought of those desperate months when she'd sought relief in alcohol and drugs. No respectable Amish man who consider her to be wife material after that.

"Just pray, Mary. Ask God for answers. Ask Him to search your heart, to show you the way. He will."

"Some days, Lizzie, I don't even know who or where God is. I don't read my Bible and often forget to pray. What does it matter? God barely knows who I am, let alone cares about me. I think I imagine God to be my father, maybe? Everything I do is somehow very wrong, not good enough, and I'm a sinner just waiting to be cast out. Out into the place where people go before they fall into the lake of fire."

She paused.

"And another thing. I feel condemned when I read my Bible. As if a finger of accusation is pointing straight in my direction. In a way, I'm already cast out, away from my family, who are all much better than I am. I'll never come up to their level."

Oh my, the things from her heart. The tangled rope of misconception and fear. Aunt Lizzie was incredulous.

"Well, I'm glad you confided in me. And I'm hoping we can continue to be open with each other. But whatever you do, don't make hasty decisions. And consider cutting off your friendship with Chester, whoever he may be. I'm not sure you can handle a friendship with a

Mennonite at this point in your life. If you were more stable spiritually, I think it would be okay, but . . ."

Her voice trailed off.

Lizzie's heart leaped as Mary suddenly lowered her face in her hands and began to weep, soft choked sounds that seemed to come from a wounded place deep inside of her. Lizzie felt disgust for her brother and his impeccable adherence to rules. Sometimes, she wondered if Mary would actually be better off spiritually if she cut all ties with her family. Could she really help the fact she was merely different?

Suddenly, a joy tumbled about in her chest. Yes. She had her own secret little army that would be called forth to battle.

She didn't have answers for this complicated puzzle, but God did. He knew that all things worked together for good for those who loved Him, and her prayers would march right along, the banners flying, the feet marching in courageous rhythm.

She touched Mary's shoulder, then rubbed the soft sleeve gently.

"It's okay, it's okay. God sees your tears, and everything will be fine. Go to bed now, and try to get some sleep."

Unexpectedly, Mary rose, and with an unfathomable look, drew Lizzie into an embrace, laid her head on her shoulder with a muffled, "Thank you. And I'm sorry."

"No, no. Don't be sorry."

She held her at arm's length, looked deeply into her swollen eyes, and said, "God cares about you, Mary. He cares much more than I can, and I love you so much. He loves you more."

But Mary resolutely shook her head.

SHE DID GET up early, after a restless night, took a good, hot shower, and combed her thick red hair into neat rolls. Today she would wear blue, a deep cobalt hue that would complement her white cape and apron.

Here she was, no longer a teenager, wearing the virginal white cape and apron, and for how long? At some point she would need to accept the fact she was no longer part of being a *rumschpringa* and wear the symbolic black cape and apron like the married women, a sign of being a maiden lady.

Aunt Lizzie smiled at her, told her she looked really nice—there was just something about a blue dress with a white cape and apron that was appealing, and Mary felt the smile forming on her face.

A quick breakfast of Bran Flakes and bananas, and they rinsed their bowls, finished the coffee, and were out the door to walk the short distance to Aaron Riehl's house to church.

The air was crisp and bright, the sun brilliant in all its spring glory as its warmth opened the rosebuds and warmed the freshly planted petunias after the chill of night. New growth was all around them—a mowed lawn, flowerbeds, the farmer's fields lush with dew-laden alfalfa and swaths of tender rye.

Vehicles crawled behind horse-drawn carriages on their way to church services. The Amish population was so thick that there were numerous services scattered across a wide region.

Already, there were at least a dozen carriages lined up on the blacktop, with more people arriving on foot. Mary parted ways with Lizzie before entering the shop to find the single girls. She greeted them all with a warm handshake, a smile of recognition, before standing beside Anna, a girl she knew was close to her own age, one who asked her repeatedly to attend her group, the Bluebirds.

Anna was sweet, a tall thin girl who had worked in Aunt Lizzie's bakery but who had always been shy, not part of the boisterous group who hung out together on the weekends.

"How was your week, Anna?" Mary asked, hoping to open a real conversation.

Anna nodded. "Good, I love my job in Annapolis."

Mary rolled her eyes. "I cannot imagine traveling that distance three days a week."

"We sleep. Talk. You get used to it."

They shook hands with others, spoke of the beautiful spring day, and Mary was glad she'd come to church. She felt a part of this gathering, knew she was known as Mary from New York, but most of them were only dimly aware of the settlement in Pinedale Valley.

The plainsong rose and fell, the German words from the *Ausbund* without meaning, but she opened her mouth and sang, the rhythm and scales as familiar as the back of her hand. She had held this same thick *Ausbund* hymn book as a small child, and would likely hold it in church as long as she lived, singing the same slow tune her forefathers had written in prison when they were persecuted for their faith, incarcerated in a dank prison in Passau, Switzerland, along the Rhine river.

The Amish people cherished their heritage, although as time went on, more and more of the younger set saw no reason to stay, to drive a horse and buggy in this day and age, creating heartache among worried parents and division in families.

Mary's mind wandered as she sang, wondering if God saw the good in this congregation, but also the good in the Hope Mennonite church? Why, if one was as acceptable as the other, was it so wrong to change? She would save thousands of dollars driving her own vehicle to the bakery every day rather than hiring a driver.

God is not mocked. We must reap what we sow.

The voice of her father broke through her musing.

She reached into the belt of her apron to retrieve a Kleenex, blew her nose softly to distract herself.

The message was inspiring, as Lizzie had promised. Encouragement flowed, and Mary was lifted up. She wondered how this minister and her father could both be labeled Amish when they held such different views, had such different approaches to life. She wiped tears and swallowed sobs as chills chased each other across her back.

Almost, she felt as she had in the Mennonite church.

But here, too, the man preaching was not really in *die ordnung*, his hair cut short, dark-rimmed glasses on his handsome face, his beard trimmed neatly. Or perhaps he was within Ohio's set of rules, but back home in New York he'd certainly be considered liberal and "dangerous," based solely on his appearance.

At any rate, she felt elevated, if only for a while, lifted out of the abyss of confusion. Did Jesus come for every single soul, even the *ungehorsam*, those who dared venture away from the narrow road their father set for them? Did He understand the frailty of humanity when He hung on the cross? According to this man, He did.

Perhaps, if she moved to Ohio, she could find peace. If she heard this kind of message every two weeks, she might feel differently about God, herself, the church . . . everything. She wished she could ask this young minister if he felt it was wrong to have felt such an uplifting at the Mennonite church.

And so her thoughts roiled, troublesome questions without answers. She got on her knees when the congregation knelt, she listened to the voice of the deacon announcing the place of services in two weeks, and she sang the last song with more enthusiasm than she felt.

After the men had set the tables, using the gleaming wooden benches on trestles, she helped spread clean white tablecloths, arranging platters of sliced homemade bread, small plates of butter, containers of spreadable cheese and peanut butter mixed with marshmallow cream and brown sugar and water boiled to a syrup, pickled cucumbers and red beets. Platters of ham, dried apple pie, and coffee completed the traditional light lunch eaten after services, a practice established many years ago.

Children dashed underfoot, women chattered, men stood in groups, visiting, waiting till it was time to be seated at the table, ministers first, then everyone seated according to age. Men and boys sat at one table and women at another.

Mary poured coffee for the minister from Ohio, but never spoke to him as she would have liked. That would be too bold, far too unconventional, unless she were speaking with his wife and he came along and joined the conversation. Mary was in awe of his wife, with that round, stiff, perfectly-fitted covering on her head, her dress, cape, and apron all the same color. She looked like a flower.

After the older men and women had eaten, the dishes were washed, rinsed, and dried before the younger folks had their turn to eat. A set of plastic Rubbermaid totes were placed side by side on a folding table, with another to set the clean dishes before they were whisked away to be put back on the table. Plates and bowls were replenished, more coffee poured, and Mary found herself across the table from one of her former friends, one who had married and moved to Lilitz, on the west side of Lancaster.

"Mary! You're back?" she asked, her face open and frank.

"Yes, I am."

"What brought you back?"

Mary shrugged. "My mother passed away. My father remarried."

"You're kidding me. I'm sorry for your loss."

Mary didn't know what to say, so she nodded and busied herself spreading cheese on a slice of bread. She folded a slice of deli ham, adding a layer of bread and butter pickles before taking a bite.

"It's fine now, but it was hard."

She thought of her mother. Who had she been, really? Her father's shadow. A hollow helpmeet with no reasoning of her own. Mary caught glimpses of her mother's own thoughts only on occasion, at broken moments in time. Sometimes she felt she hadn't had a mother, only two fathers, the one a quiet shadow of the other.

She felt an elbow in her side.

"Are you coming with me?"

It was Anna, her face pushed eagerly into her line of vision.

Glad to be away from the imposing questions, she followed Anna through the crowd, found Lizzie and told her she was going with Anna to her supper and singing.

Lizzie looked up at her, clasped her arm, and said she was very glad. Having her aunt's stamp of approval felt good to Mary, especially after last night.

THE DAY WAS sunny and warm, allowing the windows of the buggy to be lifted and secured. The doors slid back to allow the warm breezes to circulate. Anna's brother Jonas was driving, a youth of eighteen or nineteen, his face pocked with acne scars, his brown hair cut short with a

heavy tumble of bangs across his forehead. He was as outgoing as Anna
was shy, so he kept up a steady flow of questions and didn't hesitate to
make his observances known. He was also the sloppiest driver she had
ever had the bad luck to come across, the horse running in the ditch,
then straining toward the middle.

He forgot to apply the brakes while heading down a steep hill until
Anna reminded him. Then he stamped on them so hard they were
thrown toward the opened window.

"Boy, these brakes grab!" he yelled.

"It's not the brakes. It's the driver," Anna said in her soft voice.

He laughed, showing a row of crooked teeth. But there was an
endearing quality about him, a refreshing lack of guile.

"You know, you're not too bad looking for an old maid. You should
come around regularly. I bet I could set you up with someone. Or I
might ask you. What would you say if I did?"

He peered over at her with eyes alive with good humor, and Mary
burst out laughing.

"I might just take you up on your offer."

"Hey, yeah. Give me five."

He held up a hand, and she responded with a firm smack. They
both laughed, and Anna shook her head. "You know, there's a bit of an
age difference."

"How old are you, Mary? Just curious." Jonas glanced at her inquir-
ingly as they pulled to a stop at the barn.

"Guess."

"Thirty-five?"

When Anna punched him, he fell out of the buggy, laughing as he
did so. He turned to greet a cluster of boys, and the girls climbed off the
buggy and into the house.

"Sorry about Jonas."

"He's great. He's like a breath of fresh air."

"You got the fresh part right."

The house was large, the kitchen bright and airy, a group of neighbors and sisters helping the hostess prepare vast quantities of meatloaf,

some snipping vegetables for salad, others mixing sliced potatoes with sauce to pop into the oven. It smelled delicious, and in spite of having had lunch, her stomach rumbled. She would not speak of this, her consciousness about her weight like a pack on her back.

They greeted the women in the kitchen, found the bathroom, and freshened up before heading out to the volleyball games. Two games were in progress, the usual group of young people involved in getting the ball across the net. Mary took a look around and knew it would be a long evening. Everyone was so terribly young. The girl closest to her age was Anna, and she was a good five years her junior. She admitted to herself that she had come in vain hope of finding an interesting prospect, something to distract her from the magnetic draw of Chester Nolt and his church.

Had she become so desperate, wearing her vulnerability like a sweater? She felt her own blinded exposure, her need to be accepted and loved for who she was, coupled with the knowledge of the fact she could never find unending approval. Sooner or later, she would make a stupid mistake, and everyone would know she was Mary from Pinedale, completely out of her element.

Wouldn't it be better to simply step away from the Amish altogether, to make a fresh start? If she went to another church, she'd be excommunicated and would never have to worry about her former life. She'd be shunned, and maybe the finality of that would be a relief.

An excitement crept into her, tumbling her stomach. She coughed, smiled at Anna with a sudden brightness. She was an adult. She was her own person, capable of making decisions on her own. Hadn't she made a good decision about the bakery? It had proved to be more profitable than she could have imagined.

Her thoughts were interrupted when Jonas walked over and tugged her and Anna into the volleyball game. Soon she was caught up in the fierce competition for the ball. She had played volleyball often and well, so in spite of being a little rusty, she still had the ability to be a swift, calculated player.

A man who looked to be about her own age moved into the front row, swept his blond hair out of his face, grinned at her, and said hello. She blinked, swiped a hand across her eyes, and mumbled a greeting in return.

"Be ready for a mean spike," he said, all tan face and wide smile with a row of white teeth.

The lawn tilted, righted itself. Every ounce of willpower was put into use as she concentrated on the game, kept her eyes on the fast-moving white volleyball, leaped, and sent it across the net, staying on her feet to do it again. She heard a few cheers and felt a rush of pleasure. Glancing at Jonas's face, there was no doubt that he was impressed. When the evening sun was set behind the barn, the game was over, and it was time to start the hymn singing. She wondered if this was how Cinderella felt when the clock struck midnight. She'd genuinely had fun and had momentarily forgotten all her insecurities. But as they filed indoors, reality hit and she knew it was only a matter of time before these youth realized she was a fraud.

CHAPTER 4

THE PHONE MESSAGE WAS CLEAR AND PRECISE.

"You must come home, Mary. As soon as possible. Our father fell from the house roof. His condition is grave."

Mary took a deep breath to steady herself and replaced the receiver. She breathed reluctance. It oozed out of her pores. Her whole being resisted.

No, God. Not now. Don't require this of me now.

The rest of the evening at the youth gathering had been surprisingly good, and Mary had come home feeling more hopeful than she had in ages. She replayed the scene in her mind. She'd been sitting quietly along the wall, watching as Anna filled a paper plate with tortilla chips and salsa, a few chocolate chip cookies, balancing two glasses of sweet tea.

"Hello, again."

Turning her head, her breathing stopped when she saw it was him. No words formed, so she nodded, the beginning of a smile formed.

"You're very good at volleyball."

"Thank you, but I was a bit rusty."

"Same here. What's your name?"

"Mary Glick."

"Glad to meet you, Mary."

He tilted sideways, extended a hand. Mary took it. A strong grip, and then her hand was let go.

"I'm Steve. Steve Riehl."

She nodded.

"Are you from around here?"

"I live with my aunt along 340. Just out of Intercourse."

"So, you're not from the Lancaster area?"

Thankfully, Anna appeared, handing Mary a cup of sweet tea. Mary took a sip, welcoming the moisture in her dry mouth.

"What are you up to, Steve?"

"Talking to your friend Mary."

Anna gave him a look bordering on secrecy, or conspiracy, she couldn't be sure. Whatever it was, it wasn't meant for her.

"Mary's from a settlement in New York. A place called Pinedale."

At these words, Mary shrank back against the wall, feeling herself becoming small and smaller until she was a pinhead, wishing she could evaporate into thin air.

"Never heard of it."

She breathed again.

Lots of small talk ensued, and Mary had time to take in Steve's features. She took note of his large, tanned hands with clean nails, a face lined with more years than the average teenager at these gatherings, long blond hair, and small, twinkling eyes too dark to be blue, but too blue to be green or brown. He was husky, with a restless energy and a quick mind.

He loved the wilderness and hunting, felt a bit stifled in Lancaster, but here was where he worked, so he stayed.

"Mary owns a bakery in Lancaster," Anna replied.

"You do? I'll have to come check it out."

Jones inserted his presence and that was the last of the conversation. There had been no goodbyes, no promises to see you later, just a steady moving away through the throng of teenagers.

Mary was quiet on the way home, acutely aware of her own shameful attraction. Again. Why was she setting herself up for disappointment? Any romantic feelings she had experienced in the past were like the first purple crocus of spring, poking up from half-warmed soil, eager, hopeful, so delicate, only to be trampled underfoot by fate. There was no reason to think things would ever be different.

And now the untimely summons to her father's bedside.

She groaned. She paced. She lifted her hands in the air, palms up, and asked God why. Why now?

But she shared the news with her aunt, packed her bags, gave the girls at the bakery instructions, hired a driver, and left.

After a while the congested areas thinned and the mountains came into view, a distant blue haze, and then they were moving on up into the Adirondacks. She asked if she could open her window a bit, then caught the scent of mountain laurel. A purple haze along another ridge revealed the bursting buds of the small misshapen Judas trees, as her mother had called them.

In spite of having to face this catastrophe at a time she least wanted to go, she consoled herself with the thought of being in New York in spring, the sights and scents an explosion of beauty. She reasoned that perhaps God was sparing her another letdown, another disappointment, and the life-sucking heartache of having failed again.

They crossed bridges above rivers and creeks, wound through mountains and ridges with waterfalls splashing in sunlight, and she caught glimpses of flocks of geese flying in Vs, birds flying in synchronized flight patterns across azure skies.

But as they neared New York, her heart plummeted, her stomach churned. Nausea rose in her throat. She took deep cleansing breaths to steady herself, but had to ask the driver for a restroom stop before depositing her lunch.

Outwardly calm, her insides raged. She sipped a Coke, tears forming unbidden. She did not want to return. It was so simple.

She felt an aversion to the idea of her father, lying in *sark*, that state of having to be attended to. She had no idea in what shape she would find Jemima, and who would expect what from her.

But no matter her thoughts, no matter the sacrifice, she knew this was her duty. The family would expect her to do as she was told, and that was that.

As the van wound down the curving road leading to their home, Mary closed her eyes and prayed for strength. Her parents lived on Abner's farm now, with Jonas taking over the home place, such as it was, facing a mountain, tucked into steep ridges with rocky soil washing away easily. Amos Glick had squeezed a scant livelihood out of the depleted hillside, raising his eleven children on the bare minimum and God's tightfisted grace. Amos and Jemima had built a small white house on Abner's property, a *daudy* house, the house every aging person was eventually kept in near a relative's home. Sometimes the house was attached to the spacious farmhouse, called living double, or *s' anna ent*, "the other side." In this case, their home was just cross the yard from Abner's house.

AMOS'S FAITH WAS entrenched in deep personal sacrifice, the hoisting of a heavy cross, and obedience to the *ordnung*. Any doctrine smacking of liberalism was whacked down with austere measures. But for all of that, his intentions were honorable, his faith sincere, and he had done well for his children, he thought.

Except Mary. He couldn't escape this thought. Mary was the thorn in his flesh, the cross he must bear. And lying in pain, he figured the Hand of God had moved a significant chess piece in his favor, bringing Mary to the *bekentniss der vohrheit*, that area of seeing the truth. Yes. He would enjoy the fruits of his prayers before he died.

With broken ribs, a jammed knee, bruises everywhere, and two toes all but ripped away when his foot hit the cement, he was in significant discomfort. Jemima was too old to tend to his needs adequately, and the rest of the children had their own families to care for. They were needed at home, so there was no reason Mary could not do her share.

Amos closed his eyes, opening them frequently to check the clock, calculating the time she should be arriving.

MARY CRANED HER neck, her eyes hungrily taking in the astounding changes made on the farm. So many childhood memories, so many pleasant times, in spite of the exhausting rules.

Redbud trees, dogwoods, cherry all bloomed in opulent profusion, the lawns covered with windblown petals. Tulips waved in the ever-blowing wind like hula dancers, daffodils crumpling at brown edges, their dance over, their energy going back into the bulb.

Along the creek in the pasture, the watercress grew and multiplied, with mallard ducks paddling among it, grabbing tender mouthfuls.

Mary paid the driver after the tires crunched across gravel and stopped. She thanked them, wished them a safe trip home, and said yes, she'd be sure to call when she was ready to return. Hopefully it would be very soon.

She lifted the packs out of the back and made her way up the cement walk. Abner's farm had barely changed, the old siding turning from white to gray on the house, the peeling paint on the barn becoming only occasional, laughable shreds.

But the fences were in good repair, the cows were well managed, and the mules fed, so that was something. And the *daudy* house looked sturdy and fresh compared to the other buildings.

Straw-hatted boys stopped their play to stare open mouthed, and little girls sitting on downturned plastic buckets hid their faces behind doll blankets. She was ashamed to realize she had no idea what their names were. Benuel? Sarah? She had lost track.

She knocked softly. The door opened immediately.

Jemima peered through the screen.

"Mary."

It was a statement, certainly not an exclamation.

"Hello, Mima."

"Can't you call me 'Mam'?"

"Yes. I can, of course."

"Then I wish you would."

She looked in and saw a hospital bed, a thin, sallow face against white sheets, the long strings of gray white hair pasted to her father's skull, his eyes sunken, the dentureless mouth a misshapen hole in his loose jowls.

Mary repressed a shudder and made herself walk to his bedside.

"How are you, Dat?" she asked softly.

In answer, he closed his eyes and rocked his head from side to side. Mary looked at Mima, who clasped her hands on her stomach and shook her head.

"Why isn't he in the hospital?"

"We felt we could take care of him here."

Mary felt the impatience well up. "You mean you thought *I* could take care of him here."

"Now don't start. It's time you took your responsibility seriously. We need you."

All the resentment she'd managed to stuff into the past came roaring back, crowding out any affection she may have had.

Pushing past Jemima, she asked where she was supposed to sleep.

"We have a very small guest room, but it is a room, so you'll have that, at least."

Mary failed to hear the apology in her voice as she opened the door to find a double bed, a row of hooks, and a small antique dresser. A calendar was hung above the bed, a glossy photograph of a gray kitten with pink roses. The walls were painted a high-gloss sky blue, with braided rugs on the floor in shades of purple and black. The quilt was an old Sunshine and Shadow pattern, in every brilliant color, the quilting done in tiny black stitches.

Everything was immaculate, but the scent of mothballs was stifling.

"May I open windows?" Mary asked, touching the forest green window blind.

"Certainly. Just keep the door closed so he doesn't get a draft."

Mary hung her dresses on hangers, hooked them at the provided space, then put the rest of her things in the small dresser. She took a look around, sighed, and held very still. The sweet-smelling breeze brought indistinct, melancholy childhood memories with it.

She turned back to the living room, fighting an ever-deepening sense of despair. With her whole heart, she did not want to be here, but she knew there was no escape.

"Mima," came the weak, plaintive cry from the bed.

Mima scuttled over, her small feet soundless as she moved.

"*Voss vitt, Dat?*"

There was a long drawn-out groan, followed by a hideous sound of anguish. Mary's heart sank, but Mima was accustomed to his wails, so she stood patiently.

He groaned.

"What time was your last medicine?"

His voice became very strong, articulate. "That's your job."

Immediately flustered, Mima looked at the clock and counted painfully on arthritic fingers. Looking at Mary, she shook her head, saying, "I don't know."

"Oh, just give him a couple of whatever he takes. It's not going to kill him," Mary said, the howl still circling around her head, trailing anger as it moved.

So Mima brought two white pills and a glass of water with a bendable straw, hovered nervously as he swallowed, tucked the blanket around his shoulders, and bent to make sure his feet were properly covered.

Mary observed the formerly strong, feisty woman who had become father's second wife. She had been reduced to this hovering simpleton, and a shot of irritation swept through Mary. He'd done it to her mother, all his children, and now Mima. He ruled with absolute and total authority, reducing those around him to mindless, cowering servants without them even realizing it was happening. He rained threats, wielded Bible verses like they were a two-edged sword crafted to hurt (and never to encourage or build up), coerced and cajoled and meted out punishment, until eventually they all bowed before him in subjugation to his will.

No longer a gullible child, or a frightened teenaged girl, all this came to Mary in a flash of insight. She squared her shoulders, rolled up her sleeves, and determined she would not be another of her father's victims.

The one single joy of her days was Mima's cooking. Steeped in the old way, she cooked with lard and plenty of homemade yellow butter salted to perfection. She fried scrapple and homefries for breakfast, with eggs from the henhouse and thick oatmeal loaded with brown sugar and maple syrup. She flavored her coffee with the top cream from the glass gallon jar of milk from the Jersey cow in the barn and added a dollop of vanilla and maple syrup. No fake creamers for her. She bought citrus fruit by the case from Amos Stoltzfus and hand-squeezed grapefruit, lemon, and navel oranges, mixed them all together, and sugared it.

"Vitamin C, straight from the source," she said in her funny hoarse voice, and Mary remembered why she had liked her at one time.

As surely as the sun rises and sets, Amos's badgering began and didn't cease. First, he tried to gain her sympathy with pitiful moans of suffering, and when that failed to bring her into subjection, he asked dozens of questions she often could not answer. When he started in on how her life choices were depriving her of any meaningful blessings (especially a husband), she walked out the door and went to find the garden hoe.

She carried it to the edge of the large garden and lifted her eyes to the hills surrounding her. The beauty of New York provided a certain fullness in an empty spot she hadn't been aware of.

She closed her eyes and breathed deeply, felt the worn handle of the garden hoe, and allowed gratitude to wash over her. The mountains were astounding, with hidden valleys along the sides, a sprinkling of purple Judas trees, a dash of wild cherry blossoms among thousands of green leafed trees in different budding stages. A long eagle soared on powerful wings, and distant birds flew on frenzied wings as they gathered materials for nests.

The wonders of the great outdoors awakened her senses to the beauty she hadn't known she needed. Here was where she'd been born, where she spent countless hours as a child, content to accept the ways of her parents.

But the beauty was marred by reality.

Here in this mecca of God-given wonders was the law. Here she was expected to adhere to a strict, austere way of life she could never fully embrace. And there was the poverty, the lack of funds to live in the way she'd become accustomed to now that she ran her own successful business in the city. She enjoyed her comfortable room in her aunt's house, the freedom to hire a driver anytime, the ability to eat out when she chose, the days of shopping, free of guilt.

Her thoughts spun as she bent to her task, chopping at soil between rows of new pea plants, tiny spring onions sprouting long waxy stems, busy little radish tops and red beets scattered in barely visible rows. She appreciated the straight borders, knowing Mima came from generations of good gardeners.

She stopped to rest her back and spied a pair of bluebirds by the birdhouse nailed to a fence post, singing their hearts out. Sparrows twittered in the Rose of Sharon bush before bursting out in a whirring frenzy as a barn cat walked by.

Abner's farm was not what her home growing up had been. The fields fell away from the outbuildings, fertile soil in the valley between mountains, already plowed and harrowed, ready for the corn planter. There was fresh gravel spread on the muddy driveway, the lawn mowed and garden seeds sprouting.

The two small boys in torn straw hats and patched trousers came out of the house, stood on the front porch, and eyed her warily. They spoke to each other, nodded their heads, and walked toward her, their faces like somber little men.

"Hello," Mary said.

They stared at her, as if seeing an apparition, some strange creature they hadn't known existed.

"What are your names?" she asked, trying again.

Still no answer.

"You're big boys already. You've grown a lot."

More staring, but she noticed the smallest blink.

"Did you know I'm your Aunt Mary?"

A slight nod from the tallest one.

"I'm Benuel. He's Amos."

"Hello, Benuel and Amos."

"Dat says you're English, but you wear fancy Amish clothes."

"Really? Your dat said that?"

"Yes."

"Hm. Interesting. I'm Amish, though. Like you."

"We have kitties."

"You do?"

"Yes. In the barn."

"Will you show them to me?"

Eyes sparkling now, they nodded in unison, then turned on their heels. Mary laid down the hoe and followed them. The smell of silage, fresh hay, and cow manure provoked childhood memories, causing her to take in a deep breath. She took in the clean, lined walkway between cow stanchions, the freshly cleaned gutters, and felt a certain pride in her brother.

"Here. Come back here," Benuel said.

On a loose pile of hay, a gray barn cat lay on her side with a furry, multi-colored cluster of kittens around her, gazing up at them with trusting eyes. The boys reached down to take up one black kitten and held it out to her, wordlessly.

Mary cupped the small ball of fur in her hands, then brought it to her chin, savoring the silkiness of new kitten fur. The kitten purred immediately, and she held it away from her face to view the color of its eyes.

"Aw, this one is so cute. Black with blue eyes."

"They're all cute. Look at this one."

"Oh, my word. It's gray and has three white feet!" Mary said, putting down one to pick up the other.

Benuel and Amos were like proud parents, producing one little ball of fur after another, and Mary fussed and praised accordingly.

"We think we know where there's another nest, but we haven't found it yet. We have to be careful, as Dat says there are too many cats, so we hide them as long as we can."

"Too many? What happens if you don't hide them?"

Benuel's eyes fell, and he shrugged. Amos looked at Mary with the guileless eyes of the very young, but a quick shadow passed over his features.

"He drowns them," he said matter-of-factly.

Mary nodded, a vise clamping on her heart. She held the gray kitten to her face, the beginning of a dark memory forming in her head . . .

She could almost see the shafts of sunlight through the tobacco shed, dust motes swirling in the air. The smell of tobacco dust and an earthen floor. The dark interior was a place of refuge for her kittens. Then, the doorway darkened by the tall thin form of her father. His footsteps deliberate as he closed the distance between them, his long, thin fingers around her arm as he pulled her to her feet. Resisting fiercely, she kicked and squirmed, a scream forming in her throat, but never set free.

The familiar "paddling" ensued, but she never gave him the satisfaction of hearing her cry. She scrabbled wildly back at the kittens, flung herself over them, strangely silent as he pulled her off. He had to pry one kitten out of her crossed arms, and still she tried to get it away from him.

She never saw those kittens again.

She told her mother, hoping for an ally, but was told in a distracted tone, they were *yuscht kattsa*. But to Mary, they had not been "just cats." They had been her little friends, precious creatures she loved with all her heart.

A part of her always loved kittens, but as she grew, she no longer searched for the newborn ones, knowing it would end in heartache. Occasionally, when the good mousers died out, there were half-grown ones at the milk dish in the cow stable, but she never loved them too much, knowing it might end badly.

She approached her brother that evening, when she found him in the barnyard, looking after a lame cow. He had not aged, still had the youthful face of their mother, the wide, broken brim of his straw hat hiding most of his hair and all of his forehead. He straightened his back at the sight of her, a thin smile on his full lips.

"Mary."

"Yes, Abner." She cut right to the point, determined to stand up for those children in the way her mother never had. "I . . . the boys showed me the nest of kittens. I'm hoping you'll let them live. For the boys' sake. I remember Dat destroying mine, and well, you know. . . . It's not a good memory, and I'm asking you to spare them this."

He held her gaze, then cleared his throat, so much like her father.

"Mary, Mary," he said sadly.

She said nothing.

"You are still the same victim you've always been, pitying yourself if you were brought under authority. It was the will of our father those kittens were taken, and you couldn't give up to that. You still can't give up. It is the stumbling block of your existence. Straight and wide is the way for those who seek to live for the flesh, which is the road of pleasure you are on. You still don't see it."

A roaring began in her ears.

She fumbled for words.

"It may seem cruel to you, but it was an act of righteousness. To teach a child what authority means is an act of purest love, the spiritual kind. Someday, children will grow up to thank their parents for that."

She found the voice.

"No, Abner, you are wrong. Wrong! When you cruelly destroy an innocent creature that a child loves, a part of her dies inside and a rebellion is born."

"Perhaps for some. For the *ungehorsam*."

"No, for those with feelings of compassion and sorrow, normal emotions that are vital to healthy adults."

He stopped her with these words. "If you are here, Mary, you must learn to respect those who are in authority."

CHAPTER 5

SHE LAY IN THE NARROW BED IN THE EVENING, THE BLIND LIFTED to reveal the undulating tops of the mountains, like an uneven black ribbon, the lighter night sky with its smattering of twinkling white stars, a half moon like the smile of God. The sound of tree frogs down by the pond was a melodious harmony, a high note of silvery sounds of her childhood. An owl screeched, then another, and she pictured the round yellow eyes, the perfect tufted ears.

The valley was a river of fulfillment for her senses, beauty of sight and sound like an outpouring of love from God. She loved New York, loved being here in the valley, if only it wasn't tainted with the sordid philosophy, the conservative thumb squashing the life out of her as if she was an insect. Her arguments were as impotent as a worm up against a hungry bird. These people had an absolute assurance of righteousness, the confidence in their own perfection as stalwart and as unmoving as the stone walls of an old castle.

She was labeled by all as "worldly," "liberal," and looked upon with disgust and swift judgment.

Sometimes she wondered if there was some truth to Amos and Abner's words. Was her disobedient heart the reason she could not find contentment, could not marry an upright young man and succumb to his wishes? Succumb. Yes, die daily to her own mind and heart.

She felt the old familiar panic, her mouth drying out as her breath came in gasps, her heart hammering crazily. She felt the first flush of heat, threw back the covers, and sat up, her feet hitting the floor, her head in her hands. The room spun. She lay back down quickly, clutched the pillow for stability, but there was none.

Was she on the wide road to perdition, as blind as a bat, unable to take up the cross Christ designed for her? She felt a desperate need, a hunger, for real truth. What was truth?

Her thoughts tumbled, her panic increased. She broke out in a cold sweat. There were no tears, no prayers. God wouldn't hear her words if they never managed to get through the ceiling of her fear.

Alone, exhausted, she battled on, unable to control the anguish of her torment. Her father's finger pointed, spelled out her doom. Yes, she was English, owning that bakery in Lancaster, walking around with her head held high, her speech with the right lilt, imitating the worldly people she was in contact with every single day. Yes, she was *ungehorsam*, doomed according to the law.

The weight of it smashed her down into the mattress, her body crushed beneath it. Her bones turned to jelly. The panic increased yet again, and she knew she would suffocate from sheer terror if she didn't do something. She got to her feet, shakily, stuffed her feet into slippers, and groped for the door handle. She moved silently across the small kitchen, casting terrified glances at her father who was snoring open-mouthed, the pain medication giving him relief.

She drank a few swallows of water from the tap, then gripped the sink with both hands as her world spun counterclockwise.

The only clear thought in her head just then was the word "direction." She needed direction, but dear God, from whom? Where could she go? Yes, to God Himself, but He wasn't a reliable problem solver, really.

She sank into a chair and tried calming herself with slow breathing. A voice from the bed made her jump.

"Is that you, Mary?"

"Yes."

"Why are you in the kitchen?"

"I was thirsty."

"Would you put this blanket over my feet? It seems they're always cold."

"Yes. Of course."

She unfolded the light blanket, spread it across his feet, and felt an unusual sense of compassion.

Lying so alone, so vulnerable in the light of the half moon, did God look down and love him, too? Did He really love both of them, each of them so different from the other, each broken in their own ways?

"*Denke*, Mary."

"*Gayun schöena*."

She was afraid to return to her small bedroom, afraid to go outside, trapped unreasonably by her own churning thoughts. She had to calm down, go to sleep and face another day, but that thought alone brought despair as thick and heavy as a submersion in oil. Since there was nothing else to do, she returned to her bed, curled into a fetal position, and tried to pray. The only prayer she could come up with was a weak plea for help.

THE FOLLOWING MORNING, she slept later than usual, her mind gratifyingly blank. A thick fog enveloped her, and Mima finally accosted her in a harsh voice.

"Mary, didn't you sleep at all last night?"

"Of course I slept," she snapped back.

"We need gasoline for the washing machine before we can do the wash. You need to hitch up and go with the springwagon. I have to stay here."

She nodded her head in her father's direction.

"There's oatmeal on the stove" was Mima's way of saying late risers weren't fussed over. Mary ignored the congealed, cooling oatmeal and went to the barn to find a suitable horse.

Abner was hitching up a team of four Belgians, a smile on his face as he greeted her.

"Need a horse, Mary?"

"I have to get gasoline."

"We have gas. Just borrow some from us."

"Great, thank you."

"Is it for the washing machine?"

"Yes."

"You look tired. Haven't slept well?"

"Not really."

"You should go have coffee with Arie. Baby kept her up most of the night," he chuckled.

"What's so funny about that?" She gave him a hard stare.

He raised his eyebrows. "Guess you wouldn't know, still being single."

She followed him around without speaking, took the red, plastic gas can, and left.

She poured a bit into the Honda motor, then went back inside to get the hampers of soiled clothes. Mima looked up from her work at the sink.

"Back already?"

"Abner said we could have some of theirs."

"Oh. Alright then. But we can't forget to give it back."

Mary gathered the laundry, sorted it, filled the wringer washer with hot water, added laundry detergent and a small splash of Clorox before yanking on the rope of the motor. Rewarded with a quick purr, the washing machine was in gear and white sheets were thrown into the sudsy turbulence of the wringer washer.

She did enjoy this, washing the old way, dipping her hands into the hot water to lift the sheets and hold them up to the wringer, the rollers grabbing them and pushing them through, into the Downy-infused rinse water. Turning the wringer into position over the rinse water, she put them through again, into the clothes basket beneath, then to the clothesline after adding a second load into the swirling suds.

She thought of Aunt Lizzie's electric washer, powered by solar panels on the roof, a smooth, energy-efficient device for the laundry and the person doing it. A great change for housewives, many of them adding dryers, a true wonder, and a huge help on rainy days.

It was progress, indeed, and like everyone else, you had to move along with the time. Or so they said.

Did it matter?

There was no answer, no booming voice from the sky, no one to tell her if one was wrong and the other right.

To her father, all electric or alternative power was from the devil. All of it. The only blessed way to wash was with a gas-powered washing machine or, for those who could afford it, compressed air from a tank.

It was still on her mind when she hung the last load, swept the wet cement floor, and hung up the apron. She was hungry, but not willing to let Mima know, so she decided to have coffee with Arie, as Abner had suggested.

It was another beautiful spring day, the farm buildings gleaming white, the green fields and trees a gorgeous backdrop, black and white Holsteins dotting an especially pretty hillside. Mary's heart ached with the stunning view of this unspoiled land, so pure and so . . . there were no words to describe the emotion within her.

"Come in, Mary," was the answer to her timid knock.

It was Arie, in all her plump glory, resplendent in a purple cotton dress, her black apron pinned around her waist, her large white covering hiding most of her dark hair.

"I was hoping you'd show up," she said, smiling.

She looked deeply into Mary's eyes, then clucked like a mother hen.

"You haven't slept well."

"No, not really."

Her eyes went to the kitchen, the cluttered countertop, the baby on her stomach chewing on a toy. There was a variety of shoes, toys, food, and whatnot strewn across the floor. Mary tried not to show that she noticed the smudged windows, crooked blinds, a polyester cover sagging wearily from a worn-out couch.

She gave Arie a crooked smile, then sat gratefully as she put the kettle on. Her eyes traveled to the splattered kitchen window, the graying towel hanging crookedly across the door of the oven. She felt no judgment. Only the realization of how hard Arie's life must be. It was a wonder that any woman could even keep so many children alive.

Malinda watched her face.

"Excuse the mess, Mary. My oh. I'm sure you think this place is always the same. Sometimes it's half clean and in order for about five minutes after I do my Saturday cleaning," she laughed.

Mary waved a hand.

"I don't know how you do it."

"Do what? Be a wife and mother?"

"Yes. All of it."

"Why Mary, don't you know it's what God designed for us to be? It's a high calling, indeed. Is it fun? No, not always, of course not."

When the kettle whistled, she spooned two teaspoons of instant coffee into mugs with feed store labels printed on them and brought them to the table with a plastic pitcher of milk and the sugar bowl.

"Shoofly, Mary, we must have shoofly. Nothing to chase away the blues like a good shoofly."

Arie brought over the crumb-topped pie and two plates, serving Mary a good-sized slice and the same for herself. She took a spoonful and dipped it in her coffee, the very best way to eat shoofly.

They talked then, really talked. Mary told her of Abner's accusations, the kittens, her father, and her sleepless night. Malinda listened, her eyes narrowed at times, but mostly expressing compassion, or consternation.

Finally, she sighed.

"*Ach*, Mary. I often feel sorry for you. I imagine your life is so unsettled. Shuffled back and forth between here and Lancaster, with Dat's voice ringing in your ears. I just wish it wouldn't be this way."

"But it is."

"You left the second time when they didn't accept that John King, yes?"

"Yes. That wasn't right. It still isn't."

"I agree. Dat is harsh. I often feel if he could only find a middle road with you, it wouldn't have to be this way. With Abner, too. He is my husband, but between us, he's far too much like his father. I try to help along at times, but it's hard. You see, Mary, life isn't perfect, and I feel a lot of your unrest comes from living outside the boundaries your parents set for you."

"But the boundaries were unreasonable," Mary burst out.

"Were they? Or were you ruled by rebellion?"

"Arie, I'm not like the rest of you. I'm not. I can't stand to live with all these restrictions, all this clinging to trivial matters of the *ordnung*. I simply don't see it like you all do."

"You don't have to," Malinda said, quite unexpectedly.

"What?"

"We can't help who we are, and it's true, you obviously are quite different from the rest of us. If your heart isn't rebellious and you're simply being who God made you to be, why do you feel so unsettled?"

"It's all Dat's fault. He thinks I'm on the wrong path, makes up all these dire threats about hell and all the suffering and all kinds of heart-stopping fearful things that will happen to me if I don't repent. Repent from what?"

Malinda said nothing, her gaze never leaving Mary's tortured one. Finally, she raised both eyebrows, shook her head, and said, "I suppose that's the question. From what? I often try to tell Abner that God gives each of us different convictions. Each of us should be allowed to live as God calls us to. It is our Christian right, and our freedom in Christ. If we truly are new creatures by the blood of Christ, the Spirit will guide us. But Mary, the Holy Spirit will never go against the Bible, and the Bible is clear about honoring your father and mother."

Suspicious, Mary eyed her sharply.

"And therein lies the problem. To honor my father, I have to give up every ounce of the freedom you're talking about. Does God really expect me to sell my business, move home permanently, and be at my father's beck and call until some man—one Dat thinks is suitable, mind you—asks me to marry him, just so I can be my husband's servant?"

"I don't know the answer to that."

The baby rolled around on her back and began to tug at the couch cover and make short unhappy sounds. The front door opened and Benuel appeared, followed closely by Amos.

Mary smiled at the boys, asked how the kittens were doing this morning, and was met with bright smiles.

She watched Malinda scoop up the baby, open her dress, and fling a worn out yellowed cloth diaper over her shoulder as she fed her, rocking gently, her forehead furrowed in thought.

"Life doesn't have to be complicated, Mary. We can have peace by giving our will to God's will."

Mary shook one shoulder and turned her head.

"It sure would be easier if I knew what God's will for me was."

HER FATHER'S RECUPERATION was a slow painful process, but after three long weeks, Mima announced the good news. Mary could go home in a week, as long as he could get out of bed and walk on his own.

But getting out of bed proved to be no simple task for Amos. Ill-prepared for the scenes that followed, Mary lost her temper more than once, which did nothing to endear her to either parent.

Her father regularly told Mary she lacked virtue, especially when it came to patience. Mary noticed that Mima lacked patience too, though she clamped her tongue between her teeth to keep her frustration from escaping her lips. She couldn't hide her sour looks and an upset stomach on most days, though. The Maalox bottle at her elbow, she ate cracker soup and poached eggs, no doubt thinking fondly of her days as a single maid.

And Mary's father grunted and groaned, gasped and heaved as he inched himself closer to getting off the bed. Mary couldn't help but feel like he was intentionally prolonging the process. Grown children followed by hordes of little ones came to visit, upsetting Mima with muddy shoe soles and spilled drinks, crumbs and crushed pretzels. Mary's presence in the house was met with a mixture of suspicion, outright shunning, and occasionally a display of acceptance. A few went so far as to tell her how appreciated she was, helping out with Dat, saying if she hadn't done this, where would they be?

A neighbor told her she'd received a message from her Aunt Lizzie at the neighborhood phone shanty. Mary told Mima she'd be back and left quickly, before her father started asking questions. Aunt Lizzie said the bakery was falling apart without her. One of the girls messed up the ingredient order and now they had too many eggs and no flour. They had to buy flour from the local grocery store, which was much more expensive, and there wasn't enough room in the refrigerator for all the eggs. The main oven was having some issues and they couldn't get in touch with a repair person. The customers kept saying the cinnamon rolls weren't as good as usual. Could she please return as soon as humanly possible?

Walking back from the telephone shanty through a canopy of trees like a green lace curtain above her head, bluebells in the thick grass beside the road, the air clean and sharp and pure, the thought of the bakery suddenly filled Mary with dread. The cement sidewalks, the buildings stacked like Lego bricks, the constantly moving traffic and smelly exhaust. The never-ending round of hard work and dedication . . . to what, exactly?

The projected time of departure came and went, with her father refusing the walker or the wheelchair. Mima tried to gently prod him into making more of an effort, but she backed off when he gave her a stern look and then launched into a monologue about how much pain he was in and how it was Mima and Mary's duty to bear with him as long as it took. It was Mary who decided enough was enough and told him flat out she was going home. If he wanted to get out of bed, he would. If not, he could stay there, but he'd have to figure out how to change his own bedpan.

He rained down Bible verses about Jezebel and every manner of wrongdoing pertaining to women who were not in subordination to men, and the spiritual harlotry they gave themselves to. Mary tried her best to ignore him and exchanged looks with Mima, a silent agreement forming between them. Mary stood by with the walker while Mima helped him get dressed. She watched as she gently guided his legs, then adjusted his feet, then pulled him to a standing position. His face turned white, then red as he bellowed his discomfort, blaming Mary for misleading Mima to stand against him.

But he grabbed the walker on either side, shuffled his long stock-inged feet, and moved across the floor, alternately sighing and threatening that he would fall at any moment.

"If you fall, we'll call 911," Mary said calmly, which caused dollar signs to flash in from of his eyes and he stopped mentioning it.

Finally, at long last, he was somewhat mobile, and Mary could go home. But on the last evening, when the sun was setting behind the mountains, the lawn was freshly mowed, the garden a picture of perfection, and the air infused with the perfume from flowering fruit trees, she knew she would not return as the same driven person she had been before. She stood for a long moment by the front steps and listened to the cows ruminating sounds from the pasture, the swish of their tails, the soft, golden light filling her soul. She had to admit to herself that she did not want to return at all.

Her father sat in his reclining chair, his long greasy hair newly washed and combed, his face clean shaven, a somber look in his hooded eyes.

"Mary."

"Yes?"

"Come sit by me before you leave."

She was not afraid, neither was she comfortable, but she obeyed.

"I feel I have to make something right."

She waited, saying nothing.

"It bothers my good conscience that I said those things about the fellow named John King. I'm afraid I went too far that time. He is now an upstanding young man in the church, married to Sol Zook's Anna. I don't think a day goes by that I don't think of my mockery of him, and I know I must make this right. If you can forgive, I could rest in peace."

Mary wrestled with the harsh words of resentment rising to the surface but managed a weak "I will accept your apology."

"And you will forgive me?"

"I will."

"Thank you, Mary. Now my nights will be peaceful, although I still have my concerns about your soul. You were always so stubborn, and I'm afraid I didn't do enough to break that strong will."

Mary reeled with the battle to contain bitter words.

"Someday you must reveal the fruits of the born again. While you were here, I searched with a fair amount of patience but have not been able to detect any semblance of fruits of the Spirit."

"Dat, I'm sorry, but you are not God."

He slid his eyes sideways, then back again. Mary thought of a bobblehead with plastic eyes.

"I can't get past that small head covering you wear."

"This covering is perfectly acceptable where I live now, and there is no one offended by it. You must step out of the suffocating box you live in."

"Daughter, no sooner are those words out of your mouth then I know why you don't have a husband."

"I don't have a husband because you made sure I didn't get one."

"But you have forgiven me."

She said nothing.

"Well, at any rate, if I die, I want to go in peace with my family and my fellowmen, as I believe I can."

"Except for me."

"No, that's not really true. I have hope for your redemption."

Those were words not easily spoken, but it was more than she could hope to receive, so she left the home in New York that day with a softer heart and a small measure of peace. A hug and a sizable check from Mima was a true miracle, and one tugging at her heart as she rode in the back of the bus.

Why then, did tears run down her cheeks as the bus rolled through the rain, the gigantic wipers like thin arms waving the rain away?

She let her tears run unchecked. Only an occasional discreet blowing of her nose gave her away, her face turned toward the sodden landscape as the tires hissed on the interstate, sending sheets of water from beneath them.

She didn't know why she cried. She guessed it might be her father's confession, but knew, too, she needed those tears to dissolve her anxiety, the deep and lurching fear of the unknown, the lack of assurance she was on the right track. She felt her shoulders sag and all the fight leave her body, folded up like an air mattress after the air is released. She reclined her seat and closed her eyes, the sound of the wipers and the hiss of the rain beneath the tires reassuring.

She had a blissful thought just before sleep overtook her. Perhaps God had a hand in every single event in her life. Perhaps her father had fallen from the roof to allow her to make peace with her past, to be pushed into familiar surroundings and realize how much she loved New York. Or, at least the beauty of it. Not so much the people. But now she was headed home, her Lancaster home, and she knew before they hit the Pennsylvania line that she would be selling her bakery to the first available buyer.

CHAPTER 6

CHESTER NOLT SAT AT HIS FAVORITE TABLE AND CAST A SWEEPING glance across the room, looking for Mary, a twice weekly ritual taking up most of his thoughts, and a good portion of his heart.

He couldn't believe she'd gone home to New York. He'd felt God's leading, knew he needed plenty of patience and a smart strategy to win her for Christ, and eventually as his wife. He'd never felt so drawn to anyone before and felt he'd played his hand well that first evening. He knew better than to rush things, but he felt confident in their future together.

When he finally spied her emerging from the kitchen, her dress an olive green setting off a new freckled tan and her luxurious hair, the ample figure encased in a black apron, the gladness welled up and over into his dark eyes. Ah, his future wife. She came straight to see him, God be praised.

He stood up.

"Mary! Welcome home."

"Thank you."

"It's so good to see you. You're looking great."

"Thank you. What will you be having?"

He sat down hard, squinted his eyes, and gazed at the menu, seeing nothing. She waited, her gaze going around the room, her pen tapping impatience.

"Oh, just give me the usual."

She nodded. He watched her go. *Cool as a cucumber*, he thought. *Well, Mary. Two can play this game.*

One of the other girls brought his plate, which really hurt, but he was an expert at masquerade, so no one noticed. No one brought his coffee refill or noticed when he left, but he was not disheartened. He enjoyed a good challenge, and this would prove to be enjoyable, guaranteed.

But he chewed his lower lip as he drove away.

MARY FELL BACK into the usual routine as summer arrived, the heat forcing them to turn the air conditioning up, producing a whopping electric bill, but it was all part of being a business owner.

She told the girls of her plans to sell out, which was met with a mixture of wails and hard questions. She told them she had never been more certain of anything in her life, although she couldn't provide a detailed explanation. She just knew she wanted to move away from Lancaster to a place free of traffic and constant demands. Perhaps she'd go to Maine, or Rhode Island, or Utah, who knew?

The "For Sale" sign appeared in the window and Chester Nolt stopped, blinked, backed away, and blinked again. What was she thinking? This was a very bad business move, and she definitely needed sound financial advice. He asserted himself immediately, asked her to sit with him a while, and put forth every charm and persuasion he could think of.

She watched him with patient green eyes, saying very little as his monologue ran on and on.

"Are you in real estate?" she asked coolly, decidedly impatient now. She also decided she didn't like how the end of his nose twitched when he talked. Like a rabbit.

"Yes. Well, no. Sometimes," he answered.

"Are you or aren't you?"

"I advise people."

She picked at a crumb on her arm, clearly unimpressed. He felt her draw away from him, felt the need to pour it on.

"Look, Mary. You need a break to make up your mind. I'm afraid your decision has been too hasty. Why don't you accompany me to Maine when I go on business in July? Would you like that? Only for a few days of rest and relaxation. Have you ever been there?"

Ah. Interest sparked.

"No, I have not, though I would love to see it."

She bit her lower lip the way he loved, and he allowed himself to look a few seconds longer than was necessary. He had barely opened his arsenal of love weapons, and already she was falling for him . . . or at least falling in line with his plans, which would surely lead to her devotion in time.

"CHESTER THINKS I should not be selling the bakery," she told Karen, who nodded her head in agreement.

"You shouldn't."

"But I want to. I'm burned out. Food service is hard. It takes a lot out of you. And when I was in New York, there was so much nature, so much to love."

"But you left New York because you didn't like it there."

Mary said nothing. Karen was right, sort of. She had no idea why she swung back and forth like a swing, first being thrilled by the money, the bakery, her full life in Lancaster, then disliking all of that and longing for the quiet life back in New York. And there was Chester, her vow to free herself of his charms, his church, and now here she was, probably going to Maine with him. She was bogged down in a thick mire of indecision, still having no idea who she was and what she wanted from life.

Distracted, her thoughts constantly taken up about decisions having to be made, she made a pot of coffee without the coffee grounds in the filter, bungled orders, and tripped over the rug at the entry. She snapped at LeAnna for allowing the grill to overheat, was frustrated at the cinnamon rolls put on display without having risen properly.

That weekend she went to church with Aunt Lizzie and to the supper and singing with Anna and her brother. She remembered Steve

Riehl, but told herself she had just been getting desperate. He was only being nice to her, the sympathy a normal young man feels for an older unmarried girl of considerable girth.

It was a cloudy afternoon, with the low clouds and humid air before a rain, the kind of day when you know it's only a matter of time before the day turns darker and light raindrops begin to fall. The youth had set up a volleyball net as usual, with no thoughts for the weather, which made Mary grin. Those sixteen- and seventeen-year-olds thought of nothing but having a good time, fueled by youth and tons of adrenaline. Her grin turned to a wistful smile.

The rain began in earnest soon after, with girls squealing and dashing for the shop, which was already packed full of married couples with children, older women serving up huge portions of food, bending to lift massive roasters of casseroles and lasagna.

Mary stood against the wall with Anna, watching the churning sea of friends, acquaintances, and people she did not know. They were all dressed in Amish clothes, most of them born here in Lancaster County, having attended a one-room schoolhouse till eighth grade. The older ones had then gone on to begin a job somewhere, either helping at home, in shops, or at markets or restaurants.

The farms had dwindled to some extent, the economy playing havoc with conservative groups trying to make a living with horse-drawn farm equipment and the price of milk seesawing, plunging to record lows in past years, though those challenges had also bred innovation, with new ways of turning a profit, making cheese and yogurt, farming organically, bottling and distributing raw milk.

"Where there's a will, there's a way." The young farmer's motto.

"Our turn," Anna said, stepping forward.

Mary followed her, reached for a paper plate, plastic utensils. A hundred or more youth were quickly fed by lining tables on both sides with food so the youth could file along on either side, facing each other in two long rows as they filled their plates.

"Hello, Mary."

She looked up to find him looking straight into her eyes.

Yes, it was him. Steve Riehl. She went cold all over, mumbling a quick reply before moving on, telling herself to chill, stay calm. He meant nothing and who did she think she was, really? But her heart was pounding in her chest, her breath came in little gasps, and she could barely hide the shaking in her hands. Her thoughts ran out of control.

No, no, no. She couldn't allow herself to feel this way. She would avoid him at all costs. She was in no emotional state of mind to think about a relationship that would only turn sour in the end.

She pushed the hot food with her fork, a steaming mixture of vegetables and ground beef, a crisp lettuce salad, a nice serving of potato salad. But it all turned into tasteless mush by the time Anna was seated beside her. Lifting her eyebrows, Anna pointed at the uneaten food.

"Not hungry," Mary remarked, wishing away the dry mouth caused by the appearance of Steve Riehl.

"You are never not hungry," Anna said, laughing as she unwrapped the plastic utensils from the napkin encasing them.

They slid over on the bench to make room for two more girls, and Anna joined in the lively conversation the others were having. Mary bit her lip, poked the fork into the steaming casserole, and pretended to take a bite, which wasn't really that bad. She took another.

She was actually frightened when she heard masculine voices above her. She looked up to find none other than Steve Riehl with a friend, smiling down at them, asking if the space across from them was taken. Mary turned her eyes to her plate, but she'd already glimpsed the tanned face, white teeth, and long blond hair. He wasn't handsome. Not in the traditional sense. Quite rugged looking, with that hooked nose so prominent, his mouth a bit wide, a dark stubble on his cheeks and chin. Still single, but maybe in his thirties.

The young men jostled for space, then unwrapped their plastic forks and proceeded the inhaling of food. Except Steven, who buttered a roll slowly, his gaze never leaving Mary's face, her eyes still glued to her plate. No one seemed to notice, the conversation never missing a beat.

"So, Mary Glick, where have you been?" he asked quietly, thinking he'd never seen a head of hair quite in that color or abundance.

She was like a painting in his art history books. She was so different, so much more than anyone he'd ever seen. He had never really fallen deeply in love; he had come to think of himself as a lone wolf, perhaps, never to marry or be a father to children. He liked girls, always had, but never found one worth asking for a date.

All his friends were married. They all had homes of their own, children, responsibilities, mortgages, all the normal duties one took on when one chose to take a wife.

But Mary was different in a way he could not describe. His attraction to her was so out of the ordinary for him that he found doubting it easier. Perhaps he'd been lonely, more than usual, or harbored a secret longing of the heart without being aware of it. At any rate, he'd gone to the supper and singing for weeks and could find no trace of Mary. Now, here she was.

He had told his mother about Mary. His home was a sprawling white farmhouse across the macadam driveway of a white bank barn with a hip-roofed cow stable built out front, creating a T-shaped barn housing cows, heifers, work horses, mules, two ponies, two pygmy goats, and a loose flock of well-fed barn cats that came and went at their leisure. There were three dogs, a German shorthaired pointer, a black Labrador retriever, and a yapping little Yorkie who spared the larger dogs any annoyance. A henhouse was filled with Rhode Island Red chickens, and a flock of about a dozen sheep dotted the lower pasture.

The buildings weren't in the best condition, the paint graying on the south side of the barn, weeds growing along the woven wire fence. Posts zigged where they should have zagged, but it gave the bluebirds a nice tilt to come and go from the bluebird houses.

The ponies were oatmeal-colored Shetlands, fat and lazy, so spoiled the little girls had to lure them out of the barn with sugar cubes. Their mother was a sturdy build, wide across the hips, her dress straining at the snap buttons down her chest. She had a most pleasing face, round and comely, her eyes dancing with good humor, her laugh coming freely and often.

Steven was the oldest, with four siblings married and gone with families already started. Five sisters remained, school-aged or already with the youth, all blond, all active and well-adjusted children who had grown up in a noisy, happy home.

Steve's father was also a Steven. His mother had been so enamored of her firstborn with the few blond hairs on his otherwise bald head, she named him after her husband to keep the line of Steven Riehls moving right along. She loved her husband, loved the children, was a true example of glorious motherhood to those around her, and had absolutely no idea this was so. She waved away all praise, went right on with her life in her own humble way.

Yes, she hoped Steve would marry someday, but he didn't seem to be able to find a suitable girl. There was always the chance of finding someone outside the faith, which would be troubling, of course, but were the Amish really any better than their counterparts? No, indeed they were not, and she viewed parents of children who chose not to stay Amish with a great deal of mercy, as she viewed everyone around her. Compassion rode on Becky Riehl's shoulders like the cape of angels, and she found no excuse in the harsh judgment of others.

Her garden was a riot of overgrown tomato stalks, weedy rows of lima beans with a debilitating fungus turning the leaves brown, but somehow, she never got around to dusting them. The lawn was neatly mowed, but the edging was done sporadically as it seemed to be hard on her shoulders. She had to get down to the Gap Hardware next spring and purchase one of those newfangled weed eaters everyone was talking about.

The aging grandparents lived *ins onna end*, the Dutch way of describing the adjacent apartment built on to the original farmhouse. He was also called Stephen, but spelled in the old way. White hair circled the sides of his bald head, with a long white beard hiding most of his shirt front, still in good health in his late eighties.

His wife Lydia, like a beach ball with arms and legs, sat inside the enclosed porch with her embroidery, her little bird's eyes missing nothing, a small plastic dish of Cheez-its and a bottle of ginger ale at her elbow. She loved her salty snacks.

When Steve told his mother about Mary, she smiled inside for most of that week. Perhaps this was the one. But when he came home for weeks after, saying she simply hadn't shown up, she tut-tutted. She turned her disappointment over to God and was comforted. If it was meant to be, it would be.

MARY LOOKED UP to find his eyes on her face. She faltered, found her voice, and said she had been to New York. She desperately hoped he'd ask no more questions about New York. He must never know the reality of her home—Her father's long white feet with the yellowed, thickening toe nails, the calluses on his heels as thick as a horse's hooves, the scaly skin falling away from them. His greasy hair, his ruminations of fire and brimstone. Jemima and her simpering ways, the drowning of kittens. She had perhaps never felt so deeply ashamed of it all as she did in that moment.

"So that's your home?"

She hung her head, the "yes" barely above a whisper.

"I'm sure New York is beautiful. Is it in the Adirondacks?"

She looked up. "Yes. It is, actually. And I do love the landscape very much."

"So why are you here?"

She shrugged.

He raised an eyebrow.

"I'm going for dessert, Mary," Anna hissed. She pointed to Mary's plate. "Eat your food."

Mary elbowed her, but smiled slightly.

Steve was distracted then, one of his friends asking him a question, so further conversation was limited to group talk. Dessert was plentiful, the table piled with cakes and pies, puddings. And there was always the fruit salad, with its colorful display of sour strawberries and seedy kiwis, fresh pineapple unripe and sour. Fruit was not a food Mary found to be necessary, except very ripe apples or bananas. Most grapes made her cringe, but she supposed overweight people wouldn't be this size if they loved fruit salad. She wasn't going back to sit directly across from Steve with her plate loaded up with chocolate cake and pecan pie, either, so she cut a small square of Jell-O pudding, pink and unappetizing.

He appeared again, his plate piled with cake, covered in vanilla pudding, a slice of pie and fruit salad. He sat down, smiled at her before digging in.

"Sorry we got cut off before. What brought you to this area? Anna mentioned a bakery, I think. Is that why you landed here?"

"Yes . . . I mean, no. Sort of."

Steve noticed her discomfort. "Sorry, I don't mean to pry."

"No, it's okay. Sorry. I like Lancaster. Really."

He laughed lightly. "You sound like you're trying to convince yourself."

"Maybe I am. Sometimes I miss the quiet beauty of New York. I just . . . well, I don't always feel like I fit in there."

"Your parents there?"

"My father and stepmother."

"Your mother passed?"

"Yes. She had cancer."

"I'm sorry for your loss."

Mary nodded.

How could she tell him it was a mercy her mother no longer lived ruled by her father's iron fist? How could she ever allow him to see the dreadful tightfisted existence of those who lived in Pinedale?

Or was her mother happy, willing to allow the stringent rules of their community to direct her life?

Steve watched the shadows cross Mary's face, watched the dark turbulence in her eyes, until she drew the curtain of her long lashes.

She was a mystery, but he was more sure than ever that she was a woman worth getting to know.

ON MONDAY MORNING, Chester Nolt was one of the first to arrive at the bakery, wearing pressed jeans and a sky blue polo shirt, his hair freshly combed, his round boyish face tanned and healthy. He greeted Mary happily, and she responded with warmth. His heart leaped in his chest.

He asked her to sit opposite, and she waved a hand before returning with a cup of coffee and a caramel frosted cinnamon roll.

He raised his eyebrows, his warm brown eyes as smooth and restful as new honey.

She thought of the trip to Maine in the middle of summer, and the idea of it created a sparkling light, a fizz of excitement in her stomach. Oh, the lure of fresh new horizons, new experiences.

"Have you spent your weekend in happiness?" he asked.

Mary bristled.

"What kind of question is that?"

"Oh, nothing strange meant by it. Just curious," he countered.

"My weekend was good, if not happy every moment."

He knew she needed to become a born again Christian, needed a closer walk with God, according to Scripture, and if he could point out her lack of inner peace, it would be a good start. It was only through being born again that she'd find true peace.

"Are you ready for your trip to Maine?" Mary asked.

"Of course. Are you coming?"

She batted her lashes, allowed her eagerness to sparkle from her eyes, not realizing that she was, in effect, flirting. "I'm thinking about it."

He reached across the table, placed a large hand on hers.

"Mary, please do. I have been praying you would say yes."

She looked around, removed her hand.

"Remember, we're only friends," Mary said firmly. "Nothing more. I'd love to see Maine, but I don't want to give you the wrong idea about . . . about us."

"I promise to honor this, Mary."

"Okay, then I'll go."

He could barely keep from hopping, skipping, clicking his heels, and throwing his hat. He went to his job fairly bursting with success, confident the Lord was on his side.

MARY TOLD AUNT Lizzie of her plans, which were met with a frown, a worried pucker between her eyebrows, and an urge to discuss every detail.

"I don't believe it for a second. A man that age? He's looking for something."

"No, he's not."

"Yes, Mary, he is."

"You don't know him at all."

"I know his parents."

"So?"

"They don't live far from here. The salt of the earth. One of those saintly Mennonite couples I admire so much. You know they've lived a long, happy life together. It shows in their faces."

"Faces are like an open book, aren't they?"

"Many of them are, yes."

She thought of her mother, but could barely picture her face anymore. She had a pleasing quality about her, but quite often, a heaviness, a gray impenetrable cloud concealed the inner happiness that may or may not have been there. Her mother had often been a mystery, a complex whole made up of many layers. Rarely had there been a way to comprehend her true feelings.

"Mary," Aunt Lizzie said, quite unexpectedly. "I really think it would be best if you didn't go to Maine. It's questionable, spending all that time together. Alone, just the two of you."

But Mary wanted to go. She hesitated, then decided to tell her aunt about Steve Riehl, about how he'd sat with her, asked her questions. When she had finished, Aunt Lizzie sighed, a deep cleansing sigh of contentment.

"That's so sweet, Mary. He wants to know you better."

Mary's voice took on a note of panic.

"I can't. I can't risk it. You know after he finds out about my origins, he'll be repulsed, or somehow Dat will ruin things. I thought Jemima would change him, but she hasn't. The scales are tipping in my father's favor again, just the way they always do. I don't have the energy to start over again." She was rambling now, her panic mounting. "Do you know Dat sort of apologized to me for what happened with John King? But then, after I told him I'd forgive him, somehow he still made it out like everything was my fault. I just can't. I mean, part of me thinks it would be easier to leave the Amish completely, to accept excommunication and put everything behind me. Including Steve Riehl."

CHAPTER 7

THE DAY WAS BRASSY WITH HEAT, THE ROAD AHEAD SHIMMERING with it, the macadam softening beneath fast-moving tires. Mary was headed home in the front seat of the minivan, listening to the idle chatter of the bakery workers and wishing for the hundredth time she had chosen to stay home on Sunday evening.

The evening itself had been alive with a melancholy beauty, the kind of summer evening when the sound of katydids was a lilting ode to lovers everywhere, the grass dewy with promised coolness of night, the air vivid with countless fireflies.

And Steve had actually been bold enough to corner her down by the board fence at the edge of Joe Beiler's pasture, the volleyball lights and sounds dimming in the background. His pale shirt and blond hair, the height and width of him, the scent of his aftershave, his calm, relaxed manner, his words . . . all of it swirled in her mind.

He asked gentle questions, seemed to really want to know her. Eventually, they were seated on the ground, a line of dark trees behind them, the night sky still and luminous.

"You seem hesitant to speak of New York."

"I am."

"And why is that?"

She could not find a fitting answer, so she said nothing.

"Shall we change the subject?"

"We shall," she said, laughing lightly.

He laughed with her.

"You know, Mary, I would ask you out, but I have a pretty good feeling you'd turn me down. You seem a bit hesitant about a lot of things, not just New York. Are you even remotely interested in me?"

He touched her shoulder with his. She felt the heat of him, moved away quickly.

"I have nothing against you. I just have a lot of personal issues that should be sorted out first."

"First? Like, there's a chance for the future?"

"Don't make me answer that, okay?"

"Alright."

"For one, I'm not sure I want to stay Amish."

For a long moment, he was completely still. The regular thud of the volleyball, the heartbeat of the Amish youth's gathering, sounded through the night. Behind them, crickets chirped. Katydids trilled. A horn honked, then another as the low rumble of traffic moved on the highway.

"Can I ask why?"

"Oh, Steve. I don't want to drag you into my troubled life. It's too hard. You deserve better than me."

"Try me."

"You don't want to know. It's too complicated."

He waited quietly, his eyes telling her he could take it, whatever it was.

"Alright," she said, finally. "Where to start? I guess . . . well, I have a Mennonite friend. Nothing romantic at all. We're just friends. He asked me to accompany him on a business trip to Maine next week. And I'm going. I need to sort out truth from . . . I don't know, Steve. From what? I'm confused about many things, and as I get older, it only becomes harder."

"You're traveling to Maine, with a guy, alone? But there is nothing between you?" There was the slightest mockery—a hint of bitterness— in his voice.

"There isn't. Believe me."

"But you're thinking of leaving the Amish for him."

"Not *for* him."

"Then why?"

"I guess . . . I just haven't ever really felt like I belong. It's hard to explain." She looked down at her hands, then back to him, determined to avoid talking about her upbringing. "I've never been to Maine, and I think I need a change of scenery. It feels like a chance to get away and think things through."

She could hear the sound of his long exhale, then another. When he spoke again, it was in a level, well-modulated tone.

"Well then, if that's your choice, it's not my place to try to stop you. Will you be back to the singings?"

"I imagine so."

"What if you aren't? Do you have a phone number?"

She shook her head. "No phone."

"Surely there is a number where you can be reached."

"Just my aunt's."

"Okay . . . can I have her number? Or know where she lives? Mary, if you're willing, I'd feel so much better if I knew there was a way to be in touch."

"Alright. We live two houses up from Anna's quilt shop. As you're heading into town on 340."

He nodded, got to his feet, and offered both hands to help her up. She grasped his firmly and stood in a smooth, fluid motion. Quickly, she drew her hands away and held them behind her back.

"I guess this is goodbye, huh?" he said huskily, too quietly.

"I'm just visiting Maine, not moving there," she said, trying to lighten the mood.

"Still. May I kiss you goodbye?"

"No. Of course not." She turned and walked away as quickly as possible, her heart racing.

He put out a hand, called her name, but she had already reached a distance too close to the volleyball game for him to make a spectacle of himself trying to detain her.

THE BAKERY WAS slow, the heat like a thick yellow haze over the city. She still made freshly brewed tea poured over ice, fruit salads, and lettuce salads, but the baking had been reduced by half.

Two of the girls, Karen and LeAnna, were in Ocean City, Maryland. She chuckled, thinking of her father's damnation of that modern day Sodom and Gomorrah.

Why would their parents allow them to go? But why not? Likely the mothers had gone before them, that one week of being worldly. On vacation. But they were so young. She hoped the principles they had been taught would support their comings and goings. *Ach*, these wearying thoughts. She felt old.

THE MORNING OF their departure arrived. Chester picked her up at five in the morning, drew open the back of the SUV, and stashed her luggage alongside his.

The two pieces together only fed the fires of his ardor, and he smiled to himself, imagining the marriage ceremony, the car covered in streamers, well-wishers smiling and waving, and the honeymoon, the long-awaited fulfillment of his life.

They went through the drive-up at Starbucks. Mary said she'd take a chai latte with sweet cream foam, and he got a regular coffee. Mary handed him a five-dollar bill, but he pushed it away, his eyes searching for hers, without finding them.

She was being evasive, but he was in no rush. There would never be anyone else for him.

Mary was eager to see new places, if only for a few days. She was concerned about the bakery, but Aunt Lizzie was there, and business was at its lowest ebb in July. She glanced at Chester, noticed again how much she liked his profile.

They talked easily, his large hand relaxed on the wheel, his seat tilted back, so that he seemed to be lounging as he drove. The interior of the vehicle smelled of leather and air fresheners, the windows so clean there didn't seem to be glass at all.

She was impressed. She found herself imagining sharing a home together. He had the means of buying a beautiful house. She pictured a three-car garage with an opener, the clean cement on the floor, the feeling of parking the car, unhooking her seatbelt, her sandals hitting the floor, her lovely print dress swishing around her knees. Perhaps she wouldn't wear a covering. Who knew?

She'd carry her groceries through the door leading to the kitchen. White cabinets, black countertops, spotless hardwood. Expensive rugs. The world at her fingertips as she opened the computer to check her emails.

It all could be made possible with this man.

Thrilling to this envisioned life, she watched as the lights of Lancaster sped by. She knew she was getting ahead of herself, was vaguely aware that she had just told Steve that she had no romantic interest in Chester. But was there anything wrong with indulging her imagination?

"That chai any good?" he asked.

"Sure. You want a taste?"

"Oh, you don't want me to drink from your cup," he said shyly, which she found endearing.

"Here's a straw. Try it."

He did, then nodded his head. "Very good."

She smiled. He smiled back.

"I'm so glad you decided to come. I think we'll have a lovely time, you and I."

Why, just then, did her thoughts go to the long gravel driveway winding up the hill to the old homestead? The way she walked in the thick growth of weeds and grass to avoid the sharp stones hurting her feet, the dandelion stalks, so soft and hollow and waxy, catching between her toes.

Where had those moments gone?

On the wings of time, she guessed. Never to return. One childhood was what every single person received, and it was up to her to direct her good thoughts to the past. There had been good ones, but there had been many she did not care to remember.

The sheer terror of being caught in disobedience. The hand clamped on her arm, the propelling movement into the woodshed, where a real paddling was carried out, the voice of her father afterward, explaining God's displeasure, his abhorrence of anyone without honor to father or mother.

And she had trembled in real fear, for a while, until it became more important to soak herself on a hot day, setting up the sprinkling can with an attached hose, the cold water sending chills up her spine, the delight written all over her face. Discovery and impending punishment could not take away all of the pleasure, for sure.

She glanced over at Chester, the night sky giving way to streaks of light in the east. When the orange ball of heat rose on the horizon, she knew the day would be pulsing with high temperature and the sucking humidity taking away energy and stamina.

"You know it doesn't get hot in Maine. Not what we're used to. So if you brought your swimming suit, you might be disappointed."

"I didn't," she said, tight lipped.

He dropped the subject.

"We'll be going through New York, right?"

"Yes, we will. Would you like to stop at your parents' house?"

"No." Too quickly, too adamant.

She would be chased out of the Pinedale settlement by the heat of her father's disapproval. Threats and admonitions like hailstones.

No, she had no wish to be seen in this beautiful vehicle by her father or any of her siblings. She imagined their horror at her outfit. She had on a blue dress with a matching bib apron, one she'd worn years ago when she was young, fancy, and full of hope.

She would appear unclothed to her father, completely out of the *ordnung* and far from the realm of grace. A twitch began in one eyelid. She shifted positions in her seat, cleared her throat. The thoughts flooded into her head, like gashed watertight compartments.

Wailing and gnashing of teeth. They will cry for the mountains to fall on them, so great will be their fear, he had said.

She swallowed, her mouth drying as her heartbeat accelerated. She inhaled deeply, to steady herself.

Please, God, help me.

But God remained silent. She broke out in a sweat, smoothed the wet palms of her hands across her stomach. Wasn't she safe anywhere?

Chester reached down and turned on the radio. Country music drifted through the vehicle, sad lyrics about drinking beer and losing a girlfriend, only adding to the panic swiftly overtaking her.

Nausea rose in her throat.

"I . . . I need to . . . would you please pull over?"

He swiveled his head to look at her but quickly complied, bringing the vehicle to a stop. She hopped out, grasped the guardrail, and lowered herself over it as she heaved. She was aware of Chester standing by, before turning away and disappearing.

She stopped, breathed in, wiped her mouth with a crumpled tissue, and returned to her seat, laying her head back against the headrest, closing his eyes.

"I didn't realize you got carsick," Chester offered, in a slightly nasal tone of condescension.

"I'm not carsick."

"What is it then?"

"Don't worry about it. I'm alright."

They drove north on the interstate, the scenery lost to Mary, who was deeply ashamed of having deposited the chai into the weeds.

Chester turned to revive the former camaraderie, but it was lost, like a popped balloon. She had failed again. Failed miserably at keeping those torrential thoughts at bay. How could thoughts control body function? Why did this keep happening? She realized she hadn't been taking the organic apple cider vinegar recently.

Quickly, she grasped at this remedy, asking Chester to take her to the next supermarket. She thought of something she needed.

When she told him, he was completely put off. But he quickly recovered. Mary saw the way he drew the curtain on that stage, before opening them on another, the kind and caring demeanor he'd cultivated.

Locating a bottle of Bragg's organic vinegar, she purchased a plastic bottle of water, poured a bit out, and added what she guessed to be a teaspoon of vinegar. She shook the bottle, drained it quickly, then went back to Chester, who was watching something on his phone.

He turned to her.

"Feel better?"

"I do. Thank you for being kind."

He gave her a long look, full of meaning. Mary thought of a hungry hound dog, but quickly pushed the idea away. He had very soft, very expressive brown eyes, and she held the warmth with her own.

"I love being kind to you."

She said nothing, only turned her head to stare in the opposite direction.

Breakfast, however, was pleasant, with Chester being funny, expressive, entertaining. They ordered waffles and bacon, drank so much coffee they were bouncing in their seats, and Mary loved the way his eyes crinkled, actually folded into creases when he laughed.

They reached Maine in the evening and Mary had her first glimpse of the rocky New England coast. The air was salty and tangy. She took in the restless waves and screaming gulls, lobster boats and piers reaching out into the quiet inlets. The sky was as blue as the dress she wore, and Chester was quick to notice it.

They stood together at a landing, the red fishing shack below them, boats far out on the waves, riding up and down as the faint sound of the engine was heard.

Mary was thrilled, loved the wind tugging at her skirt, the unexpected scent of pine needles mixing with saltwater.

Chester gazed down at the tendrils of dark red hair and dreamt of a time in the future. She could be taught to be a bit more careful of her low upbringing, but that would all come later.

She was deeply troubled when he found a cheap motel, a blinking neon arrow on a rusted red sign with THE SILVER DOLLAR painted in black letters. There was only one room with two beds.

"No," she said firmly. "I refuse."

"But it's the only one left."

She held her head high and inquired at the desk, where they assured her there was, indeed, a room available. She paid for it herself. She pushed past him, retrieved her luggage, and bade him goodnight. Once in the room, she turned to lock the door securely before relaxing in a long-awaited shower.

The water was hot, the flow strong, so that was something. The room was reasonably clean. The smell of mold and disinfectant was strong, the carpet stained and unraveled, but if the beds were made up of clean sheets and fairly comfortable, she could sleep.

Why had he been so frugal, saving money by booking only one room, when clearly he had plenty of money? She switched on the TV, was becoming interested in a show about Alaskans, when there was a tentative knock on the door. Her heart leapt. She drew the covers up to her chin and rolled her eyes.

Again, the persistent knock.

She swung her legs out of bed and opened the door. A narrow strip of light from the parking lot fell over her face.

"Mary, I forgot to pack shampoo. May I borrow some?"

"Sure. I'll get it."

She closed the door, hurried to snatch it off the sink top, and brought it swiftly to the door, shoving it out the narrow, light-filled opening.

"May I see if your room is the same as mine? I thought you might want to have evening devotions together."

Very firmly, Mary told him they could have morning devotions in the dining area, and she was sure her room was just like his except there was only one bed.

He told her goodnight in a soft, warm voice edged with frost, and took his leave. Mary turned, sighed with relief, and returned to her show.

Her thoughts wandered back to Chester, though. She would have to be firm, as obviously romance was indeed heavy on his mind. She would have to keep clear boundaries. She thought of his reaction to her being sick, and now this . . . this intrusion on her privacy, coupled with the audacity of thinking she'd sleep in the same room with him. None of it was what she'd expected of him.

But she'd be slow to judge, quick to show compassion.

THE NEXT MORNING, he was very handsome in a black shirt and jeans, fresh from the shower, attentive, praising her punctual arrival, very soft-spoken and sincere with devotions as they sat together. He spoke in depth of grace and mercy, the flight of the soul after death, but nothing really clicked with Mary, who still viewed all spirituality with the same magnifying glass of fear and repression.

"Tell me, Mary, what do you think of the resurrection?"

She shrugged, averted her eyes.

"I don't know that much about Scripture," she said shortly.

"Don't you have a hunger and a thirst for the Word of God?"

"Well, yes, but it's hard to unravel. I mean, sometimes I feel as if it's a giant ball of yarn, and nothing will ever be clear."

"To those living in the flesh, spiritual matters are a joke."

"Now you sound exactly like my father."

"No, no. I didn't mean it that way."

And he knew he'd overstepped his bounds. He'd come on too strong last night, and now this. She was a babe, a lamb, and could only consume the milk of the Word, for now.

He took them through the McDonald's drive-through for breakfast sandwiches and then attended his meeting, leaving her at the local library in a town along the coast. He was very caring, telling her where the best restaurants were located, and saying he'd be back around three.

She wandered the stacks of books and thought through their short trip so far. What had he meant by coming to her room like that? She was wise enough to know it wasn't really about the shampoo. And what was all that stuff about grace and the resurrection?

She knew Jesus had died and rose on the third day. She also believed in grace if you were good enough to receive it. It wasn't handed out for free, like a soup kitchen, was it? Sometimes the Bible stuff could be worrisome, especially if you didn't understand it. She was well versed in the way of sin and repentance, but the rest was a little murky.

She felt very far away from Aunt Lizzie, and from her home in New York. And from her newfound friend, Steve.

Why now, in this stage of her life, were there two available suitors? She had to admit that Chester was indeed a suitor. He wasn't an option according to the rules of the Amish church, but if she were to leave the church, he would be.

Sometimes she imagined herself to be like a tennis ball, whacked back and forth on a court, never knowing the direction she would go. Unstable, wavering. Living her life according to her own terms, hurting family, disobeying parents, bounding back and forth.

She found a book about coastal birds and a comfortable chair. But it didn't hold her interest. She left the library and poked around some shops, got a turkey sandwich to eat, and sat on a bench overlooking the water. Then she went back to the shops, amazed at the local talent—rugs, pottery, intricate works of iron and silver.

She purchased a painting of sailboats on choppy water, and a pottery bowl, glazed with a black fish swimming on white water.

There was a glow to her cheeks now, her eyes sparkling as green as the water along the coast. The bell above the door tinkled as she entered another shop, one called "The Fiddler's Roof."

She forgot time as she purchased a small copper bowl, a perfect hand thrown pottery pitcher, and was contemplating the purchase of an outrageously expensive trivet to set on the stove in her aunt's kitchen.

She felt his presence, years of disobedience honing her senses, so she turned, her eyes wide, before he uttered a word.

"Here you are, finally. Do you know what time it is?"

"No, no. I'm sorry. Have I miscalculated?"

"Wildly. If you had a phone . . ."

Clearly displeased, he glared as she paid for her purchases, putting his weight from one foot to the other, sighing, rolling his eyes as she stepped past him.

"I was waiting for nearly an hour."

"I can only say I'm sorry again."

"Have you eaten?"

"Not since lunch. I suppose I was swept away by the excitement of seeing all the local art, things you can't purchase at home."

"We'll find a place to eat."

He drove them to Burger King. Duly repentant, Mary did her best to get him into a better frame of mind, but after they'd eaten, he told her the meeting had not gone in the direction he'd hoped. The deals he'd been counting on were falling through, so the trip would be cut short. Mary was disappointed but saw the intense regret in his face and assured him it was quite alright to return the following day.

"No, we're starting home now. We'll go get our stuff and then drive all night."

CHAPTER 8

MARY GAZED IN DISBELIEF. "BUT . . . I THOUGHT."

"It doesn't matter what you thought. We're going home."

"But. I was hoping to experience more of Maine. I . . ."

"Yes. I'm sure you were. And I apologize, but now my finances have taken a setback. For now."

"Of course."

She strained to absorb every moment of scenery, every glimpse of open water through fir trees, the sky as pristine and cloudless as a robin's egg. She caught glimpses of islands, boats, and always the gulls soaring on drafts of air only they recognized. She longed to experience the scent of saltwater again, the sea heaving its power against gravelly beaches and jutting rock. She wanted to turn the vehicle into the opposite direction and continue north, across the water to Canada, on into amazing lands of wilderness, where no one would ever find her. Where not one single person knew of her existence.

And the dream was born.

SHE TILTED HER seat back and closed her eyes as the last rays of sun disappeared across the land. Soft music came from the dash, the sound of fast-moving tires on macadam relaxing her. She glanced at Chester, his pleasing profile in sharp relief against the evening light.

She felt a pang of sympathy for how poorly the meeting had gone, but recognized the way in which he dealt with adversity might be a prediction of things to come.

There were memories of her father, the way he'd criticize her mother's cooking when the handle on the plow broke or a sick cow would need a veterinarian's care. How he kicked at the barn cats, sending them mewling into the air. He never gave up his own will alone, but instead devised ways of making those around him suffer as well.

"Are you asleep, Mary?"

It was a soft, gentle voice now.

"No. Not yet."

She turned her head to open her eyes and smile at him. He smiled back, then reached over and placed a hand on her knee. She quickly removed it, pressed the lever to straighten her seat, and slid her legs as far away as possible.

He chuckled. "Mary, Mary."

So this was the course she had to keep. No smile, no unintentional invitation, just a strict, caustic demeanor giving him no hope.

"Yes, Mary. I know. We are getting to know one another, and this I respect. Someday, perhaps, after you have searched the Scripture, you will be able to decipher God's will for your life. Being of considerable age for a young woman, has it ever occurred to you that there may not be a husband for you among the Amish, but that God will open new doors for you as time goes on?"

She had no answer, so she kept silent.

"I do admire your strength, Mary, but I know you will not have the courage to forge new trails by yourself. My role as your friend will be to help you see the way Jesus has for you. I know you are bound by chains of your own devising, the fear of sin and the lack of redemption, but here is where you will come to appreciate what I have to offer."

He flicked his turn signals on, then turned the wheel.

Mary watched as the vehicle bounced into a pothole on a gravel drive, past a rusted sign swinging from a green iron pole and up to a brown, single story building with grimy windows and broken, slatted blinds.

"Aunt Bertha's Eatery," Mary pronounced.

"These places are cheap, but I'll bet it has good food."

Mary smiled. The Silver Dollar, McDonald's, Burger King, and now Bertha's. She was beginning to wonder if he owned this vehicle at all.

A buzzer sounded when the door was pulled open, an insistent, blatting sound sending every diner's eyes in their direction. Mary inhaled and steadied herself as she was checked out from head to toe, grateful to be seated in a booth along the back wall.

The old formica top was worn to a colorless white where plates and elbows had been placed for years. A greasy plastic squirt bottle of ketchup was pushed against the wall next to a tower of jelly packets, salt and pepper shakers, the tops rusted and stained.

Mary felt the torn vinyl seat pinch the back of her thigh, shifted her weight to relieve it.

He pushed aside the roll of utensils in a napkin, clasped his hands together on the tabletop, then looked around for a waitress.

He cleared his throat.

"What's wrong, Mary?"

Her eyes went to his. "Why do you say that?"

He shrugged. "I thought you didn't look very happy. Just a thought."

"I'm fine."

"Do you like this place?"

She smiled. "We haven't eaten yet."

He drummed the tabletop with his fingertips.

"I'm going to miss you when we get home."

She raised her eyebrows.

The waitress arrived, a portly woman of considerable age, skin like leather, gray hair pulled into a limp ponytail, her white T-shirt stained with the day's work.

"What can I getcha?"

"We need menus," Chester said evenly.

Without a word, she pointed to the graying sign above the counter where sandwiches, soups, and fries were listed in navy blue letters. A splattering of white cardboard add-ons like chicken and waffles, hot roast beef sandwiches with fries, were taped everywhere.

Mary swallowed, could have eaten it all.

"Can we have a few minutes?" he asked.

She nodded and walked away, her backside swaying, the vast proportions moving up and down. Chester watched after her, his mouth giving away the disgust.

"She could have asked us about drinks."

Mary chose the fish sandwich and fries, added a bowl of chili and coffee. Chester ordered chicken and waffles, asking if there were free refills for drinks.

"Nope," the waitress growled.

He looked at Mary, shook his head. "See, they shouldn't have help like that. She shouldn't be allowed to work here."

"We can't be too quick to judge. We have no idea what her life is like."

She brought Mary's coffee, a Coke for Chester, then moved off with her lumbering steps, stopping to check the diner's progress at another table.

Mary wanted to remind Chester about his own choice to eat at this questionable establishment, but said nothing.

"So, tell me, Mary. What did you think of Maine?"

"I loved it, really, but I wasn't able to see much of it."

"Yes, of course not, as our time was cut short. But I'm sure you understand about my business matters calling me back home. You see, Mary, your life will always have moments of sorrow and disappointment. God has ordained it so, to make us better people, and He is testing us on how we react to these things."

Mary nodded.

Trials indeed. He had no idea the trials she'd been through. Did he understand what deep disappointment was?

"You see, we are the branches, and He is the vine, so if we stay rooted in Him, we won't grow wrong. Sometimes, though, he has to prune the vines, so that we can bear fruit."

When the waitress appeared carrying a huge tray of food, he stopped and scowled at the chipped white plate piled with an overcooked waffle and two limp pieces of breaded chicken that appeared rather soggy.

"What is this? It looks terrible."

She brought Mary's bowl of chili to a standstill, then placed both hands on the table, her face very near to Chester's, and growled. "Whaddaya expect for seven bucks?"

"I don't want this," he said, too loudly. "Take it back."

"Alright. But you ain't gittin' nothin' else."

"Fine. Come on, Mary. We're leaving."

Mary looked at Chester, then down at her food. She was hungry. Her food looked fine.

"I want to stay," she said quietly.

"Sorry. We're going."

The waitress stood as immovable as a stump, her eyes calm and willing to wait, her hands positioned on her stomach.

"May I have this to go?" Mary asked.

"Yep."

When she returned with containers, Chester stood up and started walking to the door. Mary gathered up her food, laid a twenty-dollar bill on the tabletop, and apologized to the waitress, telling her to keep the change.

The waitress watched Chester's retreating figure, shook her head, and said, "Thanks, hon."

Mary followed him out the door, winced as the buzzer erupted, then breathed deeply, glad to be outside, away from the humiliation.

They said nothing as they pulled away.

Ashamed of being the only one eating, Mary felt every ounce of her substantial figure. But her appetite took over and she opened the box and broke off a piece of fish, which proved to be quite good.

Chester snorted. "How can you eat that? That place was low class, disgusting."

"The rusted sign might've been a clue it wasn't a fine dining establishment." Mary didn't try to keep the sarcasm out of her voice.

"You can't read a book by its cover."

Mary opened her mouth, closed it again. What was the use?

"Will you share your fries?" he asked suddenly.

A stab of annoyance, but she said nothing, handed them over, and watched his large hands take half of them and stuff them into his mouth.

Mary wiped her mouth with a napkin and sighed a deep sigh, suddenly very tired and grateful to be going home. Chester was so proficient in all Bible matters, so well versed in spirituality, which left her feeling completely thrown off course by his actions. At her bakery she'd come across all kinds of customers with good and bad manners. But never, not once, had anyone displayed such boorish behavior. Sure, the waitress was a little rude, and his food didn't look great, but was that an excuse to be a jerk?

"Are you going to eat all that?" he asked, glancing in her direction and then back to the road.

"Yes, actually, I am. I'm hungry and it's good. If you want food, feel free to stop somewhere else."

After he'd shot his surprised look, he pulled off at the next exit and went through a Wendy's drive-through. He piled the console with his chicken sandwich, large fries, and Frosty, eating while he drove without offering anything to her. The food revived his spirits, and he became quite affable, entertaining her with stories of his childhood, his cousins, the countryside surrounding them. He urged her to speak of her own childhood, but she offered very little, knowing she'd already shared too much. She felt a calm clarity settling in as the hours of driving passed.

Yes, she had been lifted to new heights by the sound of singing that was alive with the Spirit, but the people were still just people, clothed in humanity, like Chester. If she left the Amish church and accepted excommunication, would the move be worth the heartache? Or would she just be immersed in a different group of broken, messed-up people? Yes, the grass shimmering in iridescent splendor just beyond the fence surrounding her was a beckoning scene, one tempting her daily. But what if, in all her starry-eyed expectation, it turned out to be just grass, the same dull shade of green growing on this side?

She listened half-heartedly as Chester explained the fall of man, the redemption for all humanity through the Blood of Christ. His voice droned on as he drove and her eyelids grew heavy. Everything he was saying she'd heard hundreds of times in church, from her father, from books, and Aunt Lizzie's Christian magazines. She knew all about the story of Jesus, but could she really help it if none of it stirred her heart?

Yes, she believed, but that wasn't enough. She had to be a good person before grace would touch her. It was all too hard, so she'd just live, doing her best, taking one day at a time.

She frightened Aunt Lizzie, unlocking the door so late at night, but after she'd clutched her housecoat to her chest, her heart slowed its pounding. She hugged her and told her how relieved she was, how happy to see her. She confessed she'd been a little afraid Mary would run off with Chester and not return. They both went to bed grateful, both rested deeply, and Mary woke to morning light.

It was Saturday and the girls could keep the bakery going till twelve and do the cleanup and lock up.

They did the *Samschdag eyavot*, that end of the week cleaning so prevalent in Amish homes everywhere. Mary swept and dusted her room before deciding to change the furniture from one spot to another, rearrange the wall art, sort and organize her books.

She threw out a pile of paperbacks, lugging garbage bags of them to the dumpster without guilt. They'd all been read and reread, torn and dogeared with brittle, yellowing pages, so she'd be fortunate to receive a quarter a piece for all of them. To pay a driver to take them to Goodwill was definitely stupid, she told herself.

A restlessness took her outside then, a need to do hard physical labor, to think about her ill-fated trip to Maine and its surprising limits where Chester was concerned. There had been no choices for her, only his, coupled with the questionable advances. She'd truly thought herself a liberal in so many ways, but traveling with Chester had brought out the conservative ways she hadn't known she still valued. And for all his spiritual talk, his actions didn't point to him being more Christ-like than anyone in her Amish circles. More and more, she was becoming convinced that leaving the Amish would not solve any of her problems.

She puttered in flowerbeds, dead-headed geraniums, pulled a few small weeds, but she felt boxed in and limited to a world where her lungs could not expand.

She sat in a patio chair, mopped her face with the hem of her apron, and decided something had to be done. She was unhappy, fenced in, watched, dissected, discussed, too old to be accountable to her widowed aunt, and it was time for a change.

But what? Where?

And there was Steve Riehl. Likely, she'd scared him away by mentioning the possibility of leaving the Amish. Well, too late now. She couldn't undo what she'd said. She watched the neighbor's fat yellow barn cat rub himself against the white fence, stretch, and yawn before walking through the bean rows. A sparrow twittered excitedly from the Rose of Sharon bush, watching out for the tender fledglings only a leap away from the feline killing machine.

She felt like doing something, anything. Maybe Lizzie would accompany her to the Tastee-Freez in Smoketown. She'd love a tall frosty root beer float, with that long-handled red spoon to scoop out the creamy vanilla ice cream. Or maybe she'd simply get a shower and lounge on the back porch with a bottle of Diet Pepsi poured over ice.

Yes, she'd do just that.

Fresh from her shower, her hair in a thick ponytail, she brought her drink to the low cast iron table and made herself comfortable on the padded lounge chair. Traffic rumbled by, but it was muted by the house between them, and she could barely hear the different sounds of ongoing traffic and cars.

She sipped her Pepsi, began one of the books she'd found on the lowest shelf, read a few pages, and stopped, looked at the cover, then turned to the inside flap and peered at the author.

She laid it aside, took up one of Lizzie's *Good Housekeeping* magazines, and flipped through it, mostly interested in the recipes, before flinging it aside.

It was too hot to enjoy anything, so she laid back, closed her eyes, and thought of leaving this place. She revisited the urge to keep going north from Maine. She felt so alive, just thinking about it.

Would it be wrong in the eyes of God to do some research, get into shape, and find some wilderness to hike through? Growing up, she'd always enjoyed hiking in the mountains surrounding the farm. She'd never gone much more than two miles, but that was something, wasn't it? It wasn't easy terrain, going straight up the mountain, through layers of leaves, sometimes the hillside so steep she had to pull herself up by grabbing saplings or tree branches. Sometimes her brother accompanied her, and sometimes Lydia or Becky.

Or she could go to Switzerland. Germany. Austria. She could go on a ship. The *Queen Elizabeth*. But not fly. Never fly. That was the rule. Flying was a modern form of transportation, one strictly forbidden.

She felt herself sinking into the place between sleep and consciousness, dreaming of places she could go.

"Hello. Hello?"

Her eyes flew open and she turned her head, then sat up too quickly. Self-conscious, her hands went to her dress, smoothing the skirt over her rounded stomach.

"I apologize, Mary."

Steve Riehl, in a short-sleeve shirt in a grayish hue, his sneakers matching, his hair disheveled by the evening breeze. Behind him, the sun had gone down, or had slid behind the small barn, leaving a golden glow across the small property.

She blinked, laughed gently.

"Nothing to worry about. I must have dozed off."

She looked around, pointed to a chair. "Sit down."

"How are you, Mary? How was your trip?"

"I'm doing great. My trip, not so much."

"And why was that?"

"His business meeting didn't go well. I don't really know the details, but he was concerned about finances and we came home after one night."

"That's too bad. I'm sorry to hear it."

"Don't be. I got to see some really nice scenery. The New England coast is quite something. Amazing, really."

"Good. Glad you got to see it."

Mary nodded.

"I wasn't doing anything this evening, and since you told me where you live, I thought I'd take a chance and swing by. I didn't really expect you to be home. But since I'm here, would you like to go out for ice cream?"

"I'm not dressed. And you don't have your buggy."

"Tied at the quilt shop."

"Oh. If you'll wait."

"Sure. Take your time."

She returned, her hair up and her covering pinned into place, a black apron tied around her waist. He looked at her, giving her a small smile, and they walked out the short drive and along the highway to his team.

The horse was the first thing she noticed. A black Friesian so big he filled the shafts and dwarfed the gray and black buggy.

His head was held high, his full mane rippling with the classic wavy hair of the breed.

"Wow," she breathed.

"Impressive, isn't he?"

"Oh my."

"His name's Knight. He's not mine. I train horses for others, and this one's not quite three years old. A stallion. He's probably worth thirty or forty thousand. Maybe more."

"How do you dare take him on the road?"

"He's insured."

"Huh."

He was loosening the reins as he spoke. He nodded at the buggy.

"If you don't mind, maybe I'll let you get in first and I'll hand the reins to you before I get in, okay?"

She nodded.

"You sure it's okay? If you're afraid, we can stable him and call a driver."

"No, if you think he's safe, I'm fine with it."

He pulled on both reins just beneath the horse's mouth, saying "Back, back. Come on, buddy. Back up."

For a long moment, Mary felt panic rising as the horse shook his head, trying to rid himself of the pressure below his bit, but Steve kept patiently working at the reverse he needed.

Finally, there was room to turn the wheels, allowing Steve a moment to hand her the reins, which she clasped quickly, and he followed up with a rapid hook of the neck rein, a few hurried steps, and a leap into the buggy, his body falling on hers as the horse went straight up, then righted himself and took a running jump forward. Mary stifled a scream of terror as they approached traffic, but Steve hauled back the reins and got him stopped at the very edge.

Of course, a line of cars awaited them, but evidently some training had taken place, the horse pawing the ground with his forefoot, quivering, his haunches lowered, preparing to leap the minute he felt the loosening of his reins.

Mary braced herself, her shoulder stiff with fear, her lower lip caught in her teeth, her eyes wide. Would they ever be able to pull out? On they came, a steady stream of Saturday night traffic. The horse hopped from one foot to another. His rump bounced up and down. He shook his head, jingling the snaps.

"Okay your way?" Steve asked.

"Yes, if we go now."

"Hang on," he shouted.

CHAPTER 9

THE HORSE LUNGED, THE BUGGY SWAYED, AND THEY CAREENED TO the left before he found his stride and moved into a glorious trot.

Mary was proud of the beautiful creature, proud to be riding behind a horse like this, receiving the stares of onlookers with a bright smile. What bliss, the parading of gorgeous horse flesh, a gleaming carriage and fancy harness.

What would her father say? He had his strong opinions of these modern-day horse sales and the deceptions of the devil, luring the plain people into a den of pride, a steaming cauldron of abhorrence.

His voice rang in her ears.

"You okay?" Steve asked, grinning at her.

"Sort of."

He laughed out loud, then really looked at her, his eyes holding appreciation and something else.

"You're pretty brave, Mary."

She smiled, and kept smiling. Somehow, she couldn't make the smile go away. It seemed as if when she tried, it only became wider, until she was laughing.

"Having fun?" he asked, looking over again.

"I could get used to this. Take some practice, though."

A red stop light loomed, its red eyes glaring. Her heart leapt.

"Ready for this?"

"Not sure I have a choice."

"Whup. Whoa, whoa there," he called out, drawing back on the reins. Mary envisioned the horse literally jumping on the back of a stopped vehicle, creating thousands of dollars worth of damage.

She braced herself for the worst, but to her surprise, the horse stood—not perfectly, but mostly he stayed in place.

She was relieved to turn at the small ice cream place, find the hitching rack under a spreading maple tree, and climb shakily off the buggy. She looked up into Steve's crinkling eyes and felt her knees turn weak.

"Not very many girls would ride behind a horse like that."

She shrugged and bit her lower lip, allowing her eyes to linger on his. *My, oh my.*

"Come on, Mary. Let's get some ice cream."

He held the door for her, stood quietly while they both looked at the big menu hanging on the wall behind the counter, then stepped back and allowed her to order. She had a tall frosty root beer with vanilla soft serve, and he ordered a full meal along with the largest banana split available. Then it was out under the soft yellow pole lights, the heady swarm of insects, and the moist, midsummer heat coming off the pavement.

"Pardon me, but I'm ravenous. I tend to have bad table manners when I'm this hungry."

She waved a hand and stayed quiet as he wolfed down one burger and half his fries. He offered them to her, but she felt self-conscious taking any.

He sat back. "Eat, Mary."

"I have all this," she said, gesturing to the tall glass.

"Nothing like fries and soft serve ice cream," he said, smiling. She smiled back, but didn't reach for his fries. "So, tell me more about your trip."

She was hesitant, but eventually the whole truth was told, except for her new feelings about staying with the Amish. For a long time, the subject was avoided, replaced by lighthearted banter, the night sky turning darker beyond the realm of electric lights. Occasionally, the sound of a horse trodding by caused the Friesian to lift his head, whinny, and become more restless. Mary voiced her fear of letting him be tied for a long time.

"That's all part of training him. You have to be a master."

"Yessir," Mary quipped.

He turned serious.

"Mary, can you tell me what you've decided?"

"About what?"

"The elephant in the room. In the parking lot, I mean."

She averted her eyes.

"You said you were thinking about leaving the Amish. I know the trip was cut short, but did you have time to think about it more?"

"Yes."

"And?"

"I don't think I'm leaving . . ."

"That's good to hear, but you don't sound very sure. Will you tell me why you were considering it?"

Mary hesitated. Steve spoke again.

"Mary, I like you. A lot. But I'm not leaving the Amish, and if you're wavering, I . . . I need to know that."

Mary's hand shook only a bit as she stirred the melting ice cream into the tepid root beer. A thousand thoughts boiled and hissed in her head, a worrisome chaos of questions without answers and only a weak faith to support the shaking platform on which she stood.

Finally, she opened her mouth and words began tumbling out.

"My family is way, way plain. Ultra-conservative, very strict. I'm the only one out of the eleven siblings to be . . . well, like this. Normal. I'm kind of an outcast, a black sheep. Being here in Lancaster, dressing like this, owning a bakery—all of it is against my father's wishes. So, I'm living in disobedience, and my father is quick to remind me of the dire consequences that await me. But when I look around at my family in Pinedale, I see no joy. Anytime there's anything slightly joyful, it gets labeled as "sin" and stomped out. Is that really the way God wants us to live? I'd almost be ashamed to take you home to New York. The

primitive way they live, the way they view the world, their interpreta-
tion of sin . . .

Now that she'd started, she found that she couldn't stop. "I'm kind
of a wreck, Steve. My stomach is a mess, and I can't seem to do anything about it. Oh, and I've got scars all over my shoulder, side, and
legs. An incident with wild dogs."

Steve's eyes went wide, but he didn't want to interrupt her.

"I almost died from a drug overdose once. It was a really dark time.
I'm clean now—haven't used drugs or alcohol or anything like that
since then."

She took a deep breath, daring to look into his eyes, which were
filled with concern, and yes, a little bit of shock. But surprisingly, she
could detect no judgment on his face.

"I suppose, to find real peace, I must go back home and succumb to
my upbringing, go live the kind of life my father wants of me."

"But the law has no power to bring peace."

"Of course it does. If I could give myself up and dress and live the
way he thinks I should, God would bless me with peace. I'm *ungehorsam*, living in unrepentant sin. And sin cannot get into Heaven. God
doesn't allow it."

Steve saw the road stretching before Mary, the road of salvation by
works, with no grace in sight. He blinked back tears of pity, as chills
raced up and down his spine. He had so many questions. Wild dogs? A
drug overdose? But they faded into the background.

*"I am the Way, the Truth, and Light. No man cometh to the father but
through Me."*

He heard the words like a song in his deepest recesses, the part of
him where the Spirit convened with the soul.

"No, you're right, Mary. Heaven will be free of sin."

"See? Everybody thinks I don't know anything about these Bible
things. I know a little."

"Yes, you do, Mary. We all know only a little."

She grasped at this straw with a certain desperation.

"You mean you don't understand it either? Like, how does Jesus dying make any real difference if we still have to keep all the rules?"

Steve realized she had never really accepted the free gift of salvation. In her own way, she was still bringing a sheep for the high priest to slaughter for her sins.

He felt a deep pity well up again and had to restrain himself from reaching out and putting a hand on hers.

She told him, then, about the singing in Chester's church, how close she'd felt to God, but actually . . .

And here she stopped and refused to say another word.

To press on would be futile, so after a few moments of quiet, he gently changed the subject, talking of his occupation as a builder, a side job of training horses, his five sisters who he adored. She listened, amazed that he wasn't running for the hills after all she'd shared. Was it possible he wasn't scared off by her past, by all her doubts and questions?

"Seriously, Mary, my sisters are the best. They think they're going to find a wife for me, by hook or by crook. It's so funny. You should see the girls they line up for me. A few of them are only sixteen or seventeen. It gets interesting."

"I bet. Well, better not tell them about me. I'm not available."

A silence fell, with only the jingle of harness rings and snaps, the slow-moving traffic and distant sound of voices. Insects whacked against pole lights and sizzled themselves to death.

"You're serious."

"I am. Listen, Steve. God's blessing cannot rest on the *ungehorsam*, which is what I am. If I did . . . uh . . . you know, go with you, it would only turn out badly. It always does."

He locked eyes with her, hoping she'd have a change of heart right then and there, but she did not. He sighed. "Okay, Mary, if that's how you feel, then I'll respect that. I won't pursue a dating relationship. But maybe you'll go for a ride with me sometimes, training horses. Just for the fun of having a companion, someone to talk to."

"That would be cool. As long as the horses aren't too crazy."

"They won't be. Knight is a little wild, but I trust him. I'd never ask you to do something I thought was actually dangerous."

"I know you wouldn't."

They rose together, put their paper products in the overflowing trash bin, and began the precarious work of getting in the buggy and safely into the line of traffic.

"Let's go the back way. It will be more relaxing, if farther."

"Oh yes. Good." Mary answered.

They had to be fast, alert, until she held the reins, the neck rope was on, and he was in the buggy, but the transition to a back alley that led to Harrison Road was by far a better choice. The night air had turned cooler, but both windows stayed open. Steve began to hum a tune, then whistle soft and low.

Mary turned to him. "Are you always happy?"

He nodded. "For the most part. Some things make me grouchy. Like my socks turned inside out and mismatched. Or coworkers. I'm not always pleasant with the younger ones on Monday."

"But you never get anxious? Like, totally unsure which direction you're headed?"

"Can't say I do."

He resumed his whistling, and when he found her eyes on his face, he gave her a reassuring look, a wide smile that soothed her more than she'd thought possible.

The countryside was bathed in moonlight, the incredible height of the cornfields like small forests. Farms dotted the rolling land, ribbons of hay fields accentuating the corn. Traffic moved in an unending river of lights on the main highway, but on country roads, it seemed like a different world.

She felt better than she had for quite some time. If only she could shake the feeling of impending catastrophe, of being in the wrong place, and the fear of being counted among the *ungehorsam*. As she watched the glossy back and rippling mane and tail in the headlights, the darkened countryside and the steady drone of buggy wheels, she did feel a certain sense of wonder at God's creation. He made this beautiful horse, made the rolling countryside and all its inhabitants. He knew the reaches of her heart and mind.

"Okay, Mary, here we are."

"Oh, don't drop me off at my house. It's not easy turning around in that small place."

"What did I tell you?"

She raised puzzled eyes.

"This is called training a horse. They have to learn to be obedient to their master."

"Like us."

He looked at her. "Well, not really. We have a choice, our own free will. Our conscience guides us, and there are a wide variety of consciences."

"I don't really get what that means."

"No? Well, we'll have lots to talk about on our next ride together. I look forward to it."

Mary smiled. She kept smiling as she stepped out of the buggy, and smiled as she wished him a good night.

SLEEP DID NOT come easily. She relived the evening, allowing herself the luxury of imagining a relationship with a happy ending, a marriage with children, and love. Whenever she thought along those lines, she thought of the Eli Allgyer family in Pinedale. The child with leukemia, little Elam. The house so full of love. She remembered the gleam on the countertops, the shine like stardust in an otherwise average house, the sense of beauty and fulfillment when she was in their presence.

This was a great mystery, how they could live in this austere community and were nothing like the rest.

Would little Elam grow up to be comfortable in his environment? She had no reason to believe he would not. He would be happy, living out his childhood, content in the faith of his parents.

She thought again of the Mennonite singing, the youthful faces rapturous with praise. Such peace. So much loveliness. She wanted to be a part of something she could not name.

She reached for her Bible, hesitated. For others, Bible reading was a comfort. For her, not so much.

It was so full of contradictions and threats, filled with arrows turned straight at her *ungehorsam* heart, pointing out all the ways she should be making improvements. Her Bible stayed unread because she could not face all that condemnation.

BUT THERE WAS a new week, a new Monday to fill her mind with pressing duties, to be physically active and listen to the bleary-eyed adventures of the bygone weekend. She did take an active interest in these pretty young girls' lives, but was always amazed at the fact they came from Amish homes. The difference between some of these girls and one brought up in homes called "worldly" was minimal indeed, but she always reminded herself she was not one to judge.

Her own upbringing had been austere, the boundaries her parents set for her absolutely suffocating, the walls surrounding her leaving barely enough space to breathe. The vast difference between these parents and her own was mind-boggling, the way they were both labeled "Old Order Amish." Cars parked at home, sons coming and going as they wished, young men free to make their own choices. Most of them eventually replaced their vehicle with a horse and buggy, became a member of the church, married their girlfriend, and lived a decent Christian life.

In New York, there would be zero tolerance for the disobedient sons, who would be asked to leave the home if he owned a vehicle or a driver's license, keeping the community pure of such worldly offense. Only on occasion would some young upstart attempt anything so brash, and usually, the disobedience was thwarted before a foothold had taken place, the praying mother and father convinced there was no hope for the soul of the rebellious, therefore instilling a deep and abiding fear of God into the wayward ones.

Caught in the crosshairs of the law, their conscience prodded into an uncomfortable crescent of damnation, the license and vehicle were confiscated, the horse and buggy brought into use, and peace was restored.

During her early teenage years, Mary moved in a gray area, never bad enough to receive the label of an outright lost soul, but not obeying, either. She didn't own a vehicle or do anything despicable. Now she was fancy in her dress and owned a business using electricity and was subject to people of the world every single day. And yes, she had never quite obliterated the rebellion and resentment taking up residence in her heart. Was she truly a lost soul now?

She listened to Karen's self-centered chatter, the sound of a siren's high undulating wail from the street breaking through.

She measured coffee into a filter, filled the pot, and poured it into the top, noticing the foggy glass pot. Someone was not washing the coffeepots the way she had taught them, a drop of Dawn dish detergent, the bottle brush used only for the glass.

"Girls," she called out.

Different levels of attention surrounded her, some wide-eyed stares, other suppressing a yawn.

"The coffeepots are looking greasy. A squirt of Dawn, a bit of hot water, and the only brush we have. Remember?"

Karen shrugged her shoulders, moved away, but LeAnna nodded.

Rose said, "Sorry."

"It's okay, we just have to remember," Mary said evenly.

The bell above the door tinkled, admitting Chester Nolt, looking extraordinary in a black suit, his hair gelled to perfection. Mary blinked, then moved across the dining room to his table.

"Good morning, Mary," he offered immediately.

"Good morning. Will it be the usual?"

He reached out to touch her hip. She stepped away, heat spreading across her face.

"Not so fast. I must tell you of the death of my beloved grandmother, a saint in her nineties. Ninety-three. She went home to be with her Lord on Friday, so the funeral is today. She was very close to my heart, and I'm in sorrow."

Mary looked into his brown eyes, saw the genuine grief, and felt a stab of sympathy.

"I'm sorry to hear it. You have my condolences."

"Yes, yes, of course, dear Mary."

There was an awkward silence, the "dear" swerving around recklessly, barely avoiding collision between them.

He pushed on. "How I would like to have you beside me at the funeral. I'm so alone for a man my age. You would be astounding in a black dress."

For a blinding instant, the need to belong, to be praised and accepted in a circle of good Christian people was so strong it was almost physical.

She longed to be sheltered, loved, consumed in a family with the bounds of understanding and sympathy. She smiled down into Chester's soft brown eyes, and thought she'd been harsh in her judgment of him. Everyone made mistakes, and he'd certainly had a disappointment about his occupation.

"Thank you for saying that, Chester. It is a compliment."

"I would so like for you to meet my parents."

"Maybe someday."

"Soon?"

"I don't know. Look, I must move on. Will you place your order?"

He looked impatient, then quickly rearranged his features to shine with complicity.

"I will wait forever, Mary."

She wrote down his order and turned, almost stepping on a tall, blond young man's shoes. Flustered, she looked up, the apology on her lips, to find herself staring into Steve Riehl's crinkling eyes, the white teeth in the deeply tanned face.

"I'm sorry, Mary."

He smiled as he reached out a hand to steady her. She swayed, consumed with a burst of gladness.

"Steve."

"Yes. I finally came to see your bakery. This is amazing."

"Thank you. Look, why don't you find a table? I have to run this order back. I'll get Rose to cover for me."

"Sounds good."

He looked around, then seated himself by a window. Clearly flustered, Mary slid the order into place, her breath coming in short puffs.

"Rose, would you cover for me? Section A? I . . . someone's here. I need to talk to him for a minute."

Her hands shook as she poured a mixture of coffee over ice, then joined him at the chosen table.

"You surprised me."

"I had a dentist appointment up the block, so I decided to stop. How is your day going?"

"It's Monday. Some tired girls."

"I guess. Oh well, we were young once."

Mary smiled, shook her head. "I was in New York, remember?"

He smiled back, met her eyes and continued to meet them. Everything faded away, and there were only the two of them sitting at this table in the golden light of the sun shining through the window, stardust and moonbeams mixing in with the wonderful kaleidoscope of rainbows and huge fluffy clouds. The only other awareness was the dull, thick thudding of her head, the soft, quick breaths escaping her body.

There was a space of golden silence as the spell was broken. She traced the marble pattern on the tabletop with her forefinger, and he gazed out the window before saying softly, "Mary."

She swallowed, admitted the fact she was thoroughly shaken.

"I'm glad to be here, always glad to be in your presence. Forgive me for saying that, knowing you don't want to hear it, but I am thoroughly impressed, for real. This little bakery is so unique, tucked into a row of old, well-preserved buildings. You must have a good business head on your shoulders. It's so much more than I imagined."

He looked around. "Whose decorating ideas?"

When she looked up from lowered lashes and said "Mine" with so much humility, almost a question to see if it was acceptable, he saw into the deepest recesses of her soul, the sight only the beginning of the patterned, mismatched puzzle of her being. He found himself teetering precariously on the edge of a cliff, knowing he would welcome hurling into space, a free fall of love, a flight of the senses.

But he had to stop, had to step back on safe ground, knowing one misstep would mean the loss of their friendship.

"You do have an eye for decorating. I like the way the antiques stand out against the white background. And these floors are the real deal, right?"

"We worked hard," she breathed, sipping her iced coffee.

A shadow fell across the table. The sound of a throat being cleared.

"Excuse me, Mary."

She looked up, to find herself pinned to the table by Chester's reproachful stare.

"Yes?"

"I expect you would accept my offer to come to dinner at my parents' house this Saturday evening, seeing as we were extremely close on our trip to Maine. I think our friendship has evolved to the point where we need to be in compliance with my parents' approval."

"But, Chester . . ."

"I'll pick you up around six."

And with no further conversation he moved away, the bell above the door tinkling its mocking little tone.

He saw her bite her lower lip, her brow furrowed as she struggled to contain her emotions. Instinctively, he stayed quiet as she breathed in, opened her mouth to speak, and thought better of it.

He waited.

"Steve, I'm . . . well, it's not what you think."

"Is that Chester?"

She nodded miserably, then burst out, "We weren't close."

He contained the viper of jealousy coiled in his chest, but Mary could see the hurt and confusion in his eyes.

CHAPTER 10

THE GIRLS AT THE BAKERY SCREECHED AND HOWLED AND TEASED unmercifully.

"He's cute!" Karen shouted. "For an old guy with long hair and no beard, he's a smasher!"

"Is he . . . I mean, are you dating?" Rose put in.

"No, no. Nothing like that. Shh. Someone will hear."

"Why was he here?"

"He didn't get anything to eat. He just left."

The truth was, Mary was sick. Sick at heart, with a sense of loss so deep it propelled her to the restroom where she sank down and put her face in her hands. Just like that, he'd gotten off his chair and left, telling her to have a good day and he'd see her around.

She could hardly accept what Chester had done. Why couldn't she have the nerve to stand up to him? She'd just been so caught off guard. Or was it God's leading?

She was thoroughly tired of Chester after Maine, but here he was grieving for his grandmother, which was sad and kind of sweet. And the truth was, she would love to meet his family. Why? She had no idea.

She thought of Steve, the way he'd complimented her on the bakery, noticing details Chester never would have. And that sensation of the prolonged gaze into each other's eyes. She'd never experienced it before. Well, whatever it was, she'd certainly lost it now, thanks to Chester, whose conniving approach was clearly aimed at getting rid of Steve.

If only she felt closer to God, she would ask Him to lead her in the right direction. But He never seemed to care, or even hear.

What had her father said? "The prayers of the unrighteous are hindered because of their evil deeds." With all her disobedience, how could she expect a plea for help to penetrate the ceiling? She felt the beginning of the heart palpitations, the nausea rising in her throat.

A thick, blinding darkness descended. The bathroom disappeared as her breathing accelerated. She sucked in much-needed air, breathed out. She got to her feet, gripped the edge of the sink as the light shone on her terrified face. She fought for control as wave after wave of panic threatened to control her. She had to get out of this confined space, but when she reached for the door, it seemed as if the handle was liquified.

She yanked at it, convinced she was losing her mind.

She stumbled, moved quickly out the back door, kicking two cardboard boxes out of her path. She pressed the emergency bar at the back door and lunged out on the sidewalk, stumbling around the building and away from everything she knew.

She had to get away, but where would she go?

As she walked, the sidewalk seemed to buckle, to split apart, leaving huge crevices for her to plunge into a wide abyss. She felt the roof of her mouth turn to sandpaper. She began to run, afraid of what the sidewalk would do, afraid of her own mind.

She was aware of the stares of passersby, aware of concerned expressions, and still she ran. The only thought was to get away. She came to a red light, the crosswalk sign with the red hand lit up. She had to stop. Her hands clenched, she leaned against an iron lamppost, her breath coming in shallow puffs.

She heard the sound of tires screeching, a door slamming, and footsteps.

Quickly, she turned, slipped into a narrow alleyway, and began to run.

"Mary! Stop!"

Wide-eyed, she turned to find Steve, his blond hair tousled in the wind.

"Leave me alone."

He reached her, reached out for her arm.

"Stop, Mary. What's wrong? What happened?"

She was breathing too hard to answer, but when she looked at the kindness in his eyes, she sank back against the brick wall of the alleyway and began to sob uncontrollably. She had no reserve, no shame, only the release of profound hysteria and an all-consuming sense of helplessness.

A sound of raw pity came from Steve's mouth, and he came close, grasped her heaving shoulders, then drew her into his strong arms.

He had never heard anyone cry this way. The weeping came in hoarse spurts, from a place so wounded she sounded almost like an animal.

He held her without speaking, feeling the tears soak through the thin fabric of his summer shirt as her face sagged against his chest.

Oh Mary, Mary, he thought. *What has caused you this much pain?* He felt a surge of protective anger. Had that Chester fellow done something to her?

He put his cheek to her hair, that abundant ripple of gorgeous red that set her apart from hundreds of others. It was soft and thick.

She drew a deep breath, then another. He provided a clean navy blue square of cloth with white paisley print. A men's handkerchief. Lifting her chin, he looked into her red, swollen eyes, the splotches of red on her freckled cheeks, applied the handkerchief and told her to blow.

She was shaking now, visibly trembling like a leaf in a storm, her eyes widened with fresh waves of terror.

"Just go, Steve. Leave me alone."

Her arms dropped away, but he stayed close.

"I can't do that."

"You have to," she choked, before sobs overtook her.

She bowed her head. Suddenly, she looked up, her expression pleading.

"I need help, Steve. Is there anyone who can help me?"

"There are lots of people who can help. But first, tell me what happened?"

She looked around.

"I don't know. It's this thing that happens to me . . ." She shook her head. "I need someone to help me."

"Okay. Here's the plan. First, we'll take you home."

"But the bakery . . ."

"We'll stop and tell your staff. They can handle things, right?"

"But I can't let my aunt find this out."

He took charge then, walking her back to the bakery, talking to the girls, giving directions to the driver, while Mary huddled into the back seat and told herself the whole thing was ridiculous, she'd be fine.

They reached her home, and he walked her to the door, then told a concerned Lizzie that Mary needed to rest, and he'd be back later in the evening.

"But I don't understand," Lizzie burst out, her eyes wide.

"I don't want to speak for her," Steve said kindly, "but I think a long nap is a good place to start."

Mary told Lizzie she just needed a cool shower, then she'd start the fan and try to rest a while before lunch. She wasn't feeling well.

"But you've been crying," Lizzie said, wringing her hands.

"I'll be fine."

It was only by the strength of her willpower that Mary got through the shower and into her room and dressed in a clean, light cotton dress.

She did deep breathing to calm herself, tried thinking fresh hopeful thoughts, but that was an impossibility at that moment. So she allowed the roiling, shouting, accusing voices to have their say.

She was condemned. Cast out. And here God was showing her the wrong ways in which she lived, by giving her two attractive men to choose from, both of them wrong. There were no right decisions for a soul living in disregard to a father's voice. Everywhere there was evil. The bakery was all wrong, the money tainted with *ungehorsamkeit*, paving the road to hell.

She had to get out of the bakery, out of the city, the Sodom and Gomorrah her father spoke of.

She would return to New York and give herself up completely this time, and so be blessed with a quiet conscience, free of sin. On and on, the ways of repentance and the planned aftermath rose and fell.

No one could help her but herself. She'd tell Steve she was going back to New York and this time it was to stay. Chester would have to be told, too.

Broken fragments of childhood scenes flitted through her mind, then. Her mother's discreet tears after her father berated her for buying a package of colorful Lifesavers for the boys. The sharp orange sparks as the plowshares hit one stone, then another, the plodding mules, and their slatted sides.

A great, overwhelming pity for those mules overtook her, and she began sobbing into her pillow. They'd been mistreated, underfed, and yet they lived in perfect obedience, plodding through the heat of summer and the ice of winter, hauling wood, her father's harsh shouts bringing them into subjection.

Even the mules were much better than she was.

She thought of her sisters' kindness to their mother, their faces lined with worry long before they should have known what it was. From the time they were five or six they felt anxious for their mother, a simple-hearted soul completely overridden by her husband as she slaved over a hot stove, a steaming wringer washer, a stony garden, and endless canning. Mary thought of the many ways they had all been punished, pounded into obedience by his forceful ways. And it had worked for her siblings. They had found the right path, set their feet on the journey he devised for them, and found peace.

Her mother told her the biggest mistake they'd made as parents was to allow her to have access to all those books. Books from the library, books for a dime from yard sales, books borrowed from classmates . . . they simply fed her fantasies, causing her to feel discontentment in the life she was meant to lead.

She'd read relentlessly, but that was not the reason she'd left. She left because she had to experience life away from the crushing dictatorship that was her father. Her siblings had all absorbed it like thirsty sea sponges, absorbed the sour verses and threats, believed the way he did, shunned every appearance of wrongdoing. And so they became blessed.

Her aunt knocked lightly.

"Yes?"

"Are you hungry? Can I bring you some lemonade?" she called softly.

"I'll be out soon."

She was alarmed at her own weakness, the way her legs did not want to support her. She told Lizzie she'd had a weak spell, and Steve had come to see the bakery, and she'd asked him to bring her home.

"Well, Mary. Was that the same Steve who took you on a ride with his team?"

"Yes, it's him."

"Is he . . . are you . . . ?"

"No, nothing going on."

"Oh, well."

She drank some fresh-squeezed lemonade but refused to eat. Her aunt watched her pinched features, her furtive, darting eyes, and thought there was more going on there than she'd say. She tried in her own gentle way to extract more knowledge of Mary's condition, but gave up after nothing was forthcoming.

When the shimmering heat gave way to the cool of evening, a horse and buggy was brought to a stop at the hitching rack, and Steve climbed down, tied his horse, and ran a hand through his hair before stepping up on the back porch where Mary sat on the glider with Lizzie. Lizzie got up, but he waved her back down.

"Don't leave."

Mary introduced them, and they greeted each other properly. Of course, Lizzie knew of his family, the way she knew everyone, so they were soon engrossed in a lively conversation of who's who, the way of most Amish folks originating and living in Lancaster County.

"Yes, yes," Aunt Lizzie kept saying. "Of course. Wasn't that Reuben's Shteff's Jonas? One of his brothers died in Mexico with stomach cancer. Had a *hesslich* time of it, bringing that body over the border. And yes, she believed his mother was a sister to Joonie Beiler's Hannah. Joonie from Gap, along the 30."

"So, Mary is your niece?"

"Yes, my brother Amos's daughter. Did you tell him, Mary?"

"I might have. I don't know."

It was wearisome, this endless circle of relatives and acquaintances, of whom Mary knew very little, so she did not contribute to the conversation. She watched a blue swallowtail butterfly on a delphinium and wondered how the monarchs were faring this year, until she heard Lizzie mention her father's name repeatedly.

"He was always like this. He never got along with any of us, as far as that goes. Caused terrible rifts in the family, before he took himself off to New York. Never amounted to a hill of beans, either."

Steve turned to Mary.

"You're very quiet."

Mary shrugged, toyed with the corner of her apron.

Lizzie got to her feet. "I said enough now. I'll let you two have your visit. Nice meeting you, Steve."

"Yes, you too, Lizzie."

They watched her walk across the patio and into the house.

Steve left his chair and came to sit beside her. He pushed the glider easily, and they rocked as the air turned into the sweet comfortable atmosphere of a summer evening.

He turned to look at her. "How do you feel?"

She shrugged. Her mouth trembled. She hated this vulnerability, this wanting to pour out her deepest, most ridiculous fears.

"Mary, you asked about help, so I've been doing research. I think for starters, you need to see a doctor. A medical doctor. I believe your problems might benefit from some medication, maybe counseling. I'm not an expert, but I'm sure there are ways to stop these attacks." He paused, wondering if he was being too pushy. "Of course, the choice is yours. I don't want to pressure you into anything."

She thought about what he was saying, but had already made up her mind. For a long moment, she was quiet, before looking into his eyes, which left him unsettled, the dilated pupils darkening the color.

"I'm going home to New York."

He felt as if the muscles of his sternum let loose, dropping his heart into his stomach.

He bent his head, trying to absorb the words.

"May I ask why?" he said soft and low.

"To find the blessing I lost when I moved here."

"And how did you lose a blessing?"

"That's what happens when you don't live your life according to your father's wishes."

And here it was, he realized. Here was the separation between his own will and that of the Spirit. He could make suggestions, but first, she might have to come to terms with her own preconceived notion of salvation.

"Will you see a doctor there, then?"

"I'll sell the bakery first. And yes. I'm open to seeing a doctor. Today was scary, Steve."

She began to talk, giving a vivid description of the bizarre sidewalks, the liquid door handle, and finally the absolute conviction she was losing her mind.

"I can't pray, Steve. God doesn't hear me on account of having lost the blessing."

"I don't understand what you mean by that, Mary. Lost a blessing? How did you lose it?"

"Disobedience. You can easily lose a blessing."

He shook his head, put his forearms on his knees. She looked at his blond hair, the wide back straining at his polo shirt, his black denim trousers with no suspenders.

"But where does your faith come in?" he asked.

"What is faith, Steve? What is it?"

"It's our personal belief that Jesus died for our sins, and that through him we are saved by the blood He shed. We can't earn salvation. Without God's grace, it's hopeless."

"I don't understand that. You mean we can go about our lives and do whatever we want and say we are saved by our faith? Do you even know how far off track you are?"

Almost, he started laughing. He sat up quickly and turned toward the wisteria growing across the railing to hide his smile.

"I'm not saying that."

And then Mary went on a long rant about the disobedience to Moses in the Old Testament, the children of Israel repeatedly suffering on account of it. Unknown to her, she repeated her father's dialogue, word for word.

Finally, she stopped.

"Or don't you agree? Say something."

"Sure, but that's only part of it. If we were all perfect, Jesus wouldn't have even needed to die for us."

She just stared at him. He sighed.

"Listen, I'd be happy to see you go to a doctor. You know, panic attacks can be from an imbalance of chemicals in your brain. There are medicines for that."

"The more I think about it, the more I think I'll be alright, now that I've made up my mind to go home. God knows my heart, and He'll give me back my blessing after I'm there, so the panic attacks will go away."

He had no idea how to counter that kind of thinking, so he didn't even try. "When you go home, will you write to me?"

She looked at him, sharply. "Why would I?"

"I don't want to lose you."

"You never found me."

"Good one," he said dryly, suddenly irritated.

"Are you mad now?"

"No, just disappointed. I had hoped you would come to see me as a potential boyfriend, suitor, eventual husband. But I guess your mind is made up."

She looked at him forlornly, but willed her heart not to give in. "I have to go back to New York. It's the only way. If I were to start a relationship with you, it would be cursed. God would never bless relationship born out of sin. But can we change the subject now? I want to tell you about my dream. Not a *dream* dream, the kind you have at night, but a dream about hiking alone in some great wilderness. Did you ever hear of Amish people doing that? Do you think it would be allowed?"

His eyes lit up. "I love hiking. In the wilderness, surrounded by nothing but trees—it's when I feel closest to God."

"So it's allowed?"

"Here in Lancaster? Absolutely. In Pinedale? I don't know."

"I'm going to do it, you know."

"*Ach*, Mary. You're not making sense. Moving back to your parents for total obedience, already planning something you're afraid they're going to forbid."

"What would you say, though, if I did that?"

"Could I go with you?"

"No, that wouldn't work. Then I'd depend on you. I'd need to do it by myself, find my own inner strength and wisdom, untangle a lot of dark thoughts. You know, find out who I really am."

She saw his worried eyes and looked away, fighting the urge to sink into his sweet gaze. She had to resist. She had to be disciplined, submit herself to the *ordnung*, finally learn to respect her father and live in submission. It was the only way to receive God's blessing and get past these debilitating panic attacks.

"Steve, I want to stay here. I really do. But it's like there's this constant voice in my head telling me I'm condemned. These episodes must be God in His mercy telling me to turn around, to repent, to obey . . . before it's too late. I've tried ignoring the voice, drowning the voice in drugs and alcohol . . . none of that worked. It just comes back, stronger than ever. I'm done."

Suddenly it hit her that she had also tried honoring the voice and returning home, only to have returned more confused than ever. But this time, she would do it right . . . whatever that meant.

Steve's voice cut through her thoughts. "But what if it's not God's voice condemning you? Mary, you might be struggling with a kind of mental illness. There is help available for that. You can get help and stay here."

"Not the right kind of help."

He was reluctant to leave, so they merely prolonged the evening by talking themselves into a circle. Steve found himself completely at sea. She had made up her mind and devised a plan, one that would undoubtedly fail. And he could do nothing to stop her.

MARY SOLD THE bakery to a young English couple, who were truly from England, who would turn it into a tearoom, complete with all kinds of fancy pastries and a wide variety of teas. Mary consoled many disappointed customers, had a tearful farewell party at Pizza Hut with the girls, a long explanatory talk with her aunt, who tried to talk her out of going back to New York and failed. When she told Chester Nolt she was leaving and why, he shouted redemptive verses at her until his face was quite red, then resorted to half-hearted apologies before taking his leave.

Before she sold the bakery, she searched online and found a home in Pinedale to purchase. It was a small house tucked on the side of a hill with a gravel drive winding through fir trees and across a small wooden bridge. Her eyes took on a new light, her cheeks bloomed with color as she wrote a letter to her father, letting him know of her decision.

A tender moment with Steve wrenched at her heart, and for that evening, she regretted her decision. She stayed in his embrace, told him she cared about him, of course she did, but this parting was a necessary part of her journey. He promised to visit, and she looked deeply into his kind and gentle eyes and found the beginning of her destiny.

All her siblings, every last one of them, heartily supported her decision. The winter had set in by the time she had settled on her property, but finally, she held the keys and buggies full of family members came by, each of them armed with soap and rags and buckets.

Her father was strangely aged and rickety, an old man with a cane that bore most of his weight. His long hair was white, his beard containing only flecks of gray, his eyes watery and without good vision.

He said he was glad she had made the decision to come home, he only hoped it was done with the proper attitude, and that her house would be in the proper *ordnung*. She smiled, said it would.

She painted and scrubbed, laughed and joked with her sisters, climbed the ridge behind the house with her adoring nieces and nephews, felt an old stifling burden lift, and knew she had come home, a true prodigal.

Her little house was brown with a newly shingled gray roof, a front porch, and a few outbuildings, one of which her brothers renovated into a small horse barn. Abner had a good brown Standardbred mare for her, and she'd purchase her own buggy soon. There were lilac bushes and untrimmed yews surrounding the porch, a stone chimney and two bedrooms, complete with an open floor plan and a kitchen island. Two low windows looked out across the front yard to the fir trees and the winding driveway. The floors were genuine oak, which she refinished for hours on her hands and knees, working alongside her sisters-in-law, who promised to bring patterns to make plain clothes. Mary slanted them a look which seemed to tell them to back off a bit. She was here, wasn't that enough? Did she really have to change her entire wardrobe? But she recognized the rebellion in her heart and conceded, saying yes, she'd need patterns.

The joy of being home yet away from her father's daily croaking admonitions was almost too much. She sang as she worked, she whistled and twirled her way through her days, then subscribed to the local paper and began circling "Help Wanted" ads, which were rather scarce, the way everyone did everything online these days.

Winter closed in, snow fell, and the temperatures dropped. Wind howled and shook her little dwelling. She stoked the wood fire, sat in her new glider rocker with the beige cushions, and waited for her blessing.

CHAPTER 11

Snow CONTINUED TO DRIFT AGAINST THE HOUSE BY THE FORCE OF the strong winter winds. Mary still sang as she browsed through cookbooks and used new mixing bowls and spoons, made cupcakes, and piped vanilla frosting on them the way they'd done at the bakery. Occasionally, she wandered into the living room to stand unseeing across the distant mountains covered in beautiful shades of white, gray, or blue. She pictured Steve, his tender eyes alight with his feelings, and wondered why he hadn't preached at her the way Chester had. She knew he hadn't agreed with her decision to go, but he'd been kind about it, and in the end, he really seemed to mean it when he held her in his arms, congratulated her on the new home, and said he hoped everything would work out exactly as it should.

A sense of well-being pervaded her cozy house, and she began to feel content in a way she hadn't thought possible. Now she had listened to her conscience, had pleased her father and Mima, and had created happiness in the family by returning to the fold. She had finally given herself up, and righteousness rested on her doorstep.

She laughed out loud at this, thinking how the doorstep was covered in about three feet of snow.

She loved everything about New York winters.

She made friends with her nearest neighbor, an aging woman named Jessie Byers and her husband Art. Jessie was the boss, a tall, thin stick of a woman matched by a tall, fat husband who wore his hair in a graying ponytail and owned three motorcycles. They were devout Christians who clasped hands at every meal to thank their Heavenly Father for His bounty, they put Mary to shame, the way she often found herself eating alone at her kitchen island without praying.

Jessie took Mary to town in her rattling white Jeep, slipped and slid up the driveway, turning the wheel furiously from left to right and back again, laughing uproariously as Mary hung on.

She found cleaning jobs for her, five- and six-hour jobs that made up to thirty dollars an hour, which made Mary feel better about the state of her bank account. She put a quilt in frame, receiving a dollar a yard from a quilt shop in Shermandale, Missouri. Her sisters made new coverings for her, which she flat out refused, saying she'd wear bigger ones but this was unnecessary. They had a good laugh about it, and Mary put on her larger covering, looked in the mirror, and told them she appeared to be very matronly.

But she loved her sisters, and it felt right to please them, so she sat down on her new glider rocker with the beige cushions and waited for her blessing.

Jessie came over on snowshoes and thumped and yelled on the front porch, giving Mary an awful jolt. Her heart beat so fast she began to suspect a panic attack. *Please God, no. Don't let it happen.*

Jessie wore a backpack containing a loaf of raisin bread and a jar of apple butter Art had made in the fall. Mary made a pot of coffee and ate four slices with apple butter and sharp cheese, listening to Jessie's stories of the exploits of her sons stationed in North Carolina, doing something for the military.

Mary listened halfheartedly, until Jessie began telling her about the pack of coyotes circling barns, slaughtering any animal they could get ahold of. The winter was exceptionally harsh, and they were ravenous, so she'd have to be cautious, going to feed her horse. Mary's thoughts flashed back to the wild dogs that had attacked her and she felt a shiver run through her body.

She visited her sisters, the brown mare taking her surefooted time over hills and through low places, whistling lightly under her breath as she absorbed the perfect beauty surrounding her. Her sister Lydia's house was depressing though, painted a sickly glossy green with torn plastic window blinds sagging across fingerprinted windows, African violets in every stage of life and death, potted in Bush's pork and bean tin cans without bothering to remove the wrapper. Dead stink bugs went belly up between them, and a confetti of black mouse droppings took up much of the shelf space as well. A faint odor of urine permeated the entire house, due to a plastic bucket of soiled cloth diapers soaking in water.

It was simply their way of life, Mary reasoned, tentatively washing her hands at the sink before joining her sisters at the kitchen table covered in faded oilcloth.

They drank a cheap brand of instant coffee laced with raw milk, the sugar bowl set in the middle, a plate of sugar cookies and one of peanut butter cookies, which had been pressed down with a potato masher the way their mother had always done. Mary couldn't help comparing the lavish brunches they enjoyed at Susan's house, or Ruthie's, but that was in a different world, a different time.

As conversation flowed, Mary followed the comings and goings of the community, largely unchanged from what she remembered of years ago. She couldn't bring herself to agree with their narrow-mindedness, at all, but she did a great job concealing her disapproval. She was heartened by the shared sense of humor, felt a great and homey belonging, and wondered if this was the promised blessing.

The sisters told her she was the talk of the community. Pinedale was alive with stories of her past, the ways in which she had rebelled, going so far that she even traveled in Amish boys' cars.

Mary's face flamed and her eyes stayed on the tabletop as waves of shame and regret washed over her. If only they knew everything. No, they couldn't absorb the awful truth without casting her out. At which point was she actually forgiven? When did the erasing of sin begin? She was here now, was doing all she could to be perfectly free of pride and fancy clothes, and she had finally pleased her father. Surely she had earned forgiveness.

Sometimes when she looked in the mirror, she could barely comprehend that this matronly person wearing a large covering and a dark-colored dress with a belt apron pinned around her waist was actually her. No bib apron, no pretty colors, and certainly no colorful sneakers. Her legs were covered in black stockings, with plain black shoes.

She couldn't say that she liked the image that she saw reflected back at her, but she did love her new home. And she truly loved New York, the way she always had.

Her sister Miriam looked her up and down.

"You're ashamed, *gel* Mary?" in a tone both kind and condescending.

"Yes," she answered meekly.

"Oh, course you are. Shame brings repentance, Mary, and that will not go unrewarded. We're just so glad you came to your senses."

"Yes," Lydia chimed in. "And all you need now is a chappie."

Mary smiled, but the smile was merely a drawing away of her lips from her teeth. *No, she thought. No, I can't go as far as that. Do I have to?* She could be content staying single, but she could not imagine submitting to a man who expected her to birth and raise a slew of children and stand by meekly as he beat them and drowned their kittens. She could not, *would not* do it.

The old familiar nausea rose, her heart pounded. She toyed with her coffee cup to distract herself. *I have done so much, I have been obedient. I have the blessing.* She repeated the words in her mind over and over, willing away the waves of nausea that continued to rise in her throat.

"Yes, Mary. You are at the age where no single young man of marrying age would ask you likely, so we're thinking along the line of widowers. What a blessing to ease the loneliness of a widower and take on his children. The poor lost little sheep. Yes indeed, God is calling you loudly to such a role."

They all nodded to one another meaningfully, while Mary's face turned pale and sickly. She reached over to lift a little niece to her lap and reached across the table for someone's used handkerchief—never napkins, paper towels, or Kleenex—to wipe the thick, drying mucus from the little girl's nose. A cold sensation spread across her lap, and she realized the child was soaked through her cloth diaper.

"She's wet, Annie," Mary said quietly.

"My bag's beside the couch. The one on the right."

Mary lifted the child and went to change the diaper, finding the bag and the graying, torn pre-folded diaper tucked inside. She felt pure revulsion. Couldn't they wash their diapers properly at least? Well, perhaps Annie did her best, taking after their weary mother, who barely managed to keep her head above water.

Why was she herself so different? Or would she simply not be able to give herself up to the lifestyle expected of her? She swallowed her panic by sheer force of will. Regaining her composure, she finished changing the child, then returned to the table.

"She's already being broken in," Annie laughed, which resulted in broad grins and knowing looks. Mary smiled, but it was a smile edged with sadness, an insecurity clouding her eyes.

Rachel watched the shadows chasing one another across her eyes, then sat up straight, thumped her marbled black coffee cup on the tabletop, and said they needed to stop teasing Mary. All eyes went to the sister who had the nerve to call all that attention to herself.

"Perhaps Mary has no longing to raise a brood of children for some needy man who doesn't care about her except as a help in raising his family and keeping his bed warm."

There were horrified gasps, then. A faint, "Rachel."

"I mean it. Mary should not be pushed into a situation in which too much is required of her."

Mary felt the lump in her throat, her nostrils burning as she struggled to retain tears of relief.

Approaching frightening uncharted territory, a silence hung thick and suffocating, all of them unwilling to tread on dangerous ground.

"Well, no matter," Lydia said brightly, steering the course away from the unspeakable. "Annie, did you bring those patterns?"

A hand in the air, slapped down on a substantial knee.

"*Ach*, I forgot. Should have written it on the back of my hand."

And the day was saved.

Driving home, Mary was lost in thought, the steady slap of the britchment coming down on the rounded haunches of the dependable brown mare relaxing her, erasing the nausea and moment of erratic heartbeat. She supposed it would take a while to settle into a substantial blessing, but at least she'd been able to keep from a full-blown panic attack. Was the nausea created by her own unwillingness to go where she didn't want to? Was her heart still too stubborn?

She needed to get her mind into a healthier state, but she had no idea how to go about it. She missed her mother on days like this, but had no idea what she would have told her, having lived her whole life on the perimeter of her mother's heart. Had she ever truly been close to her? Had any of the siblings?

A deep sense of sorrow settled across her shoulders, for the missed opportunities of having been close to her, to share her feelings, her disappointments at losing her friends to her father's disapproval.

Her mother had never known Mary's rage, had never seen the cold resentment mushrooming into rebellion, had stood by quietly and supported her husband's decisions. He had spoken and she had obeyed. It all boiled down to obedience, no matter the state of the heart.

She brought the reins down lightly and chirruped to the small brown mare as the winter sun slid lower in the afternoon sky. Shafts of light appeared between heaps of gray clouds, turning a forested ridge into an ethereal sight, the fir trees laden with golden snow. An eagle glided low above the trees, its wingspan of amazing proportions. She caught a glimpse of its snow-white head and yellow beak.

The wild creatures were hungry, the white-tailed deer reaching for soft bark, pawing the snow for a taste of frozen vegetation, the occasional cache of acorns. She thought of Jessie's warning about coyotes.

She'd have to purchase a gun, much as she disliked the idea. She'd ask her father the next time she visited. He'd know what kind of a sensible rifle or shotgun she might need.

As she turned up the snowy drive, the sight of her small brown house filled her with joy. She loved it. It was as amazing now as it had been when she signed the sheaf of papers at the settlement office.

The purchase of this house would not have been possible without the profit she made from the building she'd sold in Lancaster.

Guilt sometimes pervaded her days, cropping up like a swarm of hornets. Was it okay to make over a hundred thousand by purchasing and selling? Did God think her dishonest?

She stopped the horse by the small barn, stepped down, and flipped the reins out of the window, brought them together and slipped them through the silver ring, made a knot, and went to unfasten the britchment snap from the shaft. The mare lifted her head, her ears pricked forward. Mary sensed the movement behind the line of trees without actually seeing it. A bolt of fear shot through her.

Quickly, she went to the other side, loosened the harness from the shafts, and led her into the small barn. Skittish now, the horse had to be held firmly in check as she quickly loosened buckles and snaps, pulled the harness off her back and onto the steady hook provided for it. She'd need a *cha-shank*, the closet made for a harness, with doors and a latch, but it could wait till one of her brothers had time to build one. They'd done so much already.

"There you go, Honey Do," she said, putting a rounded scoop of horse feed in her trough. "I have to come up with a better name for you."

She brought a square of hay, placed it in the deeper part of the trough, then pushed aside the black forelock and smoothed the white star beneath it with her fingers.

"You are a honey, so Honey you will be," she said, smiling.

What a good thing, she thought. Self-sufficient. Stabling her own horse, pushing the buggy into its own area, closing the swinging door and latching it. She pushed away the fear of whatever wild animal she might have heard with was ecstatic with thoughts of her own accomplishments.

Not very many Amish girls my age have acquired what I have.

Her father's words rumbled in her mind and her pleasure melted away.

Hoffart. Hochmut. Selbscht lob. Every German word pertaining to pride and the love of material things slammed into her conscience.

She hung her head as she picked her way along the shoveled walkway. Her brown house seemed to reach out with open arms to envelop her into its embrace. As she stepped up on the wide front porch, she reached for the straw broom propped in the corner and swept away the accumulation of windblown snow. Movement caught her eye. A chill went up her spine. A thin graying dog, then another, stood at the line of trees, watching her.

A silent shriek tore at her throat. Suspended in time, she tried to move swiftly, but her feet seemed to be encased in cement.

She was literally unable to move as wave after wave of terror swept over her.

Another dog appeared, then another. The largest one took a step forward, its large ears like triangles. The key. Under the mat. She had to get the key. The problem was, she couldn't move. In her mind, she relived the horror of the feral dogs' attack, years ago. Torn and bleeding, she'd been hospitalized, the experience still vivid as she stood, trembling.

I must get the key. I must do it.

The leader of the pack took another step, then lowered its head and sniffed the ground before lifting its nose, testing the many scents in the crisp afternoon air.

With a hoarse cry, Mary flung herself to her knees and scrabbled wildly for the key. She located it with ice cold fingers, stiffened and clumsy. Her head spun. She reeled as she almost lost her balance, clinging to the doorknob as she searched for the keyhole.

Please, please.

It wouldn't fit. She glanced wildly over her shoulder. No, no. There were more than four. A pack. They were moving, closing in, so close they moved as one animal. The key was upside down. She turned it over. It seemed to stick, so she jiggled it, and was rewarded with the satisfying click of making contact with the necessary lock. She turned the key, felt it give way, and wrenched the doorknob. She fell through to the rug inside the door and swung it shut behind her, leaning against it as her teeth rattled in her jaw. Slowly, she went to the window and peered around the frame.

They'd reached the walkway, all six of them. Long-legged, lean, with hairy coats covering empty stomachs, their fur in matted bunches of brown and gray, their yellow eyes containing a desperation.

They snuffled close to the ground, lifted noses to inhale the foreign scents of leather and horse, then turned and loped down the drive, as if they had an appointment elsewhere.

Mary began to breathe normally, but the trembling stayed for a while longer. She hung up her coat, put her bonnet on the closet shelf. She needed some form of protection. She thought longingly of her telephone at Aunt Lizzie's. How nice it would be to call someone now, to tell them about her fright and hear a comforting voice on the other end.

Had they been wolves or coyotes? They seemed smaller than wolves but bigger than coyotes. She wished she could pull up pictures on the internet to compare.

Perhaps she should get a dog. This idea circled around her mind as she made a pot of soup, browning ground beef, cutting carrots and tomatoes, slicing cabbage. A dog would warn her of lurking predators and help scare them away. A big dog, an imposing presence when it was needed. But to have a real companion, she'd have to start with a puppy.

Puppies were trouble. They needed to be housebroken, they chewed furniture, they destroyed things, they whined and cried. Oh, she wasn't sure. And they shed. They smelled. She was a meticulous housekeeper, couldn't stand dirt and dust and hovering dog hair.

Amish people were not given to canine affection, especially not large dogs. No one kept big dogs in their homes, letting them snuggle in bed or curl up on the couch like another member of the family. English people loved their pets, treated them like children, but that wasn't the Amish way—at least, not in Pinedale.

Could she do it? What would her father say? He'd think it very odd, think her a spendthrift. Too English. "Keep the dog outside," he'd grumble. "He'll get used to the cold." But as much as she loved a tidy house, she also knew she couldn't let any animal suffer outside in the cold. Domestic dogs weren't bred to withstand the elements in the same way that wild dogs could.

As she threw in a handful of chopped tomatoes and stirred the contents of the pot, she breathed in the appetizing scent of simmering meat and vegetables, shivering involuntarily at the close call.

She really did need a good watchdog. Maybe in spring.

As she sat alone at her table with a steaming bowl of soup with saltine crackers, a small dish of applesauce, and two red beet eggs, she couldn't help but bow her head with an overwhelming gratitude.

God was indeed looking out for her, but she also needed a common-sense plan for the remainder of the winter months. She had to feed her horse, now christened Honey, and walk to the mailbox. The mail. She'd forgotten about the mail.

She could not go now, in the gathering dusk, with those creatures hanging out in the area. Wolves, coyotes, dogs, whatever.

She thought of a potential weapon. The broom? A rake? A bread knife?

Suddenly, she wished she could talk to Steve. He'd know what to do. Perhaps she needed a husband instead of a dog.

But no, she was here now. She was no longer a fancy young Lancaster girl with dreams of marrying someone like Steve. He would think her dowdy, old and large and plain, her thick wavy hair brought into stern rolls, flattened and tightened, her covering hiding most of its beauty.

For an unsettled moment, the question taunted her. Was this who she truly was? Deep inside, was she fulfilling her destiny by pleasing her family, giving up the hopes and dreams she would not allow herself to cherish?

She was glad she had never encouraged a dating relationship with Steve, so there would be no heartache this time, no bitter resentment against her father. Steve would find someone else, they always did.

But as the evening wore on, she became increasingly restless, and found herself pacing the living room, stopping occasionally to stare unseeingly out of the long windows into the dark night, thinking of sturdy walls and the roaming animals somewhere out there in the snow.

She almost felt sorry for them, their stomachs aching with hunger, their eyes desperate with it.

She searched the bookshelves, but could not find anything at all that stoked her interest. She picked up her Bible, thumbed the pages without actually reading anything, knowing she'd find no solace if she tried.

Bible reading was mostly for the Chester Nolts of this world, men with high IQs who could understood what it all meant. She'd be ashamed to tell anyone how she really felt, although Steve had been the one she'd been most honest with. He had not made fun of her, but simply didn't see things the same way.

She took a long, hot shower, fixed the fire for the night by adding a few heavy chunks of wood, turned out the light, and went to bed, shivering between the flannel sheets before warming slowly. The weight of the thick comforter felt wonderful, and she was becoming drowsy when she remembered to pray, sincerely thankful for the sturdy house, the safety of its four walls, and the little barn housing the horse, Honey.

SOMETIME AFTER SHE'D fallen asleep, the wind picked up, sending twigs and pinecones skittering across the frozen snow, bending the tips of fir trees like synchronized dancers. Smoke from the chimney rose and was hurled across the night sky. Across ridges and mountains, the deer curled tightly beneath giant oaks in patches of brush and beside fallen logs, the deep snow serving as walls of protection. The pack of coyotes roamed the hills till they fell in pockets of deep snow in ravines and hollows, put their noses below their hind legs, their thin tails wrapped around lean, hungry bodies, and tried to sleep.

In the morning, Mary, armed with the garden rake, her pale face and frightened eyes darting from right to left, slipped and slid on her way to the barn, returned safely, and made herself go to the mailbox, arriving there completely out of breath and absolutely terrified. She grabbed the few envelopes and, using her rake as a hiking pole, she moved as fast as possible up the slippery drive, her skirts whipping around her legs, her face numb as she approached the welcoming porch.

Thank you, Lord, for this, she thought.

A statement from the bank. A plea for money from St. Jude's Hospital. And an ordinary-looking white envelope with neat, block writing and no return address.

Her heart leaped? Could it be? Would he have written?

She went to the kitchen drawer for a paring knife, slit the top of the envelope, pulled out the pages, and quickly found the signature.

Aunt Lizzie. She sighed, steadied herself, and began to read, the disappointment sagging into a kitchen chair along with her.

CHAPTER 12

SHE WENT TO MRS. GRAHAM'S HALL CLOSET AND GOT OUT THE
vacuum cleaner, the floor mop, bucket, and two clean rags, one to
polish furniture and one for the bathroom. She sniffed, enjoying
the aroma of a toasting blueberry bagel. It was not her breakfast,
but belonged to the tall, thin woman named Gina, who lived in
this house in a wooded development for the middle- to upper-class
English people who lived lives of ease, or so it seemed to Mary. Heat
pumps created a constant, level temperature of seventy-two degrees,
light flooded rooms at the flip of a switch, warm garages housed late
model vehicles. No woodstove to coax into life, no ashes to take out,
no horse to feed or propane tank to change.

"So, how's it going for you out there by yourself, Mary?" Gina called
from the kitchen. Mary stopped halfway up the stairs and shrugged,
before realizing Gina couldn't see her. Feeling foolish, she called down,
"Good."

"I don't see how you can stand it."

A coffeemaker whirred, grinding coffee beans. Mary went her way,
lugging the cleaning tools step by step, not sure how to answer that
blunt observance.

She entered the bathroom, groaned inwardly. She picked up clothing, dropped them in the hamper, raked filthy towels off racks, wrung
out sodden washcloths and threw them in after the towels. She sprayed

the tub with cleaner, then the two washbasins, before starting on the enormous mirror with window cleaner.

Gina appeared in the mirror.

"You know, you need to get out more. You'll lose your mind out there in the sticks. I cannot imagine. Would you clean Erin's electric toothbrush? It looks as if it needs it."

Mary nodded to let her know she'd heard.

"I like it out there."

"But you don't have a telephone."

"I know."

What would she say about the coyotes, the wind of the previous night, the garden rake? She decided to keep it to herself.

"I just don't know how you do it."

"If you're not born and raised this way, you don't understand it, I guess."

"I guess. Would you move my nightstand and get the floor underneath real good? I dropped an earring back behind somewhere, and I don't want it sucked up. Oh, and when you get to the downstairs bathroom, would you do the tub? We had guests."

Mary nodded, caught her eye and smiled.

"Thanks. I'm leaving."

Gina never offered information about her comings and goings, never mentioned what time she'd return. She simply left, and Mary was on her own, which suited her just fine. Her mind wandered as she worked, going from room to room, admiring the fine furniture, changing sheets, making beds, polishing, dusting, sweeping, filling the house with the scent of Pledge furniture polish and Murphy's oil soap on the hardwood floors. Mary often thought of the downward turn of her status at the bakery, having been the owner, the boss, the manager, giving orders, not taking them. She had certainly become a faithful servant, bending and bowing, scraping the floor with humble "Yes, ma'am," "No, ma'am," "Anything you say, ma'am."

But it had been her choice, and her cleaner conscience was proof enough that it had been the right one. Although Aunt Lizzie's long, interesting letter, with news of the community, left Mary missing parts of her previous life. But she was no longer young, and all that was behind her now. When she caught her reflection in the mirror, she could barely comprehend this was really her. She appeared middle-aged, like a mother of at least six. Well-rounded, her gray belt apron pinned into place, a navy blue dress with plain sleeves, it appeared her life was basically over, as far as nice clothes and hope of a husband went. But she hummed and whistled as she worked, taking pride in rugs looking like new, polished floors and countertops, gleaming bathrooms and spotless appliances. She grabbed a few minutes to eat a granola bar from the stash below the coffee maker, drank a bottle of water, and continued.

Six hours later, she clutched two crisp one-hundred-dollar bills, lifted her tired feet into Gina's Infinity, and was whisked home to her little brown house.

"That lilac will have to go," she commented.

"I'll trim it next year," Mary said. "Thank you, Gina."

"Thank you. Three weeks?"

"Yes, that will be the fourteenth then."

"Bye."

Mary lifted a hand and watched as she turned around and moved down the snowy drive, carefully. She sighed, turned to let herself in the front door, and immediately put wood on the fire. The house was cold, the few red embers in a bed of ashes all that remained from the logs she'd put on that morning.

She sighed again. One job down, three to go later that week. Her days might not be full of excitement, but at least she hadn't had any full-blown panic attacks lately. She had proved her own resilience, was still proving it, but had to admit, a certain lethargy marked her existence. But, she reasoned, happiness was not as important as obedience.

On Sunday afternoon, she hitched up Honey, her level of anxiety keeping her moving swiftly, eyeing the garden rake at regular intervals.

She'd heard them a week ago, or had it only been a few days? A long drawn-out howl, followed by a chorus of jolting yips and barks. Jesse told her they weren't wolves, just a pack of starving coyotes, but it was best to stay on guard.

She traveled the distance of five or six miles to her father and Mima's house, Honey trotting along as if proud to be pulling the carriage, Mary keeping her eye out for coyotes. A warm lap robe kept her comfortable, gloves on her hands, and her black shawl and bonnet worn just the way her father approved, the bonnet large enough to cover all of her hair and part of her face.

She was greeted with genuine welcome, her father clapping his hat on his head as he thumped out the snowy walks to help her with the horse. He gripped her hand, his eyes filling with tears, as he told her how much he appreciated her coming to see them.

Yes, she knew he did, but what he really appreciated was her shawl and bonnet, the sturdy leather shoes and heavy black stockings.

She let her hand be crushed enthusiastically by an effusive Mima, smiled, and said yes, she'd take coffee with cream. Then she folded her shawl and put her bonnet on top, arranged her large covering, and allowed herself to enjoy the feeling of acceptance and belonging.

Yes, this time she was doing it the right way. She was an honor to her parents. She had repented, changed her ways, and therefore the blessings were flowing.

"Oh, Mary, you are a sight for sore eyes. So humble, so sweet of you to come for a surprise visit," Mima gushed.

Her father's voice was thick with emotion, his smile wide and genuine, his eyes wet with unshed tears.

"Ah Mary, I feel as if I have seen the promised land, and now I can rest in peace when I leave this world. Truly, God has answered our prayers, and we are not worthy of this blessing."

Mary bowed her head, receiving the benediction.

Mima cooked a pot of salted potatoes, fried ground beef, and made milk gravy, opened a jar of string beans and one of stewed tomatoes. She had prepared food for Sunday visitors, a bowl of vanilla pudding with a chocolate center, orange Jell-O with shredded carrots and crushed pineapple, an apple cake with walnut and caramel icing, plus a golden pumpkin pie with a brown top, baked to perfection. Good old-fashioned food, the dishes she remembered as a child when they visited Grusmommy Kinnich. Mary's father seemed to have morphed into a much better version of himself. He laughed, spoke, smiled, and made jokes.

God's goodness sat at his table in the form of his wayward daughter having returned into the fold, gloriously bedecked in the traditional shawl and bonnet.

Before she left, a shadow crossed his features, however, and he said although he was pleased beyond belief, he still felt he needed to be honest with her and extend a gentle reminder.

Mary arched her eyebrows. Her back stiffened, expecting a blow.

"They say you have white blinds in your house, Mary."

She nodded. "I do."

"And why, may I ask?"

Mary shrugged, felt cornered, betrayed.

"Our *ordnung* is green blinds at our windows. In the bedroom and bathroom, we have fabric, ruffled blinds, but only halfway up the frame of the window, for privacy. They say you have fancy ones in your bedroom, which does not sit well with me at all. It shows you still have much room for improvement, although, as you so well know, I see the good changes you have made, and I am so grateful."

Bile rose in her throat. Her face turned crimson with irritation. She opened her mouth, but knew the release of bilious words would only prove regrettable.

Her ears burned with fury.

"Mary."

Mima's hand was placed on hers.

"Mary. Dat is only looking out for your soul."

All caution was thrown away. Without a thought in her head, a volley of words burst forth.

"So if I have green blinds, I'll be good enough to get to Heaven, but if they're white, I won't? Dat, I come here looking like my grandmother,

and still, still I'm not good enough. I will never be good enough for
you. Never."

Shouting now, spittle flew from her mouth. Every red hair on her
head seemed to bristle, and her green eyes blazed.

"Now Mary. There is no reason for you to become angry. Yes, you
have made a great change, and one for the better. But as we are only
weak mortals and prone to the lust of the eyes, I feel I must do my duty
and never rest on my laurels. I wish you would take into account the
rewards of true obedience that bring a great and lasting blessing."

Mary shook her head, over and over.

"Dat, I don't know if it's possible. If I change my blinds, it will only
be something else. Someone will find a shiny rock in my driveway and
you'll tell me I'm too fancy."

"Don't speak to me like that. I'm only showing you the way to *full-
kommheit*. The way of the blessing."

It was only by the force of her own determination that she told
him demurely she would do what she could, never promising to change
anything. They parted in peace, her father well pleased with the humble
display of subordination. But in the buggy on the way home, tears of
frustration overflowed from her eyes and ran down her shawl.

She should not have come back to New York at all. She should have
listened to Steve. Nothing, ever, would reach the unreasonable pinnacle of his expectation. If she changed her blinds—she honestly had
not known the *ordnung* said anything about blinds—he would merely
request something different.

"Resting on his laurels." *His.* As if this were all about him winning
some kind of righteousness contest.

The beautiful snow-covered ridges seemed to disappear, replaced by
graying hills devoid of vegetation, a barren wilderness cursed like the
Dead Sea. There was nothing for her here in New York. Nothing.

Her future stretched out with no radiance, no light to guide her,
a string of hard labor cleaning up after the more fortunate, pocketing
her cash to pay her bills, going to church in crowded houses with her

dull siblings and their urine-soaked litters. She loathed them all, these soft-spoken, righteous adults awash in their own holiness.

She was still crying when she came up the winding drive between the fir trees. Through a haze of tears, the brown house with the almost black roof with the wide porch reached out and drew her in, patted her back and brought comfort. She stopped crying as she stabled Honey, pushing the buggy into the shed and swinging the door shut. She stepped up on the porch and turned to look at the sun sinking behind snow-covered hills, creating a golden orange glow in the lavender sky.

She crumpled newspaper, added kindling, and lit the fire, holding her hands to the warmth before crossing her arms and turning to look at the blinds. They weren't white. More like beige. What was wrong with beige blinds? She remembered the Allgyers' kitchen, the clean sunshine, the light in that house. Light walls, floors, tablecloth, the light of love and understanding. A willingness to see.

She made a cup of tea and sat on a chair, contemplating this fresh dilemma. It almost seemed as if her father's opinion was like an idol, more important to her than God Himself. A shrine in which she lost herself again and again. Or was it? Was she so far away from God that she couldn't see clearly without her father's guidance, but bungled through waves of fog and blinding clouds?

She took a deep breath, then another, and waited for the pounding of her heart, the shallow breaths and dry tongue.

But nothing happened.

She awoke at eleven fifteen, the house dark and cold, the fire having burned itself out. She lit the propane lamp, stuffed more newspaper and kindling into the firebox, and lit a match, groggy with sleep.

The visit with her parents came back to haunt her, followed by a sickening assurance that nothing would ever change. If only she had someone to talk to, anyone who would understand.

She brushed her teeth and took a long hot shower, luxuriating in the fact she could use all the hot water she wanted. This small pleasure, at least, had not been condemned. And at the end of the day, she could also choose the color of her blinds, and whether to get a dog, even if those things were met with disapproval.

And she knew without a doubt she missed Steve. Quite unexpectedly, she was filled with longing, a certainty of what she wanted. What she was entitled to. And it was the loving arms of another human being, a safe haven, and this house made into a home. With startling clarity, she knew the loving arms were not just anyone's arms.

They were Steve's.

An impossibility? Probably. But God told Abraham to go forth into a strange land and his seed would be like the sand of the seashore.

His wife and he well past the time of childbearing. And he believed God, and it was counted for righteousness.

Was that belief called faith? Was that the missing ingredient? She'd prostrated herself at the altar of her father's unreasonable expectations far too long, had counted obedience to him as righteousness.

He had exploited her conscience. He had taken away her understanding and replaced it with his own.

It was only a weak light in the stifling darkness of misconception, but it beamed steadily. It was small, but it would never waver, and never leave her.

MONDAY MORNING BROUGHT Jessie flying up her driveway in the battered Jeep, stopping by the doorstep and laying on the horn. Mary hurried to the door.

"What?" she called out.

"Your lady called. Sheila. She says the weather's bad, or gonna be. She's not coming to get you today."

"Oh. Okay."

"Look, you gotta get a phone. I don't want to keep running over here. Go tell the bishop you're gonna get a phone. I gotta go. Art's all flustered about the firewood. Storm's coming till late this afternoon. We'll check up on you."

Mary lifted a hand, watched her go back down the drive. Far away, she heard the plaintive whistle of a train, probably the one going into Carson's Ferry. The air was still and heavy, her breath clearly visible.

She turned to go inside, when an unexpected jingle of happiness washed over her. She fairly bounced across the living room floor to the coffeepot on the gas stove. Pouring a cup, she added sweet cream and toasted a bagel.

Oh, the day was rife with possibilities. There was wood to stock under the back porch roof, the horse to feed, a new recipe to try, and perhaps a letter to write. If she could summon the courage to write it.

God was in His Heaven, and yes, He was. She believed He was there. She felt this was real. Her father and Mima lived in their house with their green blinds, and she lived in hers with her lovely beige ones. And it was okay.

Probably. Hopefully.

She couldn't go too fast. She had to take little steps at first or she'd return to. . . . She honestly didn't know what. Something gray and dead and depressing. Something so useless it made her anxious, powerless, useless.

She chomped happily on her bagel, then put another one in the broiler, and waited till it was nicely browned.

She began to hum the song stuck in her head, then whistled it very soft and low. She began to weep, but not on account of sadness, more of an unbearable beauty somewhere she couldn't reach.

She stood in the middle of the kitchen and told herself she was unstable and mentally unsound, which really was funny, so she laughed.

No one would care if she laughed. It didn't matter. So she fed Honey, stacked wood all morning, went back into the house, and made date, nut, and raisin cookies that were so good she ate five or six, she couldn't be sure.

And she did write that letter, after three false starts. On lined tablet paper, in her best handwriting, she wrote about her life, keeping it short and simple. She described the house and the plain clothes she wore, so he wouldn't be shocked if he came for a visit.

She told him about the coyotes, her need for a dog and a phone shanty at the end of the drive. She signed her name, sealed it, addressed it, and applied a stamp, then propped it against the jar of spaghetti for three days as the biggest storm of the season dumped another few feet of snow. But she was prepared, safe and warm with good neighbors around her and the newfound something—a feeling she couldn't quite name—that things would turn out to be alright.

HIS SISTERS BROUGHT the mail into the house and hid that letter, hinting around until he didn't believe there had been one at all. They laughed until they bent over and slapped their knees. He caught bib apron strings and told them he would have to resort to serious arm twisting.

But they got a promise to help with the new pony out of him, before brandishing the letter with wild leaps around the kitchen. He clutched the letter from New York and withdrew to his room, where he stayed no matter how they pounded and begged to know what she wrote.

His mother gave him a long steady look when he finally came into the kitchen, after the girls were sound asleep.

He checked the perimeter of the kitchen to make sure no girls were lurking in corners. Going to the coffeepot, he felt the outside with the palm of his hand, before turning the burner knob. He stood back, crossed his arms, and asked, "Mom?"

"Yes, Steve?"

"What would you say if I went to New York?"

For a long moment, she said nothing, then turned to meet his eyes. "*Ach*, Steve. Do you think it's good?"

He shook his head, gave her a small smile. "I don't know."

"You do know she has quite a history. The thing most worrying is back when she was so out-of-control. Lizzie hardly knew where to turn. Then back and forth to New York, and last was this Mennonite stint. She hardly seems to be a stable young woman."

"She isn't."

"Then why bother, Steve?"

"I don't know why I bother. Well, maybe I do."

She lifted her eyebrows and waited.

"Do you believe sometimes God calls us into service and we don't understand it very well?"

"I do. But we have to be very careful that what we think He wants isn't all tangled up with what we want and can't let go."

He nodded.

"Well, she doesn't live at home. She actually did buy her own property, so if I go, I won't be chased off. But think about her courage, Mom. In the face of all her turmoil, she actually did make money on that bakery and bought a property. She's amazing. Not very many girls would manage that."

"It's true. I'm just not sure, Steve."

He sighed.

"Why don't you wait a while? Keep praying?"

"I have been praying."

"God's time is not always ours."

He turned his back to pour a cup of coffee, then turned to sit at the table.

"You know, we always look for that perfect partner. One with all the right qualifications. Every parent wants their children to have the perfect relationship, the perfect marriage. But I feel God's leading."

"It is His leading, Steve?"

"I believe it is."

Their eyes met and held.

AND SO, HE booked a bus ticket, told his mother to pray for him, packed clothes in a well-worn duffel, and bade them all goodbye on a Saturday when his sisters were all at home, lined up like observant crows with bright eyes and knowing smiles. Annoyed, he still grinned, waved, and was gone.

In the bus, he relaxed as the wheels turned on the cold macadam, the engine thrumming deep inside, a soothing sound. He tried to stay positive, told himself over and over this was the right thing to do, but could not rid himself of niggling doubts. He thought himself too bold, then dismissed that with the fact that she had written to him first. It wasn't quite an invitation to visit—more of a newsy update on her life. But still, she'd written. And besides, she was unlike most other girls, and perhaps open to a more unconventional approach.

He tried to picture her face, to remember the essence of her, but it had been too long. She said she was dressed in plainer clothes, which would do nothing to change her beauty, he felt sure. She was Mary, the one he had found, the one girl still holding his interest.

Whether it was truly the will of God would remain to be seen, but if he would be blessed by God's leading and their relationship ended in marriage, he would count himself the most fortunate among men.

As the trees waved their bare branches in the strong gusts of wind by the side of the road, he felt as if they were bystanders ushering him on.

CHAPTER 13

He told the Uber driver he had the address, fumbled in his wallet, and produced it with an apology. He'd kept him waiting, and perceived the impatience, but found him quite amiable once they were on their way.

The driver had moved here from Boston to be close to his girlfriend and her family, but hadn't been prepared for the culture shock. It was like moving backward fifty years, he said. And these Amish people and their horses and buggies on every turn of these narrow country roads were nothing short of a traffic hazard.

"Like, man, I don't even mean it as an insult, but Jeez."

Steve grinned, nodded.

"It's quite alright. I suppose for someone accustomed to city life, this is a change for you."

"It's a change, alright. What creeps me out most is how dark it gets. Like, it's black, man. Black."

"Even with the snow?"

"Snow doesn't mean anything. It's dark."

The road gave way to a narrow pot-holed one, winding in and out of hollows and along snowy hillsides. Stop signs loomed unexpectedly at unforeseen curves, the road leading up steep hills and down again.

Ahead of them, Steve saw the familiar gray rectangle of an Amish buggy with the brilliant red-orange "slow moving vehicle" emblem in stark relief. When they passed on the left, Steve was surprised to see a sweat-stained horse lunging exhaustedly into his worn collar, his thin neck outstretched as his feet dutifully plodded along.

Steve slanted a look at the driver.

When they reached their destination, Steve felt his heart pounding. He could feel the color draining from his face. More courage was required of him than he'd thought possible. As they wound their way up the snowy drive, he was struck by the small brown house tucked beside a tree-covered ridge. Idyllic. It was the cutest thing. His heart raced, and he stammered when he tried to speak.

"Your friend at home? Better check," the driver commented.

"I'll be fine."

He paid, got his duffle, and stood, sizing up his surroundings as the car moved off with a slight swaying motion as the tires slid on packed snow.

Board and batten siding, a deep front porch, tall front windows. Whoever had built this little house had certainly done well, the exterior blending into the forest.

Ah. Mary, Mary.

A great warmth enveloped him, an unexplainable happiness for her. Had she found a measure of peace?

Resolutely, he walked the short distance to the porch, noticed the flagstone on the floor, the heavy door, the concrete urns on each side.

He lifted his hand and knocked.

The door opened slowly, the bewildered face belonging to the one he had missed more than he knew.

"Mary."

"Oh."

Almost, she closed the door in his face, but she steadied herself, her eyes wide with the shock of seeing him.

"Oh. Oh my."

A hand went to her mouth. Then, gathering her senses, she said, "Steve. Hello. Come in, please."

And he stepped over the threshold into the cozy living room lit by the flow of the afternoon sun and the dancing of a million pieces of stardust. He thought he might never want to leave again.

When she turned to him, he extended a hand.

"Hello, Mary. How are you?"

She felt his strong grip but extricated her hand quickly.

She nodded. "I'm fine. Doing well, in fact."

Self-conscious now, she touched her covering, smoothed her hair. A hand went to the belt of her plain gray apron.

He searched her face, surprised to see the healthy color in her cheeks, the golden glow with the smattering of freckles, her eyes barely concealing her self-awareness, the shame of her appearance.

"You look as if New York suits you," he said, smiling.

She shook her head. "You shouldn't have come."

"Don't say that."

"But. . . . *Ach*, Steve. I'm not the Mary you knew in Lancaster. I . . . I look like your grandmother."

"It's okay, believe me. You're still the same Mary to me."

"But. . . ."

She shook her head, took in his Carhartt coat with a hood and zipper, the gray hiking boots, the yellow shirt and black vest.

His longish hair was tousled, and yes, he was hatless. A deep sense of loss took away the gladness she'd felt at the sight of him.

"Steve, I . . ."

He stepped forward, asked her to look at him. She refused.

"Well, I'm here till Monday morning, so do you have a place I can put my duffel? If you don't, we'll just set it here in the living room, and I'll be quite comfortable on the couch."

"But you can't stay." Panic edged her voice.

"Why not? Do you have plans?"

She shook her head. Her breath came in gasps.

"Will you have unexpected visitors?"

Again, she shook her head, mute.

"Look, Mary, you wrote that letter."

"Yes, but I didn't think it would bring you to my door. You can't stay here. It would never be allowed by my father or by the rest of the community, really. I mean, I hardly know how else to say it. You can't. I mean, you can't sleep here."

"I'm sorry, Mary. I should have written to ask before coming. I didn't happen to see any hotels on the way here. Could I perhaps stay with a relative?"

"No!" The thought of him seeing the way her family lived was horrifying.

He was aware of her conscience being directed by the severity of the circle in which she moved. He felt like a fool, putting her in this difficult position. And yet, he really didn't see any other option now that he was here. Unless . . .

"Shall I stay in the barn?" he asked without a hint of mockery.

"Don't be silly," she answered quickly. "There's a small guest room, if you want to place your belongings there. On the right. My . . . uh . . . my bedroom is on the left."

Dressed in a dark purple dress with a gray apron pinned around her waist, her large covering concealing most of those abundant red waves, he decided she was, in fact, dressed like his grandmother. But somehow, on her, it was charming.

"Coffee? Tea?" she asked.

"Coffee would be great."

The kitchen was small, but so perfect, with quality oak cabinets, a hardwood floor, quietly and tastefully furnished. The back door looked out on another porch, the window above the sink spotless, adorned with small brown pots of ivy. He was relieved to see she owned a gas stove and a small gas refrigerator, which meant they allowed that much.

She had her back turned to fill the coffeepot, so he could not see her face, which was being heated by a furious, unwelcome blush of epic proportion. She took a deep breath and opened the refrigerator door to hide as much as possible. He had certainly caught her off guard, arriving unannounced, looking every inch the true Lancaster young man, dressed in expensive clothes, way out of the *ordnung* according to her father. He'd never pass inspection. He didn't belong here. And what had possessed her to write that letter?

A moment of insanity, that's what. She shuddered inwardly.

He simply was not allowed to be here.

When he returned, his coat and vest were missing, and he was in his stocking feet. Panic rose, a deepening despair coupled with the pounding of a heart bursting with raw fear. She sat heavily in a chair, her chest rising and falling as color drained from her face.

"Mary. Is something wrong?"

"No. I'm just going to step outside for a minute."

Oh, the relief of cold air flooding her nostrils. She sucked in the frigid, moist air that gave her renewed life. Her hands shook as she tucked them beneath her arms.

She heard the door open. He stepped out on the porch.

"Are you okay?"

"Yes. Just give me a minute, please."

When he turned to go inside, the knowledge of how unwell she really was hit him like a sledgehammer. He could see the whole picture in a flash of wisdom, reality slamming him. She was here, had brought herself into subjection, still blind and fumbling, still unaware of who she really was. *Dear Lord, this is up to you*, was his last thought before he sank into a chair, exhaustion seeping into his being, the task at hand a steep cliff he had no strength to scale.

He did not look up when she entered.

"I don't know what to do, Steve. You shouldn't have come."

"I won't stay long, Mary. I have a return ticket for Monday at nine forty-five."

"You can't go outside."

"Why not?"

"Someone might see you. Neighbors. Word gets around."

"Alright. I'll stay inside."

That statement seemed to relax her, give her enough confidence to resume the ordinary task of procuring cups and cream.

"I'm sure you're hungry. It will soon be suppertime."

He was, in fact, ravenous, but told her he didn't want to be a bother.

The coffee was hot, strong, and thick with cream. She brought a plate of cookies, without speaking. An awkward silence hung between them.

Finally, he cleared his throat, took a deep breath, and began.

"Mary, can we merely be friends? Catch up on our lives?"

She looked up, hope rekindling the light in her eyes.

"We can, I believe."

"Tell me about yours."

"There's not much to tell. I love my little house. My father is happy, says he can rest in peace when he dies, so that's, you know, something. I mean, that's what I wanted when I moved here. I clean houses now. For English people."

"Do you enjoy that?"

"Yes. Well, for the most part. It pays my bills."

"But are you happy?"

"Sometimes. Not always. But life isn't all about our own happiness. If we can give ourselves up, happiness forms naturally."

He nodded in agreement.

"You . . . must think I look ridiculous."

"Of course not."

By all outward appearances, they were ill matched as a couple, but he knew now more than ever, his life would somehow be dedicated to her. She was in every fiber of his being, although he did not fully understand it. She was here dressed in all the right clothes on the outside, and he suspected there was a roiling mass of pain and confusion on the inside. The craziness of humanity struck him, the hurts we inflict on one another with no awareness whatsoever, all while feeling satisfied and righteous.

And so he smiled, offered to help her with supper.

"If we were in Lancaster, I'd offer to order pizza."

Instantly, her shoulders stiffened. "We can't do that."

"Of course. I was just saying . . ."

"I have some leftover chili. And I could make grilled cheese sandwiches?"

"Perfect."

The sun slid toward the mountaintop as they sat down together. He went to the living room to stand by the windows, commenting on the gorgeous view, and she absorbed the sight of him standing in her living room.

I can't have him, she thought wildly. *I can't. What came over me to think I could? It all started when Dat lovingly mentioned my fancy blinds. I was rebellious, and the devil had a foothold. I must have the power over my own desire. I must replace those blinds. Obedience is the way to truth.*

He turned, his fair hair like a halo, his yellow shirt a beacon of light. She could not look.

"You're one lucky girl, Mary. It's really beautiful here. I can see why you love New York so much."

"Right?"

"Oh, absolutely. I could easily live here myself. Is there carpentry work available?"

He watched her closely, and recorded the stiffening of her shoulders, the edge to her voice, her eyes clouded with fear.

"I . . . no, not that I know of."

"You would not want me here?"

She told him, then, in a straightforward manner, there was no way he could live here in Pinedale. Not now, not ever. And when she wrote that letter, it was merely missing an old friend, and if she'd realized he'd come to visit, she'd never have written.

"I don't believe you," he said, as they sat on the couch together, a whole cushion length between them.

Shocked, she turned to face him, her eyes wide.

"But you have to. It's the truth."

"Is it, Mary?"

"Of course."

"There was something between us. You know that. We both know."

She shook her head. "All that was ever between us was the human desire and self will we need to conquer. We have to see that. We are not meant for each other at all. Look, I'm not going to talk about this. I have to feed my horse."

She got up, moved to the clothes rack to take down the plain black coat and scarf, then let herself out the door without another word.

He walked back to the small guest room, put on his coat and shoes, opened the door, and followed the path in the deep snow outside. He remember her warning then, and glanced around to make sure no neighbors were in sight. The odor of fresh hay and horse feed greeted him, and he smiled when he noticed the absence of manure, only a clean scattering of wood shaving. The barn, like the house, was organized and spotless.

"What's your horse's name?" he asked quietly.

"This is Honey. A lovely little mare from my brother Abner."

"He gave her to you?"

"I'm making payments, but it was very kind of him."

"It certainly was."

"You think so, right?"

"I would say so."

She seemed glad of his approval, saying her brother was a good husband and father, a true man. Guilt and shame were stuffed away as she hid the troubling knowledge of drowned kittens and an exhausted wife bearing children every year. She must stay true to the path she had chosen, could not be misled to another road filled with confusion.

"I would enjoy meeting your family, seeing their homes, actually, the rest of the community. Do you have church tomorrow?"

"No. You couldn't go. You don't have your church clothes."

"I brought them."

"Well, you can't go."

Back outside, the moon had risen, the night sky filled with its pale yellow light, countless stars scattered across a vast area, the snow adding to the beauty of the night.

Without realizing, she closed the door and took up the garden rake.

"What? Why are you carrying a rake?"

"Oh. It's . . . well, I guess I rake the snow when I'm bored."

He laughed, a rich unrestrained sound that caused her to giggle.

The humor eased the tension, and a companionable silence settled between them. He asked if she wanted to go for a walk, which she considered, but told him about the warning of coyotes.

"You won't be hurt by them. They're extremely shy."

"How do you know?"

"I've been around."

"Hmm."

"Come on, let's walk."

She nodded and they set off, their breath coming in little white puffs in the freezing night atmosphere, the snow crunching beneath their feet.

"So many hills and valleys. Must be hard to farm here," he noted.

"Some of the more well-to-do farmers paid more for land and own more level acreage along the river between these hills. My father, well, I told you all that. It was a hardscrabble kind of life, I guess. But they live in a nice grandfather house now. It's different than it used to be. I mean, he's different."

Steve chose to stay quiet, wondering how true that was. She babbled on nervously. "I mean, Mima, my stepmother, really cleaned him up. He's actually better looking. His hair is clean, and he seems more gracious or something. He approves of me now, which gives me lots of peace. And I try to understand his way of looking at . . . well, things."

She hesitated, then continued.

"I mean. I do love him. I wore my shawl and bonnet to their house a few weeks ago, and it meant so much. To him, not so much to me. He said he can rest in peace now. But I did tell you that. So as long as I can please him by giving up my own will, I can live my life with a free conscience, knowing I am an honor to my parents. I mean, I try to be."

She gave a small laugh.

"He did say something about the color of my blinds, but it was said out of love. I mean, he wants what is right for me."

She sighed, before rambling on about green blinds and the forefathers requiring obedience.

"Let's turn back, Mary. I'm getting cold," he said suddenly.

"Fine with me."

Once inside, she told him about the rake and the coyotes, how real her fear had been. Seemingly, honesty was winning, at least in a few areas.

They sat side by side then, and talked, really talked, far into the night. Eventually, Mary slid to the floor, and Steve sprawled on his stomach on the rug, cups of coffee between them.

Mary laughed and cried, admitting she was trying very hard to find her way, finally relaying in detail the fury when her father approached her about the blinds.

"If you change them, what will be next?" he said.

"Exactly!"

"Leave them," he said forcefully.

"Steve, you stop. You are *fer-fearish*, pointing me straight down the road to perdition. You know that. We are Amish people, and a certain respect and obedience is expected of us."

"But this is ridiculous."

And they argued, in a healthy way, airing their views until Steve told her she was not being truthful, not being herself, and that she came very close to living a lie, which infuriated her.

He smiled into his forearms, his blond hair tousled over his forehead while she told him he had far too much nerve, acting like he knew anything about her, a perfect stranger. And he told her she was by no means a perfect stranger and never would be.

"What's that supposed to mean?" she snorted.

"I think you know."

"I told you, we are the world's most unlikely couple. I don't even think of you as an attractive suitor."

"Yes, you do."

She challenged him by asking how he could think he knew her better than she knew herself, and he shrugged his shoulders and pretended to fall asleep.

Outside, the high yipping of coyotes sounded, followed by the eerie howls of primal animals.

"They sound close," Steve remarked, opening his eyes, getting to his feet, and going to the window. She followed him. They waited in silence as the moon slid lower toward the mountain.

"There," Steve said suddenly, pointing.

Down by the road, along a snowbank, first one, then two more shadows trotted by. Lean, long dogs, likely without sufficient food for too many days.

"Poor buggers," he said soft and low.

"They kill deer. Why pity them?" Mary asked.

"Guess I just do. They're God's creatures, same as everything else."

She nodded, thought of beaten dogs and drowning kittens, of faithful mules lacking nutrition, and cows with hammer marks on their hip bones. And obedience pounded into young lives.

He was standing too close, the way she caught the scent of his aftershave and the fabric softener in his shirt.

She stepped away. It was late at night, the devil's hour, when he stalked around seeking whom he may devour, and she had come dangerously close to his skulking ways.

He chuckled.

"Why did you move?"

"Because I'm going to shower and go to bed. Goodnight."

And that was precisely what she did. He was just drifting off when he heard a light tapping on his door.

"If you don't have enough covers, there are more in the closet."

"Thank you," he said, smiling.

HE GOT UP early, expecting his usual early morning shower, surprised to find a light in the kitchen and Mary standing with her back turned, a cascade of wavy red hair caught in a loose ponytail on a white robe.

It was a heartbreaking sight, and one he had never expected to see.

He turned away, suppressing the urge to go to the kitchen, speak of his love.

He showered, donned clean clothes, a flannel shirt of navy blue and his black Sunday trousers, then went to the kitchen and sat on a chair, lifted one knee to strip a sock over the foot.

"Good morning, Mary. Did you sleep well?" he asked casually as he rolled the sock over his heel.

"No. But good morning."

"Why didn't you sleep?"

She shrugged. "Who knows? Maybe because it's the first time I had a guest, I don't know."

They drank coffee together like a married couple, talked about Pinedale and its inhabitants, the neighbors and the ladies she cleaned for, the air between them cleared of falsehoods or guilt.

During the night, unseen forces had broken barriers, and Mary allowed herself a small reprieve. Reluctantly, she admitted to herself that for the first time in a long time, she felt like herself.

CHAPTER 14

THEY FRIED SCRAPPLE, MADE PANCAKES AND EGGS, TOASTED HOME-
made bread, and ate together at the kitchen table, the sun hidden by a
thick cover of clouds. There was no wind, just a frosty stillness broken
by the occasional call of a bird.

"Do you want to have devotions, Mary?" he asked when the meal
was finished.

"You mean read the Bible together? Chester did devotions when we
went to Maine, but I didn't think Amish people did that."

"You're serious?"

"Well, of course I'm serious. My father never did any of that. He
read the German evening prayer and that was that. We didn't read our
Bible, especially not in English. Go ahead if you want, but I don't think
I'll join you." She thought of how Chester had tried to explain the Bible
to her that morning in Maine, and then considered how wrong it had
been to take that trip at all. It made her feel a little ill.

He said nothing. Devotions had been a morning ritual for Steve,
always. Bible reading, taking turns around the table to read verses, then
singing a few hymns, sometimes in English, other times in German.
Although he had known there was great diversity among his people, it
was hard to accept the lack of taught morning devotions.

They cleared the table and washed dishes while the gray clouds
turned to churning white ones, and then the sun broke through, creating brilliant light throughout the house. He sat on his bed in the guest

room to read a chapter in Romans, then went to the living room to find Mary fast asleep on the recliner, her covering on the table beside it.

She didn't wake up, so he lay on the couch and drifted off himself, alarmed to find it was past one when he awoke.

Less than twenty-four hours before he had to leave.

Mary said they had to stay inside, too many teams traveled past on a Sunday, and if she got caught, she'd likely have to confess in church. Steve was incredulous, shaking his head.

"It's the way it is here," she said, tight-lipped and defensive.

"But what about us, Mary? I know you say nothing will come of this, but what if I go home and the first thing I want to do is turn around and come straight back? I can guarantee you that's how it will be."

For a long moment, she said nothing. Finally, she sighed.

"Steve, I don't know. I cannot go back to Lancaster, and you are never going to fit in here. One look at you and my father would run you off. There is no 'us,' as you call it. Isn't there some special girl in Lancaster?"

"Is that what you want?"

"Yes."

But later that evening, she said no, she wasn't sure if she wanted him to pursue someone else. Then she said again they would always be friends, but not dating, not a dating couple.

He told her she wasn't being fair, that she was giving mixed messages, but she insisted there was no way they could be anything but friends.

He went for a long walk. He needed to clear his thinking, he said—he promised he was not doing it to be rude or disrespectful. She watched him go and immediately felt a sense of loss.

When he returned, it seemed as if he had reached an agreement with himself. He'd been so sure of God's leading, so sure of Him working this out somehow, but for now, he had to admit defeat.

He could see no way through.

This invoked a greediness in her, a longing to have her own fair share of happiness, and why shouldn't she? "Sometimes," she confessed, "I don't know why I had to come here, why I sold the bakery."

Bewildered, heartsick, no longer sure of his own answers, without the courage to cling to what he thought God had clearly shown him, he spent the evening in near silence, while she poured out her deepest fear: Being found unworthy when Christ returned.

"I'll tell you what, Steve, and this is the truth. If it was only God, Jesus, whoever, and me, I could live happily and forever in Lancaster with you. But it's that sickening sensation of living on the wrong side of the tracks, and the condemnation of being disobedient.

"Is my father's sadness greater than the grace by which Jesus saves? Sometimes I feel as if I'll go mad with never being able to find the whole answer.

"I live here now, dress ultra plain, and am pleasing to my family. This is truly living in self-denial. Do I have the blessing I long for? I honestly don't know. I haven't had a panic attack, so that's something. Sometimes I'm even happy. I love my home. It feels good to have my father accept me."

Then she went on to tell him about her glimpse of the faith of Abraham, how righteousness was allotted to him by believing what God told him, then obeying his belief.

"I don't personally believe I have to dress like this to please God, but my father does, so . . . I don't know. I get all mixed up. But for one space of time, a light shone through and I understood about faith, felt all lighthearted and sure of myself, sat down and wrote that letter. And then went straight back to worrying about what my father would think if you came."

He nodded and told her he understood. Perhaps it was best that they parted ways. Maybe God had someone else in mind for each of them, or maybe He was calling them to singleness.

She nodded, agreeing. "We can do this, Steve. It's not like we're giggling teenagers with crushes and no idea what real love is."

He nodded. "Yes, Mary. I believe you're right. We'll try it and see what happens."

But on Monday morning, with the Uber driver waiting in the driveway, the parting was almost more than they could stand.

In the end, he crushed her to him, held her as if the thought of releasing her was unbearable. She sobbed on his chest, and his tears were mixed with hers in the universal language of love.

She watched him walk away, put his duffel in the back seat, climb in, lift a hand, and the vehicle moved away through a haze of tears. She flung herself on the couch and cried great gulping sobs of frustration and loneliness, then sighed, sat up, and wiped her eyes, telling herself it was the right thing to do.

She would be blessed beyond anything she could imagine. She'd given up the bakery, her home in Lancaster, and now Steve, so surely the riches of her blessing would be forthcoming.

THE DAY STARTED off well enough, her wringer washer filled with hot water and detergent, the extra towels and washcloths on the line, the house dusted and swept. She had just dozed off when the insistent blare of a car horn awoke her. Irritated, she got off the chair to find Art in the Jeep, yelling about Jessie wanting to know if she wanted to ride along to the library.

"Why not?" she yelled back. "I'll go."

Why not indeed. She needed a few good books to fill her mind. She would fall in love with the characters, take a healthy interest in someone else's life, and forget all the drama that had just taken place.

She put on a clean apron, fixed her hair and adjusted her covering, grabbed her purse, and rode to town with Jessie.

"Did I see a young man walking down the road? I would almost have taken him for Amish except he wasn't wearing a hat. And I think he was wearing a Carhartt. Hooded."

"Dunno," Mary mumbled, suddenly interested in the scenery on the right.

"I don't know, Mary. I'd be sure and lock my doors. I'm telling you, you need a dog."

She chose a few books, one of them about a long hike a woman took alone, thinking that might hold her interest, the way she'd often wondered at someone like that. They certainly had courage, these lone hikers.

They stopped at the IGA for a few groceries, then went to the local Quick Mart for gas, with Jessie keeping up a lively chatter about local gossip, logging accidents, the price of a dozen eggs, and the stupidity of New York's governor and the country in general. Mary nodded at the proper intervals, grunted approval or said "Seriously?" or "Really?" when an answer was expected, but her mind was mostly occupied with Steve.

His facial expressions, the way he ran his hand through his hair, his laugh. And that navy blue flannel shirt. Oh my.

What a married couple they were, she in her bathrobe, he sitting there drawing his socks over his feet. Oh my. And what would her father say? He would be outraged, then sullen, after which she'd receive the lecture of her life.

She opened the book about the hiker named Audrey, became so engrossed in the story she didn't go to bed till past twelve, and that after a weekend of barely any sleep. So when Karen Baxter pulled up to the house and lay on the horn, it was all she could do to be civil, disliking the way her polished nails were far too long and slim and red on her fat fingers with the vast assortment of rings. No wonder she didn't clean her house.

The house was small, but opulent, the Sub-Zero refrigerator in dire need of a good cleaning, so she spent an extra half hour, dragging herself from room to room. But, as always, at the end of the day, she felt a sense of accomplishment as she received a crisp roll of bills, and this time it included a twenty-dollar tip.

Unfadeend gelt instantly came to mind. Her father would call it "unearned money," which was another sin. But she had earned it, the way those refrigerator shelves gleamed. Still, her father's scowl lurked in the back of her mind.

Would she never be free?

STEVE WENT BACK to Lancaster and told his mother she must have been right, and he would have done well to heed her advice.

He described Mary's home in glowing terms, but ended his account by telling her how Mary wavered from one position to the next, and was still held in the grip of her father's dictatorship.

"Then it's best for you to forget her," his mother said.

Every word was a dagger to his heart, the hurt making him actually wince. He knew his mother meant well, thought she was probably right, but the hurt was there, just the same.

Wisely, she saw the damage she'd inflicted, laid a hand on his arm, and said, "Steve, you know if it's God's will, neither of us can alter the course. So I'll keep praying, and so shall you."

Those words were like a drink of cold water to a man dying of heat and thirst, allowing him to whistle soft and low as he drove the horses, resuming life with a peaceful heart.

SPRING CAME IN late March, flirting deceptively, wearing yellow daffodils and purple crocus, batting her eyelashes with soft fragrant breezes, then moved away to allow cold winds to howl in from the north, bending the shivering flowers in its wake. Mary piled wood on the fire and grumbled to herself, thinking how long and how arduous these New York winters truly seemed to be.

Sometimes she felt as if she would have a permanent scent of Mr. Clean about her, emanating from beneath her fingernails and from the palms of her hands. But losing a few pounds here and there amounted to something, didn't it?

Jessie brought the message one morning. She was needed at home. Her parents were both very ill, the family debating whether they should be taken to the emergency room.

So she shut the draft on the stove, fed Honey, packed a few clothes just in case, and bounced off with alarming speed with Art at the wheel of the Jeep.

She found her sister-in-law Emma hovering over her father, the house reeking of homemade tinctures, the windows streaming with high heat and humidity from the kettles of steaming water. Onions lay in slices on ceramic plates, glasses of warm grape juice with bent straws littered the counters. She joined Emma, alarmed to see the pronounced rise and fall of her father's chest, the high wheezing of every breath.

In the bedroom, Mima lay quietly, her white sleep cap tied beneath her chin, a stained flannel nightgown clinging to the steamed onion poultice on her chest. Her round face appeared much younger, relaxed, as if the sickness was becoming.

Mary shuddered. This was not good.

"Emma, where's Abner?"

"He was in about an hour ago."

"They need help, both of them."

"Are you sure?"

"I am. Dat is very sick. Is he even conscious?"

"He spoke earlier this morning."

She found Abner in the house, eating graham crackers with peanut butter and with milk.

"Abner, I think it's time our parents had medical help."

He chewed and swallowed. "Who will pay for it?"

"He has some money laid by. That's what we'll use, of course."

"I hate to see it go to waste. I believe it's the flu."

Mary counted to ten, calming herself before replying.

"Abner, they're too weak to get in a vehicle. We need an ambulance."

"Are you going to call for one?"

"No, you are. I'm staying here with Lydia."

After what seemed like hours had passed, the howling of the ambulance siren sent chills up her spine.

As the flashing red lights sent pink shadows on the walls, she held the door for the two men dressed in navy blue, the red logo on their pockets bearing the name of the firehall where they originated.

They spoke quietly and went to her father, whose eyes opened wide with alarm, followed by a thrashing of his arms and legs, a twisting of his face, a resounding "No-o-o." A hideous, rasping wail of denial.

"Mr. Glick, everything will be okay. You'll be fine," the man named Scott intoned in a soothing voice.

Again, the long drawn-out sound, a hollow refusal of medical care. Abner stepped forward.

"I believe my father wants to refuse treatment, and we need to respect his wishes."

Instantly, Mary stepped up. "No, he needs the help."

Abner nodded. "Yes, Mary, if he wishes not to go to a hospital, we need to obey."

"But he needs antibiotics. He needs a doctor's care. Please!"

The EMTs stood, then went ahead with the required protocol, recording blood pressure, taking his temperature, inserting an IV, the life-giving solution he so badly needed.

Mima went willingly and was gently laid on the provided stretcher, which was almost more than Mary could take. She pleaded with Abner to allow them to take their father.

Undecided, Abner looked down at his father, who had apparently lost consciousness. Upon Mary's insistence, he, too, was laid on a stretcher, his unbelievably thin frame heartbreaking in its helplessness.

Abner rode along, his face red with anger, resistance setting his face in stone.

And Mary stayed with Emma. Malinda joined them, her face drawn with a lack of sleep, the concern for her in-laws an act of love and caring.

"*Ach*, Mary. I'm so glad you came."

Mary smiled as she clasped her sister-in-law's hand.

"I'm glad you sent a message. I'm just worried for both of them."

"You think they'll be okay?"

"I don't know."

If they regained their health, it was the will of God; if not, then that, too, was the will of God, so they would give themselves up.

Together, they cleaned, aired out the scent of boiling onion and homemade herbal tinctures. Small brown bottles of oils were put back on the bathroom shelves, bedding was washed and aired in the sweet scent of flowering trees.

Malinda brought the two toddlers, a five-year-old, and the baby, seated herself on her father's rocker, and promptly began to nurse while the remaining three sat quietly on the couch with a stack of Mima's Little Golden books. Mary listened as her wide cheeks accentuated the opening and closing of her mouth, words of praise for Mima, how long she'd cared for their father before falling ill herself.

Emma, thin as a rail with her hair plastered darkly to her head, nodded as she scoured the sink, countertop, and stove, her red, large-knuckled hands in constant motion.

"Yes, the day she became his wife, she did us all a favor. Can you imagine Dat without her? Someone would have their hands full."

Mary stopped the rhythmic drawing of the broom, her mouth dropping open in surprise. She, in fact, knew exactly what it was like to care for him, but she never thought Emma would speak in such a way.

"Oh, but Emma, it is our duty to care for him."

"Duty patootie. He's a cranky old man, and I for one, would have a hard time of it. I never did one thing right for him."

"Emma! I'm shocked."

"Well, be shocked, then. I can't help it. He never liked me."

Mary stopped sweeping. A hysterical mixture of incredulity, of laughing and crying, welled up inside of her.

"You mean it's not just me?"

"Of course not. It's you and half the community."

"But you are in the *ordnung*. I thought it was only me, on account of not obeying his words."

"Of course I'm in the *ordnung*. We all are. We believe in the rules of the church. But that doesn't mean he's satisfied."

After the floor was scrubbed on hands and knees, Mary emptied the bucket, rinsed it, replaced it beneath the sink, and hung the microfiber cloth over the side of the rinse tubs. A row of succulents in all stages of growth were potted in small plastic containers, all painted white, a testimony to Jemima's eye for beauty and order, her own small corner of creativity. A wave of understanding nudged her to the narrow windowsill, where she reached out to touch the small containers. As she'd thought, they were single serve yogurt containers, spray painted, a thing of frugal prettiness.

Oh, Mima. I know, she thought. *We're squelched down, repressed, and yet we create and find beauty.* She thought of her bedroom in Lancaster at Aunt Lizzie's house, the disassembling of beauty, the disposing of forbidden wall art, cushions, and rugs. And yet she'd acquired more, pieces of tasteful furniture matching the cottage vibe of her small brown house, arranging things of beauty, a place where she was surrounded by things that made her happy. She'd decorated the white walls of the bakery with fine antiques, doubled her money on them when she sold it, and was still searching for items now.

Would this, too, be added to her father's list of sins?

And now Emma's disclosure. She vowed to get to the source of those painfully honest words.

She sniffed as she returned to the kitchen. Hungry, as usual, she found a pot of home-canned vegetable soup on the stove. Malinda opened a jar of canned hamburger meat. She grabbed an onion from the bin in the pantry and proceeded to chop in furious hacks with a paring knife.

Emma wiped the storm door window with crumpled newspaper, the old remedy for spotless windows. She used a bottle of vinegar water with a spray attachment and crumpled paper, costing only pennies and creating better cleaned windows than Windex and paper towels, or those horrendously expensive Norwex cloths that were all the rage in Lancaster.

Mary smiled, thinking of her own accumulation of Norwex cloths, all stacked neatly in a drawer, a lavish lifestyle well hidden from eyes that judged, eyes that sniffed with disdain.

The thought of God seeing those cloths, knowing her checkbook showed the alarming amount for only two of them, made her hope no one would ever have the privilege of snooping into her financial affairs.

Did God care about what you used to clean windows? He knew how much she spent, but would He hold it against her on the day of judgment?

Emma finished, pitched the ball of newspaper in the trashcan, then set the bottle of vinegar water on the turntable beneath the sink.

"Well, now they can come home to a clean house. Malinda, open that window by the sink. We need to air this place out. It's a wonder they didn't die just from all these onions."

Mary stared at her.

"Don't look at me like that, Mary. I'm just saying what I think."

Mary sighed, sank into a chair.

"It's just that I have never heard you talk like this."

"Hm. Well, I have lived here in Pinedale with my father-in-law for many years, and I've decided it's time to voice my grievances. I tell my husband as much, whether he wants to hear it or not."

"But . . ." Mary shook her head.

"What?" Emma asked, stooping to pick up a few children's books.

"I thought you were all one big, happy family. All pleasing to Dat, all complying to his wishes, all winning his hard-earned approval."

Malinda nodded. "We are. I mean, we do."

She reached behind her ample waistline to adjust a straight pin.

"Abner and I don't have a problem. If you respect Dat, he treats you well."

Emma drew her mouth in a straight line and didn't answer. Mary looked from one to the other, feeling as if she could slice the tension like a freshly baked pie.

This was, in fact, extremely interesting. She would love to question Emma, knowing how she, Mary, had always felt like the sole black sheep, the outcast, and now it seemed as if there was one in the inner circle, one of the obedient members. Or was there?

Perhaps her father didn't mean his words to be perceived the way Emma took them, knowing she was thin and brittle, perhaps a bit waspish, and her father's severity chafed at her own views.

As if Emma had been mulling this reply for too long, she snapped suddenly. "Yes, Malinda. You can say that for yourself. But I choose to have a mind of my own. This thing of having large families should not be the father of the groom's choice. And I'll have you know, Malinda, on our wedding day, he told Jonas of his views on that matter, and I can't forgive him for that."

Malinda gasped audibly. "Why Emma, you must. If you can't forgive him, you can't be forgiven. It says so very plainly when you say the Lord's prayer."

"That area of marriage should be between man and wife, and he had no business meddling in our affairs."

She set the pot of steaming vegetable soup on a cast iron trivet in the middle of the oilcloth-covered table, which promptly puckered up beneath the heat. No one seemed to care, so Mary let it go, watching as Malinda herded her group of children to the table, crumpling saltines in their dishes and ladling out the steaming soup.

CHAPTER 15

WHEN MARY STOPPED AT THE HOSPITAL'S FRONT DESK AND WAS told her father had been moved into the intensive care unit, alarm rose in her chest. She found four of her sisters, dressed in plain dark colors, their black capes and aprons covering their shoulders, chests, and necks, the loose aprons disguising any shapeliness. A neat stack of black bonnets was on an end table, and homemade carpet bags containing a variety of hand sewing were set by each one's chair, a testimony to industrious hands.

She was greeted warmly, but with a gentle admonition about the missing cape and bonnet—a gentle pat on her arm and a lenient "You'll remember as time goes by."

She remembered walking the streets of Lancaster, swinging along in sneakers, her long skirts and black bib apron, her hair in the latest style, her white covering small and heart-shaped.

Sin. It was blatant sin.

But just a few times, she'd felt like someone of consequence, a woman of substance, without the fear of wrongdoing. But it was never long before she was back to searching her own conscience, dreading the consequences of every potential sin.

She sat side by side with her sisters as crochet needles clicked and embroidery thread was drawn through white muslin in wooden hoops, their mouths drawn in concentration as they prayed for the health of their father. When a middle-aged couple entered the waiting room, no one acknowledged them, no one met their questioning eyes except Mary, who gave them a smile of friendliness.

A nurse appeared with Rachel and told them two more could see their father now, so Mary accompanied Lydia through doors that swung open at the touch of a square button, down a sterile hallway alive with brightly dressed nurses and interns, wheeled carts and hums of machines. They entered a dimly lit room with lighted screens, beeps, a confusing mass of tubes and plastic wire. His face was as white as death. His long, thin hand lay atop a white sheet with a needle inserted in the sunken, pallid vein, the skin dry and scaly. His eyes were closed.

They stood, unsure, their arms crossed for protection from the sight of this man who was their father, the man they had always feared. It was unsettling to see him lying so helpless, dependent on the latest medical technology, run by the electricity he so condemned, dressed in the universal garment all hospitals provided.

Mary had a terrifying thought. She broke out in a cold sweat. He had placed great importance on fabric and color, homemade shirts with plain buttons, the black vest with hooks and eyes, and must he now face the Savior dressed in no less than the garment even the unbelievers wore?

She trembled, her heart raced. A confusion of thoughts created a pounding in her temples. She coughed, reached out to cling to the foot of the high, narrow bed.

She felt a hand on her back.

"Are you alright?"

She nodded quickly at the kind nurse.

He must not die. Not now. Not before she discussed this with him. He would live. He wasn't that old. She needed to understand a few things. The nurse brought a small glass of apple juice, said she'd feel better when she finished it.

Lydia placed a hand on her father's, said, "Dat."

His eyelids quivered, then slid open, only to close again.

Pity welled up in Mary, followed with a rush of alarm. He could not die. She needed him to answer a few questions.

Lydia stepped aside. "*Komm*, Mary."

So she stepped up, placed a tentative hand on top of the taped needle putting life-giving liquid into his veins, and thought how awful, how sad—these hardworking hands, these earnest, righteous hands, so still, so helpless, unfairly thrust into the world he so despised.

Tears welled up and spilled over.

"Hello, Dat."

Again, the eyelids quivered, followed by a mere shake of his head. He opened his mouth, closed it again.

"We're here to visit, Dat," Mary choked.

There was no sign that he'd heard, so Mary took her hand away. To stand beside his bed brought a bit of solace, but eventually Lydia led her away, her face showing no emotion and Mary desperately choking back her own.

The doctor arrived, introduced himself, and came straight to the point, saying the lung infection had entered the bloodstream, creating a condition called sepsis, and his heart was not as strong as he'd like. He assured them they were doing everything possible, which the sisters thanked him for, in turn.

They sat in stunned silence, then. Their father was very ill, but each one showed no emotion, only a resignation, the news borne stoically. Except for Mary, who had her own turmoil to sort through.

Suddenly, Rachel said he didn't seem as if he was actually going to die, and Lydia agreed, saying he'd pull through. He always had.

They took their carpet bags and their bonnets, found their way to the elevator, and were carried to the third floor. They found Mima's room and almost burst into laughter. There she was, her bed propped as high as it would go, her whole head swallowed up in a gigantic white sleep cap tied beneath her chin, watching television.

Her eyes lit up at the sight of them.

"Look, girls! Come look. It's something called the Discovery Channel, and it's lions and elephants and stuff. I didn't turn it on, the nurse did. But oh my, it's amazing."

In varying degrees of guilt, they turned in time to see a lioness stalk a herd of wildebeests. They held a collective breath as she went slowly forward, gasped as she pounced, after which they all came to their senses and told Mima to turn it off.

It was television, a *verboten sach.*

Mima rang for the nurse in attendance, who cheerfully did as Mima requested and left the room. Mary touched her shoulder, asked how she was doing, followed by each sister in turn.

Greeted warmly, genuinely happy to see the children of the man she had married, Mima informed them of her condition. She had pneumonia in both lungs, but already the antibiotics were doing their work, and she felt stronger, although she was fairly certain she'd be in for a few more days. She shifted happily, and Mary concealed a wide grin, knowing the minute they walked out, the television would be put to life again.

Going to the car, Rebecca said evenly, "I think maybe there is more to Mima than meets the eye. *Hesslich.*"

And Mary thought it was true for all of them, wasn't it? She started to giggle. "I guess it's a good thing she has that big *schlofe copp* on."

To which Lydia answered sourly. "She had better. To have her sins forgiven."

But Mary thought of Mima's childish enjoyment of the Discovery Channel, her curious mind suddenly elevated to the wonders of nature in faraway places, and was happy for her.

But of course, she did not tell the sisters.

She was dropped off at her house, glad to go through the warm brown door and into a quiet home of her own. The rewards of being the owner of her very own house were far too many to count, and gratitude welled up as she put the kettle on for a cup of tea.

Alone with her thoughts, she kept going back to her father's condition, the end of his life, and the readiness to meet the God he had always known and obeyed. The importance he placed on being a firm believer of the *ordnung.* Would it be enough? Or did it go hand in hand with receiving the blood of Christ to atone for his sins?

Did he have sin? Or did obedience chase it all away?

She cast a glance at her Bible, the almost new, rarely touched book of answers for every Christian. If she was very honest, it only confused her more than ever, so she left it closed, a nice decorative touch on the end table.

Over and over, she asked God to spare her father's life, to allow him to return with Mima, allow her to question his ways, to find a deeper understanding of the mysteries of the afterlife. She wanted to tell him how she had done what he wanted, had a free conscience in front of him, dressed and lived for him, and felt an increasing emptiness every single day. Sometimes she thought she might have reached the long sought-after blessing, and then it evaporated again.

She thought of Steve. What would he say about Heaven, about what it took to truly be saved?

THEY WERE CALLED to the hospital, the granite gray six-story building called Parkview Health, overlooking a grand park on the banks of the Huegenot River, the Adirondacks like a long line of sentinels watching over the comings and goings of life along its meandering banks.

He was awake, though extremely weak. Still in the intensive care unit, he was hoping to leave for another room with Mima.

No one told him Mima had gone home on Thursday. In short gasping sentences, he told them to hold fast to what was right. To stay in the *ordnung*, as it was the way of the cross. He said there was a small booklet in the lower left-hand corner of his desk containing every direction and detail for his funeral. "In case of my death," he gasped.

He closed his eyes, and the only audible sound was the rasping breath, his chest rising and falling. His long thin fingers plucked restlessly at the white sheet covering him.

Finally, he said in painful spurts, "Live righteously in the way I have taught. Let no man deceive you."

There were sincere acknowledgments of this advice, murmurings of assent. When he spoke again, it was hard to hear the labored words.

"There is something more, but I can't seem to grasp it."

They swayed forward, impatiently wanting more.

But he had fallen asleep.

DURING THE NIGHT, a cold rain was driven against the north windows, waking Mary from a troubled sleep. There was something, some noise. She rolled on her back and lay very still. The steady strumming of rain. For a long moment, she convinced herself it was nothing, then heard it again.

Someone was by the front door. A scraping.

There it was. A rapping, scraping, sliding sound. The pounding of her heart was loud in her ears. She had to get up, but seemed frozen. She should have listened to Art and bought a dog.

Slowly, she heaved her feet to the floor, sat upright.

She took a deep breath, a step toward the door.

The clock in the kitchen glowed, the hands at the one and twelve.

She jumped when the strange noise began again.

She stopped, held her breath, then moved soundlessly to the window and peered around the wooden trim and down to the stone floor.

She realized it was a small creature. A rabid wild animal? What should she do?

Then she heard a hoarse cry, a real child crying in desperation. Quickly, she moved over, unlocked the door, and yanked it open. Her flashlight's beam moved over a green and white striped T-shirt, torn jeans, bare feet, long black hair in sodden strings, and a dark face containing glistening black eyes.

"Missus?"

The question was spoken between sobs and hiccoughs, the one word going straight to her heart where it took up residence. She stepped out on the porch and bent over the wet, huddled form, one hand beneath the sodden back and one beneath the knees. A child. It was a small child, perhaps three or four years old.

Quickly, she lit the propane lamp, amazed to find the small brown face watching her every move. She sank down beside him, deciding it was a boy, and asked his name, before noticing the pronounced shiver, the chattering of teeth clacking together. She brought a few thick towels and wrapped him tightly, rubbing gently to dry him.

He began to cry in earnest.

"My mom. I want my mom," he sobbed.

"We can find your mom, if you tell me who you are."

"I'm . . ." he choked on a sob. "I'm Tiger."

"Tiger? Your name is Tiger?"

He nodded.

"Would you like a warm bath?"

He shook his head, his eyes going wide with fear.

"Then let me get you a blanket, to warm you up. I'll be right back."

She wrapped him in the oversized blanket, sat on the glider rocker, took him in her lap, and began to sing. The sobs quieted. She bent her head and sniffed the soaked black hair, which gave off a mild odor of soap and little boy hair. If she had a phone, she would notify the police. But at this point, it seemed more important to warm the child up than to traipse to Jessie and Art's place to use their phone.

Tiger's eyes were getting heavy, drooping slightly at the corners, his small form relaxing. This now, and her father gravely ill. An hour at a time, although she knew there would be no sleep for her. When she was positive he slept, she carried him to the guest room and laid him on top of the quilt, leaving the door open.

She must have dozed off only for a few minutes, awakening to a dull, gray morning light. Time to find the parents or guardian of this little guy.

Poor child. She could only imagine the terror of the night for someone as small as him.

She felt a presence rather than saw one, startled into being fully awake.

"Did he come back?"

She sat up, swung her feet over the edge.

"My dad. He said he'll be back."

"Who is your dad?"

"My dad."

"Do you know his name?"

His eyes were large and round and very worried.

"He said we were going for a ride, and we went. Then he put me out of the car, said to wait, he'd be right back."

"Okay, Tiger. You're safe here until we can find him. Would you like some hot chocolate?"

His brow wrinkled as he thought about it, then nodded his head quickly.

"Mm. Yeah."

His long dark hair was matted and tangled in back, his dark face not very thin, just normal-sized, with almost perfect features.

She knelt by his chair, plied him with simple questions, but could gain very little helpful information. His house was white, but a whole lot of other people lived in it, too. Upstairs and beside them. His mother's name was Mom. She worked but he didn't know where. His dad only came sometimes. He came for a visit. He worked, too.

She persuaded him to bathe, then washed his clothes and hung them by the heat of the woodstove, before making pancakes.

He ate, but only a few bites, saying he wanted his mother.

"Okay, Tiger, we'll find your mother. When your clothes are dry."

There was a chill in the air as they started out, but by the time they reached Art and Jessie's house, they were warmed by exertion.

"What now?" Jessie asked, her way of greeting them.

"He showed up on my porch last night."

"Good Lord."

She turned, yelled. "Art? Art, come here."

Art stumbled out of the kitchen, his hair disheveled, and looked from Mary to Tiger and back to Mary. Mary answered his questioning eyes by telling him and Jessie the bits and pieces she had extracted from Tiger.

Jessie shook her head.

"I dunno. I just dunno. You can get tangled up in a real mess sometimes, cases like this."

"Well, she can't put him out," said Art.

"No, she can't do that."

"Would you give us a ride to the police station?" Mary asked, which was immediately met with nods of approval.

"Yes, yes. That's the thing to do. Probably should have gone as soon as you found him, but that can't be helped now."

So Mary found herself bouncing to town with Art and Jessie , with Tiger beside her in the back seat. She thought he should probably be in a car seat, but that couldn't be helped. It was a short ride, anyway.

The police station was in a low brown building with a massive brick sign in front, glass doors, and low glass windows with no blinds. A thin red-haired woman took them to a room off a long hallway, the scent of old cigarette smoke and something like smelly feet permeating the stale air. Photographs dotted the wall like giant flies, along with a New York road map that was littered with round-headed pins. A picture of an obese police officer and his glum-looking wife and children was carefully preserved behind glass in an ornate silver frame, flanked by various awards and honors.

"It stinks in here," Jessie commented loudly.

Art held up a finger. "Sh."

"Don't tell me to be quiet. It stinks in here."

Tiger blinked, leaned hard against Mary. She put a protective arm around his shoulders.

The officer was big, very round with his leather belt drawing him in what appeared to be two pieces: an upper policeman and a lower one. Kind, though, and very helpful, he fingerprinted, took hair samples, asked questions, and said that if Mary was willing, she could watch Tiger until someone else was found.

"I'll have to talk to CPS—Child Protective Services—and they'll run a background check and stuff, but I don't imagine it will be a problem. They can fill you in on the paperwork and all that."

Mary found a lump forming in her throat when she bent to ask Tiger if he'd like to stay with her for a while, and he nodded brightly, saying his dad would be coming back soon.

The officer raised his eyebrows.

After Mary had spoken to the woman from CPS and signed some papers, she was told they could leave and someone would follow up with them soon. They stopped at a store to buy socks, underwear, a couple extra shirts and pairs of pants. Then they went to IGA for cereal, milk, bread, and some food Jessie insisted any kid needed—Froot Loops, graham crackers, apples, frozen chicken nuggets, Juicy Juice, and ice cream bars.

Tiger didn't smile, but his eyes looked pleased.

Mary spent a long, fretful day, wondering how her father was and trying to entertain the lonely boy who kept repeating the same question about his father ("When will he be back?"), sometimes weeping softly into the couch cushions.

Mary felt frustrated and alone, without an anchor to keep her thoughts at bay. What if no parent was discovered, or it turned out they didn't want their little boy back?

Was she up to giving him the love he would need, and would he have to be Amish if she was his guardian? Could a single girl even legally adopt? She didn't know.

She took him along to the barn in the evening, where he raised large fearful eyes to the horse towering above him and refused to feed him.

Back inside, she made chocolate chip cookies and allowed him to help, but that distraction was short-lived and it wasn't long before he was whimpering again. She watched the clock, hoping someone, anyone, would show up.

When Jessie arrived in the late afternoon, her face was tight. She ushered Mary into the bedroom and spoke in a hushed voice so Tiger wouldn't hear.

"They might have found him."

She mouthed, "The dad?" Mary raised her eyebrows, her heart beating too fast, too loud.

"Drove his car over a bridge."

Oh no, Mary thought. Surely the mother or grandmother, someone, would come for him. She had felt real pity for this sweet boy, but today had been stressful, and she knew she was not ready for this amount of responsibility.

"How could he, over a bridge?" she asked, suddenly angry at such a display of childishness.

"Did I say bridge? I meant cliff. A cliff. Into the stone quarry. Still no news about a mom."

She paused. "Oh, and your dad is about the same."

That, at least, was good news.

Mary shrank inwardly, wondering if she would have to be the one to tell Tiger the news, if the time came. She knew the Amish children were not protected from death but learned to accept it at a young age. People were dead when their heart stopped and they no longer breathed, but the soul was taken up to Heaven.

"Don't say anything," Jessie whispered. "Nothing's confirmed yet."

Mary shook her head, saying of course she wouldn't.

She took a week off, found toys at thrift stores and a few indoor garage sales. She purchased books, a few cars and trucks, sand toys, and a hefty ten bags of playground sand. One warmer afternoon, Mary built a sandbox, ruined her lower back lugging and dumping the sand into it, then stood back as the delighted boy began to shovel and fill containers.

Jessie watched Tiger while Mary went to the hospital to visit her father, then became discouraged when he took a turn for the worse. The antibiotics were doing the work, but his heart was not strong enough to keep his organs functioning properly; his kidneys were now in stage four renal failure.

Mary asked the questions she sought answers to—about sin, the afterlife, how to be obedient enough to avoid the everlasting lake of fire—but in his illness, his answers were jumbled, and she found herself more confused than ever.

With the added responsibility of this poor child, she decided to put her questions to rest. She had to focus her energy on Tiger.

CHAPTER 16

WHEN HER FATHER TOOK HIS LAST BREATH, THERE WAS NO ONE TO see, not even Mima. He died alone, on a windy night in May, when Mima had gone home to get some rest, the night nurse making her rounds when the alarm sounded. They had all expected it, but when the time arrived, it was still a shock. The finality of it simply rocked Mary's world, and she sobbed into her pillow at night, putting on a good face for Tiger's sake during the day.

As was the custom, Abner and Malinda's farm was swarmed with community members who cleaned barns and sheds and the house, preparing for funeral services. Mima and the eleven children, their spouses, and many grandchildren sat together in the house for two days, dressed in black. Meals were prepared and served by volunteers as the children wrote the obituary and arranged the funeral services. It was all done like a well-oiled machine, everyone seeing to his or her duty, working together in the way they had been taught.

In her grief, Mary left a message for Steve. She didn't have the energy to wrestle with whether it was right or wrong to do so, and she needed a friend.

THE DAY OF the funeral was a beautiful spring day in New York. A breeze ruffled new green leaves, sent blossoms on fruit trees drifting to earth, covering the ground in a soft white layer. The sun seemed to add a touch of benevolence, a heralding of things to come, leaving that which was behind, the cold and the fury of winter.

Mary sat with her family, her red hair brought into subjection, her covering large and made according to New York requirements.

Hundreds of friends and relatives crowded into the large equipment shed, most of whom Mary didn't know. How precious, though, the arrival of Aunt Lizzie and her girls, the husbands so neat, so cleaned up. She felt a sense of embarrassment at her own appearance, but Lizzie gathered her warmly into an embrace of loving kindness, followed in turn by each of the girls.

The tears flowed for Mary, and wise Aunt Lizzie recognized their tears for what they were, though most did not. Everyone in Pinedale commented on Mary's grief, how hard it was for her to lose her beloved father, and it was such a good thing she had him to point her in the right direction. The prodigals were always grateful to their benefactor. It had been proved over and over.

As the funeral service was conducted, Mary wept silently, but constantly. Memories of childhood, so many years of confusion and pain, the endless effort to win his approval, the overwhelming responsibility of Tiger, even the fact that Steve hadn't left her a message in return . . . it all swirled together into a tangle of overwhelming emotion.

Her father was gone now. Who would tell her if she got off track? She wasn't especially weeping out of love for him, but he was a necessity, in a roundabout way. Yes, he had ruined her relationships, and yes, he'd created an anger unlike any other, but he was her father, and he had always been her compass, pointing her toward obedience—even when she hadn't wanted him to.

Now she was alone in the world—except for Tiger, who wasn't really hers at all. Her father would be laid to rest beside the remains of her mother, and on the day Jesus returned, their souls would rise up to meet Him with joy.

The long funeral procession wound through the hills and valleys, across gurgling streams and new lambs frolicking in fresh pastureland.

The solemn darkness of the gray and black buggies was a stark reminder that frail mankind must return to dust.

On the windswept hilltop, the black-clad group bowed their heads and watched as the plain wooden coffin was lowered, able young men shoveling the clods of wet earth on top. Children wept for Doddy, but her siblings remained stone-faced, controlled. Mary lifted swollen eyes to find Aunt Lizzie smiling at her. A great longing to throw her arms around her, to be hugged and loved and understood, came over her like a warm breeze.

At the funeral dinner, she made small talk with eager relatives, found her father's brothers were nothing like him, Aunt Lizzie the center of their attention. It was indeed an eye-opener, this new understanding of her own traits so unlike her siblings. They sat with Mima after the funeral, when only the workers remained, setting everything right, washing floors and windows, putting away leftover food.

Mary thought Malinda's house was likely cleaner than it had ever been, but would return to its normal chaos in days. And on the sidelines, women would talk. They would cast meaningful glances, lower their voices, and say what everyone was thinking. Malinda was no housekeeper.

"Oh my, no. Did you smell her bathroom? That diaper bucket? Did she even know what a toilet brush was? *Siss yuscht hesslich.*"

"Her mother wasn't like that. Oh, but her sister Suvilla is no better. *Ya vell.*" Mouths snapped shut with indignation, consciences awakened, they quickly made excuses. Shouldn't talk like that, but each went home and poured a liberal amount of Comet into their own toilet bowls and swabbed with a vengeance.

MARY RETURNED TO her own home. Mima stayed on in the grandfather house, but made plans to return to the home of her childhood, in the beloved area between two mountains. She had done the will of God, had been a good companion to Amos Glick, had cared for the grandchildren when the need arose, but now she would return to her family. She had many good memories of Pinedale, indeed, but some not so good.

Did anyone truly understand the man they married? She had set out to change him, indeed she had, but in the end, she was the one who had come under subjection. His power remained a mystery, but she had good hope for his soul, and yes, she had loved him, had cared for him when the need arose.

CPS came for Tiger. Finding the mother had been no easy feat. She had fled from the violent acts of her husband and tried her best to disappear so he couldn't find her. But she was waiting for Tiger now, with his grandparents.

Mary hugged him, her heart filled with the caring she'd developed since he'd been in her home. She would always remember the softness of his T-shirt, the silkiness of his hair, the sweet little-boy scent of him. As tears rose to the surface, he kissed her cheek, drew back with large serious eyes, and told her he'd be back with his mom for a visit.

She watched him go with the woman from CPS and climb into her car. Mary stood in a haze of overpowering emotion. She wept for her father, for the fact she might never have children of her own, and for the long, dull weeks and months ahead of her. She realized now how badly she wanted a child of her own, an opportunity that might never present itself in her lifetime. No, she didn't want a dozen children and a husband who ruled with an iron fist, but she did ache for the experience of being a mother. With her father gone, would she be able to have a relationship with a young man of her choosing?

Her sister had nudged her side at the funeral service when the minister had spoken of a parent's teaching remaining with you till death, and now when life had fled from her father, his words would ring louder than ever.

But he wasn't here. The question burning in her conscience was to decipher between her own desires and God's leading.

Yes, she was attracted to Steve, wanted him badly. Was God in that feeling, or was it merely the lust of the eyes and the flesh? And now, it felt like God had sent Tiger, the little lost boy, just to tease her, to remind her of what she was missing out on in life. Was it possible that, because of her disobedience in her younger years, she had missed out on God's blessing forever?

MAY TURNED INTO June, the pea blossoms dropping off as the tender pods developed on sturdy green stalks, upheld by the chicken wire strung between two wooden posts pounded into the ground at each end. Mary's mother always yearned for a setup like this for her garden, but she never had one, her father saying it wasn't necessary, that the peas were just fine without a support for their vines. Every year, when the pea pods were rounded and Mam had pronounced them ripe, the children had been ushered into the wet, slimy pea patch, the vines tangled like family arguments. They hoisted dishpans and buckets, lifting vines and grasping wet peas. Skirts and aprons received the dripping pea pods, and before half the morning was gone, they were thoroughly soaked, the sun already hot on their shoulders. Mary's sisters bent their backs and worked hard without complaint, while Mary fumed her unspoken rebellion, split pea pods and ate them raw, threw empty pods at twittering sparrows, and dreamed of telling Dat to get a bucket and come see how miserable pea picking was.

Now, Mary loved to be in her very own garden on a fine summer day. If she put up chicken wire, it was no one's business but her own. It was a joy, picking handfuls of peas, watching the nuthatches and juncos come to the feeder by the garden, everything bathed in morning light. She felt a sense of renewal, where possibilities awaited her, the sun warming her shoulders.

Two five-gallon buckets full later, her back hurt, her legs ached, and her shoes were soaked with mud and dew from the vines, but she could look forward to sitting in a clean chair on the back porch to shell them. She washed her hands, dried her feet, and donned a clean apron before settling herself on the comfortable chair she'd chosen for the job.

All around her, God's beauty became alive. The deep green of the surrounding forest, the brown, black, and gray of sculpted tree trunks, the lawn freshly mowed with a border of shrubs and flowers. She'd dug her borders the way Aunt Lizzie had taught her, and planted many things she had bought at the local greenhouse. She would never tell her sisters how much she had paid for the boxwoods and yews, the arborvitae and icy spruces, the daisies and phlox and lavender.

As she split pea pods with her thumb, raked them out in one swift, fluid motion, listened to the peas hit the bottom of a stainless glass bowl, her thoughts were taken to her childhood home. As children, they'd sat on the broken porch floor, the gray paint peeling like dead tree bark, sitting on folding chairs her father had salvaged from the dump. Scattered around them were plastic calf starter buckets and beat-up bowls, wooden bushel baskets for the empty hulls. There were a few straggly pink petunias planted too close to the porch, the long grass growing haphazardly around them. They had never dug borders, and certainly never spent a penny on expensive shrubbery.

As a child, these sparse surroundings were all she knew. Really, it wasn't until she went to Lancaster that she'd seen another way of life and realized how primitive her own was.

Her father had told her that the lust of the eyes was from the spirit of the world. The devil had shown her earth's luxuries, which were not for the Christians on the narrow road to Heaven. And for a while, she had turned a deaf ear, gone on her own way and carried a sense of disdain for his idealistic views. But now, seated on a cushioned wicker chair, a cement urn of geraniums by the doorway, the knowledge of having spent four hundred and twenty-nine dollars for the chair and close to a hundred on the urn, could she justify the purchases?

Yes, she had a changed heart, changed clothing, but oh how she still loved things of this world. She did. She loved nice things, decor for the porch and the lawn and the interior of her house, and now her father was not here to judge her decisions.

"Hello? Yoo-hoo! *Bischt da-home?*"

Mary jumped, got up quickly, scattering pea pods.

"I'm here. On the porch," Mary called out.

Mima's rounded face appeared at the back screen door, her black bonnet framing the wide welcoming smile. Dressed in the widow's black, she looked particularly austere, but her expression was warm and friendly.

"Well, Mima, it is certainly good to see you. I was just pitying myself a bit. Pea-shelling always makes me reminisce."

Her hand was caught in a firm grip, then covered with the remaining one, Mima's eyes alive with love.

"I'm so glad, Mary. I've thought of you so much since the funeral, then told myself perhaps there was a reason you were on my mind so much. Mary is lonely, I thought, so I came and sure enough, your peas are ready. Give me a bowl."

"I certainly will. And coffee. Have you already had your coffee this morning?"

"Of course, but I'm ready for another cup," Mima said, beaming.

It was so good to sit in the warmth of the golden sunlight, discussing her father's death, the funeral, the relatives, and the great diversity of Amish folk from all over the states. Peas were split, raked out with thumbs, as words flowed easily from one to the other.

"So, tell me, Mary, are you handling the grief okay?" Mima asked, searching Mary's face.

"I don't know if it is grief," Mary said honestly.

"But you loved your father."

"Perhaps."

Mima said nothing, unsure how to respond as she took in the beauty of the backyard.

Mary eyed her with a piercing gaze. "Did you?"

"Did I what?"

"Did you love him?"

"Yes. Yes, I did. Certainly at first."

Realizing the courage it took to announce this, Mary prodded her on, but Mima shook her head, saying he was a good man, and it was wrong to discuss the shortcomings of one deceased.

Mary dumped a small bowl of shelled peas into the larger half-full one, sat back down, and reached for a handful of pea pods. She sighed, letting her breath out in a long, slow whoosh.

"Is it wrong, Mima? Or are we just trying to avoid the truth?"

"What is truth?" Mima countered.

Mary was completely caught off guard, was rendered speechless by Mima's honesty.

"I mean," she went on. "After living with him these few short years, my view of God seems to have been distorted. Not that it's wrong, necessarily. But well, it's difficult to talk about this without dishonoring his good name. He was a good man, if a bit . . ."

Mary leaned forward, her willingness to share evident in the brilliance of her green eyes.

"Go on. I will understand."

"It's just that—and I have gone over this a hundred times in my mind—it's almost as if I lost sight of aspects of God. Over time, I was blinded by the sight he used, as if I was consumed by his way of interpreting the Scripture, his narrow-minded way of using it to judge everything and everybody. He was a powerful man, one well versed in Scripture. He read it constantly. He lived a life of self-denial, there is no doubt."

Mary nodded. "That power still rules my thinking."

Mima said softly, "You, too? I often wondered."

"There is simply so much I don't quite understand, and I was growing spiritually, just coming to the point where I wanted and needed him to explain things so I could be more fully obedient to him and obtain the blessing he so often told me I lacked."

Mima pursed her lips and squinted her eyes.

"I mean, I'll never be perfect, but I have to try. He admonished me about the color of the blinds in my house, and I haven't changed them yet. But when I do, I believe I'll be closer."

"Closer to what?" Mima asked, her voice taking on a sharp tone.

"I'm not sure. To obedience? To God's blessing?"

"And you really believe the Lord's blessing will be upon you after you change the color of your blinds?" Mima burst out.

"No. Not really. But maybe? Yes, it might, because I'd be one step closer to following the *ordnung*."

"Mary."

The kindness in her voice brought quick tears to Mary's eyes.

"You don't know what you believe, do you?"

"Sometimes I do."

"Do you still get those panicked spells? That sour stomach?"

"No. Well, sometimes. Not as often as I did when I lived in Lancaster. That was why I moved back. They kept getting worse."

Mima said her husband was dead and gone now, and she did not want to dishonor his name, Lord knows, but the man had taken her for a loop. Now that she was alone again, she had a little more perspective again.

"He kept a tight rein on his own will, was an expert at self-denial, but not in some areas. He had a terrible temper."

"I know. As a child, I knew."

"So here it is in a nutshell. He ruled through fear. We were—are—afraid of wrongdoing, afraid of being caught out by him, and afraid of God. His God is fierce, demanding. But the Bible tells us we're all sinners and it's only through Jesus's sacrifice that we're saved."

Mima threw caution to the wind, her voice picking up strength.

"Yes, by all outward appearances, we are the perfect family. You, the last prodigal, returned to the fold. But are we? Mary, the bickering in this family is out of control. You have no idea. Especially the daughters-in-law, who fairly hissed at the sight of him. I don't know how long Malinda could have taken it."

She paused. "But I've said too much."

Mary eyes opened wide. Her mouth dropped open. She shook her head in disbelief. Finally, she found her voice.

"Was that why no one else cried at the funeral?"

Mima shrugged her shoulders. "That's not for me to say. Your father despised emotion, in public or private. He had an iron hold on his own, except when it came to anger, so he expected it of others. Tell me, Mary, why did you weep?"

"It's . . . it's hard to live life without him. Who will guide me?"

Mima was shocked. "Who, indeed? Mary, Mary."

After having been held captive for too long, subject to the voice of judgment and condemnation, Mima was coming back to the faith of her childhood. Faith in a God who loved her—a sinner—enough to die for her.

Mary lifted perplexed eyes. "Who, Mima?"

"Why, Mary. God, and Jesus, and the Holy Spirit. The Comforter is come, and he will show us all things."

"Now you sound like my old friend Chester Nolt, and he sure wasn't all that great."

Mima chuckled. "Stop looking for answers in imperfect men."

"I can't find God, Mima," she burst out. "The Bible scares me. God is silent and distant and points His finger at me every single day. I live in fear of His return, knowing I am not ready. I try, I try so hard to do what is right, but with every change I make, there is always something else I need to do. I'm not good at self-denial. I like nice things."

She slapped the arm of the chair she was sitting on.

"I saw this at Lowe's. I had to have it. It's lust. I finally get victory over my fancy clothes, then I buy this chair for way too much money. And I'm afraid I'll never manage to get to Heaven."

She was breathing hard now, her chest rising and falling.

"My brothers and sisters would never spend money for a chair like this. They'd take one look and recognize it for what it is. A temptation."

"Mary, it's a chair. A very nice comfortable chair for you to enjoy. Do you feel guilty in front of God? Is it forbidden by the church?"

"Yes. No, I'm not sure. I don't know. God would want me to take the chair back to Lowe's and give the money to the poor."

Mima slapped the arm of her chair, her eyes crinkling with delight.

"*Ach* my. I can't believe we're having this conversation. One of my stepdaughters. You seem like my own child. And I wish so much I could help you to see, but I think you must find it yourself. There is no one in a better position than one who seeks the truth, but you must adjust your eyesight to the One above."

She lifted a crooked forefinger, jabbed at the porch ceiling.

"You were raised in fear, rebelled against it, hated your father then, and finally found your way back. But fear is still your master. You are brought into subjection by it, but it will never fulfill you.

"Oh, I know full well. He had me convinced of it. I was like a disciple to his harsh views. Mary, I helped run off the young man in your life at that time. When I dared go up against your father, it did not go well with me. So I gave up, the way a good housewife is expected to do."

Mary nodded, averting her eyes.

"Well," Mary sighed. "I'm old now. I must try to give my own will up for God's and forget about a husband or children."

"You never know what God has in store." Mima placed a hand on Mary's arm. "But first, you need peace in that soul of yours. Your father was a God-fearing man, but he wasn't perfect, and he was never going to bring you peace. You'll have to look straight to God for that. I will pray for you every day of my life."

"I wish you'd stay here."

"No, you won't find peace with me either. You need to put your trust in an invisible God. Not me. Or anyone else. Every human being will eventually disappoint you. You know what you should do?"

Mary looked up.

"You should travel somewhere, go away for a spell."

"I have often thought of doing just that, but I don't have the nerve. Where would I go?"

She nodded then, answered her own question.

"Actually, I have dreamed of . . . well, I read this book, where a young woman went on a long hike alone. It was life-changing for her. But it would take planning, and money. And I'm not exactly in great shape, either."

"Why would it take money?"

"The gear. The time off work. The food. I don't know. I probably won't do it. Would the church even allow it? Do you think it would be safe?"

"Probably. Depends on where you'd go." Mima shrugged.

"Well, it's just a daydream."

But she'd owned and operated a successful bakery. She had dreamed of that, and actually done it. Then again, that had only ended in the worst panic attack of her life, causing her to make the decision to come here to New York.

She could not always run when things went sideways, could she?

Mima watched as emotion displayed itself across her face, the shelled peas in the bowl worried with restless fingers. Her plight was serious, and there was a long battle ahead of her. To be raised without faith was one thing, but to be raised with a substitute for faith quite another. Sticky tentacles encircled her questioning mind, her eyes half closed with the dread of an angry God who disapproved of her every move, coupled with a strong will and a liberal view of so many things, traits handed down by genetics, perhaps. A mixture of circumstances, who knew?

But if Mary were to find a suitable young man, there was no doubt in Mima's mind, the relationship would be bound to fail unless Mary was more settled in her own mind.

But she'd said enough already. So she shelled more peas, brought up the subject of Abner *sie* Malinda being in the family way again, and how was the poor woman ever expected to keep her head above water.

CHAPTER 17

THE FOLLOWING WEEK, SHE DROVE HONEY BACK TO HER FATHER'S residence to help Mima pack her belongings. It was a hot day, the summer wearing itself into July, when the sun's power produced discomfort for man and beast.

She slowed her horse to a walk going uphill, the white foam building up around the britchment and along the traces. As Honey lunged faithfully into her collar, Mary watched a pair of bluebirds in flight, coming to rest in a barberry bush beside the road. Such a beautiful blue. She felt sorry for the poor birds, having to light on those prickly branches.

Her mind was pleasantly empty this morning, after a good night's rest after a long evening's work, pulling out the pea stalks and hauling them away with the wheelbarrow, then removing the posts and chicken wire.

She'd tilled the soil and planted lima beans afterward, the way her mother and Lizzie had always done. She wasn't sure if it was a good idea here in New York, with the shorter growing season, but she'd give it a try. Lima beans were not her favorite vegetable, but she liked them in vegetable soup, with cabbage.

She hummed a tune in time with the buggy wheels, then thought about installing a telephone in a shanty at the end of the drive, permissible by church rules and a very handy arrangement. She used Art and Jessie's phone now, but wasn't sure if she had always been welcome of late, the way Jessie was always in the middle of some important task or other when she knocked. She guessed that, too, was common sense, the church allowing neighborhood telephones so as not to disturb the neighbors.

She couldn't build a phone shanty by herself, so she'd have to purchase one from a shed builder, she supposed. Or ask Abner and Jonas, which would likely be met by opposition.

It didn't seem real, walking through the door of the *Daudy* house to find him gone. He really had passed on, which was a bit hard to digest, really. Although, after Mima's visit, she could work through her grief with more understanding, recognizing the tears as those of deep disappointment that things had not been better.

Oh, but it was true.

Mima came up from the cellar, a large men's handkerchief tied around her head, the front of her dress stained with dust and dirt.

Her eyes lit up at the sight of her.

"Oh hello, Mary. *Komm rye.*"

"How are you, Mima?"

"Good. I'm doing good. Just working hard to get ready."

She flopped into a chair, nodded at the tea kettle.

"Go ahead if you want tea or coffee. It's too hot for me already."

Mary looked around, said she'd gotten a lot accomplished.

Mima nodded, took the corner of her apron to wipe her forehead.

"Abner and Malinda have enough on their plate without me yammering over there for help. Some of my siblings are coming tomorrow, for what that's worth. They'll be a huge boost."

But Mary was only half listening, falling on her knees by a box of her father's possessions. The wooden backscratcher, the small wooden pen holder he always had on one side of his desk. Stacks of diaries, old journals, deeds, and paid bills. A bag of marbles. A Ziploc bag of paper clips, small nails, eraser stubs.

A stack of blue men's handkerchiefs, never red ones. Red was the devil's color, he always said. Far be it from him to have the devil's color in his own pocket. A hook of resentment caught her unaware, slicing across her mind. When he told her that, she was in third or fourth grade, and he removed all her red crayons from the well-worn box she owned. She refused to eat red apples and became nervous when her face turned red from the cold. She stayed far away from a classmate when she or he turned up in red clothes. She pictured red horns and a forked tail from the individual wearing the fateful color.

So many things were deemed sinful. Skipping to school on a bright morning was brought to a halt by a rebuke from her brother, followed by a sister saying she could see Mary's knees. Mary's black stockings had been drawn up to her knees, secured by a length of elastic sewn into a garter, so tight it was a miracle they didn't cut off her circulation. She told her mother if she didn't make new garters her legs would fall off right below the knee and how would they like to push her to school on a *reddaschtul*? Her mouth was smacked a stinging blow by her mother, but she held her head up high and refused to show pain.

As she sorted through her father's things, she found a small blue book, the one terrifying her most through all of her childhood. It was called "The Heart Book," or in German, *Hotz Büchly*.

Her father often took her on his knee and showed her the ancient depictions of death and life, of Heaven and Hell. Drawings of angels, the real holy ones who came to carry you away when you died, and the hovering demon with split hooves and a tail. The fear of all spiritual matters took root in her small heart back then, the droning voice of her father explaining Hell in full detail—a never-ending lake of fire was too much for her sprouting senses, so she told herself it wasn't real.

Denial was survival for her in those days. If you didn't believe it, it wasn't really true.

"You're being very quiet," Mima observed.

"Just going through stuff," she answered quietly.

And here was the cigar box with pens and pencils with business logos. Zimmerman's Horse Dentistry, Logan's Plumbing, Beiler's Horse Shoeing. There must have been a hundred of them, all saved, kept in a box.

She sighed, picked up a handful and released them. She thought how her father's bones would return to dust long before these plastic pens began to break down in a landfill somewhere. Here was his photoless ID card. Absolutely no picture of himself anywhere, no graven images.

She'd let her brothers take care of all this.

She pushed the box away with a sense of finality. So many worthless items to dispose of, but she guessed if it brought him a sense of accomplishment, it was worth that much. To be frugal, a good steward of his finances, had been his highest goal, and certainly he had done well, saving every pen and pencil.

She called out to Mima, "Tell me what to do."

"Oh, you're busy going through his stuff," she answered.

"No. I'm done. Nothing to see."

"He didn't have much, did he?"

"No."

"Does it make you sad?"

"No, not more than anything else."

But it had. An impending sense of doom settled over her. What was life here on earth if all you had to show for it was a cigar box full of pens and pencils, a mortgage on a crumbling farm in a valley filled with rumblings of God's wrath and human sin?

Why did anyone ever bother trying? The sun rose each day and set at night without fail, the four seasons came and went, and man struggled on, only to take his last breath at the hands of a cruel disease. Between the covers of your life's book, what was there? Lost in thought, she became aware of the beating of her heart, the acceleration like a frantic sparrow now, the fluttering wings increasing her fear. She tried to concentrate, tried her best to draw deep, even breaths, thought of rippling water and calm summer breezes, but was engulfed in waves of terror. Sweat poured off her face, her mouth dried out like a wind-driven leaf.

Mima stood over her. "Mary!"

Gasping, lunging for the bathroom door, she threw herself in and slammed it shut, lowered the lid of the commode, and sat down. She put her head between her knees to stay conscious as waves of dread rolled over her. Inky waves of blackness, thick and suffocating.

The door was thrown open. Mima was there, rubbing her shoulders, saying, "Mary. Mary."

She began to cry, then, huge gulping sobs of despair and loss. And Mima stayed, rubbing her shoulders, her presence keeping her centered, bringing her back from the precipice.

"Tell me what brought it on," Mima pleaded.

But Mary choked on her sobs.

Mima led her to the back porch, where the shade protected them from the blazing sun. For a long moment, they were quiet, as Mary's sobs subsided, then stopped. She sat up, wiped her face, but kept her eyes downcast. A thin barn cat appeared out of nowhere, arched its back, and rubbed against the webbed lawn chairs.

Mary reached down and rubbed a palm across the cat's back, a deep shuddering breath escaping her.

Mima waited.

"It's so hopeless, Mima. Life is hardly worth the effort we put into it, really."

"Don't think like that, Mary. Please don't. You scare me. I'm afraid I'm deserting my post, going back to my old home. You need someone to stay with you. Won't you please see a doctor, at least to get over the worst of this?"

"This? What is this? What is wrong with me? Is it my heart?"

Mima shook her head.

"Come with me, Mary. Come stay at my house in the valley."

"No, I can't. I have jobs. The housecleaning. I'll be fine."

"You aren't well, Mary."

"I'll be fine."

AT HOME, SHE took a long soothing shower, changed into clean clothes, and relaxed on the pretty chair, her thick red hair drying in waves of color. The geraniums moved very slightly in the breeze, bringing the scent of tilled soil and decaying vegetation.

Here was a measure of stillness, here on her own property, surrounded by cool forest, even in the middle of summer's heat.

She must stay here, away from memories she would never fully understand and had no power to control. She knew Mima meant well, knew her words were meant to be helpful, but it only stirred up a deep confusion, especially coupled with solid evidence of her father's ways.

Where had that thought come from, that wondering what he had left behind? Of course life was worth living. She must bring her thoughts into subjection, must control that part of her brain.

For so many unknown reasons, she didn't really know God. Of course He was up there somewhere, watching her. He knew her sinful ways, could see her disobedient heart, but she had no clear idea of who He really was—except, perhaps, someone to fear.

She wondered seriously for a moment if Steve would contact her if she changed the color of her blinds and sold this chair. Oh, and the urn. Would God's blessing finally reach her if she obeyed the law to the letter? Mima didn't think so, she could tell.

Well, Mima didn't know everything.

For now, she was grateful for the measure of peace she found here in her own backyard. Perhaps if she had no other blessing, she could begin by being thankful for tiny things.

Opening her eyes, she watched a blue butterfly with black outlines on its wings hover and dip above a lantana bush, a perfect combination of colors against the backdrop of green forest. She closed her eyes and whispered, "Thank you," hoping God would not find her silly.

AT WORK THE following day, she listened as Mrs. Combs told her about her husband's drinking at night, the way it was beginning to affect their relationship, turning the music up too loud when he made dinner at seven.

"He just gets weird," she moaned, sinking onto the leather sofa, her head in her hands. Her hair was loose and disheveled, her eyes bloodshot and swollen as two hard-boiled eggs, her T-shirt loose on her skinny frame.

Mary pushed the dust cloth steadily across the piano, lifted a pile of sheet music, dusted underneath, and replaced it.

"Here. Give that here."

Mary obeyed.

"I'm hiding this. He doesn't need to go pounding on these keys at night. He drives me crazy."

Mary didn't comment, going on with the dusting, carefully lifting costly items and replacing them.

"Did you clean the hall mirror?"

"I did."

"You know that Windex doesn't work real well."

"I know. I use window cloths."

"What are they?"

Mary explained, was met with a snort. "Never heard of such a thing. How can windows be clean without soap? They're not. Fold your paper towels better. Like this."

Mary watched patiently as she demonstrated the proper usage of Bounty towels, which would always, always leave lint and streaks on her windows, then listened as she described her husband's alcohol-induced singing as he cooked, the way he created an argument as they ate, and how she always had to praise his cooking, even if it wasn't all that great.

Mary thought of Amish housewives cooking every single meal with no help from their husbands and then milking cows in the dairy barn after.

But Mrs. Combs didn't realize this, and her own set of problems were very real to her, so she listened.

"Don't you have a boyfriend? Aren't you ever getting one? I mean, it's unusual for your kind to be this old without being married."

"Yes, it's unusual," Mary said, quietly.

"Well, maybe you're better off. Men are just trouble. Anyway, I gotta leave. I'm getting my hair done, then yoga. Oh, would you clean the inside of the microwave? I warmed a dish of spaghetti and got it too hot."

Mary couldn't bring herself to answer, so she nodded.

"Okay, see you."

For thirty dollars an hour, you did what you were told, never talked back without due respect, and washed windows with Bounty towels and Windex, even if they left streaks and lint. You also used Clorox on the bathroom floor even if you would never use it on your own floors. You were grateful for the ride to and from work, knowing every handful of cash would be your means of survival.

You also didn't ask which was the most sordid fate, a husband you couldn't stand or no husband at all. You stayed quiet and knew your place in the order of things.

She smiled at her reflection in the hall mirror.

Yes, she was no longer a teenager, for sure, but she wasn't all that bad, either. In summer, she was a bit golden, her freckles complementing those red waves.

As she moved into the computer room, she dusted, swept, and wondered how her future would pan out. She had no joy in thinking of the coming days, of fall's approach, even the long winter ahead, but knew she must make an effort to go on. If only she had a goal, a challenge, she might find a purpose in life.

She thought of Tiger. Where was he now?

Tiger and Elam. She often thought of Eli and Sarah Allgyer's house, the golden aura of perpetual sunshine, the love and healing surrounding this child with leukemia. The antiseptic scent of the hospital hallways, the pale face surrounded with love. And then the small lost boy named Tiger.

With all her heart, she hoped Tiger was safe, secure in his mother's love.

She supposed the two boys had been in her life for a good reason, but had not been able to explain anything, even to herself.

She'd often heard the saying that everything happened for a reason, but how was a person expected to understand? She placed a kitchen chair below the microwave, stepped up on it, and peered inside, finding splattered, dried-on tomato sauce.

She shook her head, stepped down, and drew a sinkful of hot water, added a long squirt of dish detergent. She swirled a clean rag in it, wrung it out, and stepped back up. It was slow going, but eventually, the interior was shining, with no trace of tomato sauce. She glanced at the clock, knew she had to speed up to finish in less than an hour.

Would her whole life be a series of cleaning days?

She would practice gratitude, would appreciate her house and garden, her family and friends, the beauty of New York, and yes, the ability to have a successful cleaning business. Perhaps if she did that, she would finally find the favor of God.

On the way home, Mrs. Combs told her the house always smelled so good when she was finished, and how she appreciated the open windows in each room as she cleaned. With central air, it just gave the house a fresh feeling in summer. Mary smiled, felt compensated for her hard work, and knew why she continued to work for Mrs. Combs.

As they drove up to her house, they met a taxicab pulling away, a black and yellow vehicle with a white top across the roof of the car.

"Looks like you have company," Mrs. Combs remarked.

"Hm." Mary answered.

She was given a wad of cash, a confirmation about the coming date to clean, a smile and a wave. Mary took a deep breath, then stepped on the porch and into the house, finding nothing out of place, no one lurking about. She opened the back screen door and found Steve, looking a bit uncomfortable, his duffel bag on the chair she'd purchased at Lowe's.

She stopped, her eyes wide in her startled face.

"Steve?"

"Mary."

He stepped forward, extended a hand. She took it. They shook hands formally.

"I took a chance to come see you. I couldn't bring myself to come to your father's viewing, but I wanted to extend condolence."

"Thank you."

She nodded at the chair. "You're staying?"

"If I may."

She snorted unbecomingly, slanted him an exasperated look.

"You know you can't stay here."

"Why not?"

"Because of my father. Well, his voice. My family, the rules. The church."

"Mary, we are friends. I have no plans of saying or doing anything immoral, not even questionable. I was just hoping we could talk."

"Oh, do we? Now that my father is dead and gone, safely six feet under, you think New York has changed for the better?"

He said nothing, but squinted his eyes as he surveyed the backyard in the brilliant afternoon sun. Birdcall was everywhere, the drone of bumblebees on hollyhocks, the swish of cornstalks in the small garden. The leaves from the poplar trees created dappled shade by the porch.

"I'm sorry you feel that way, Mary. I know I should have come when he passed. You did leave a message, and I'm grateful. You'll have to call me a coward for not coming when you needed me."

"I didn't need you. I don't now. I'm fine."

"Good. Glad to hear it."

He paused, looked at his duffel bag, straightened his shoulders, and took a deep breath. "Alright, if that's how you feel, I'll get my bag and hitch a ride back to the bus station. I was hoping to come to an understanding somehow, but that doesn't seem possible, so I'll take my leave."

"I didn't say you had to go."

"You sort of did, actually. Do you want me to stay?"

"How long?"

"Till Sunday."

He could see the conflicting emotion, the biting of her lower lip, the anxious eyes going to the corner of the house, as if her father's ghost had already appeared to warn her of her hazardous position.

She looked at the chair, the worn rocker beside it, evaluated the cost of telling him to sit down, after which her eyes went back to the house corner. He saw the raised eyebrows, the tense shoulders, before she lowered them, shook her head, and sighed.

"*Ach*, well, you may as well sit down. Let me get some iced tea."

He sat. A quick prayer bolstered his courage. He realized the need to make these few days count, to win her trust in a very short length of time. To see her step through the screen door had certainly cemented his feelings for her. Her face, her voice, the fullness of her figure—it was all the Mary of his dreams, and all he ever hoped to have. She had so much strength, a hidden reserve of good, if only she would have the faith to see it.

If only she could see the true way of Christ, free from the disabling fear that bound her. But how could he show her that without seeming like he was tempting her into sin? It was daunting, but he would never forgive himself if he didn't give it all he had.

CHAPTER 18

SHE RETURNED WITH A TRAY ON WHICH SHE'D PLACED TWO TALL glasses of tea with ice cubes tinkling, a plate of pretzels, and slices of yellow cheese.

She eyed him apologetically. "I'm hungry after housecleaning."

"Of course. Don't you want more than a few pretzels?"

"There is a casserole in the oven."

They talked of mundane things then—the weather, his work, the garden, the shorter growing season. Mary sipped her iced tea, broke a pretzel in half, added a slice of cheese, and ate it hungrily.

"I'm starved."

They both laughed, which served to clear the air between them.

"Now tell me about your dad," he said, his eyes crinkling as he watched her face.

So she did, starting with the call for help, the situation she'd found in the small house, and the hospital stay for both him and Mima. Often, her eyes would be lowered, or slid away uncomfortably, her apron picked up and folded into pleats, the agitation clearly visible. When she stopped, he watched her face until her eyes found his.

"Mary, you've been through a lot. Grief is never easy, and I'm sure you loved your father."

"I did. I do. His words ring true, now more than ever."

"That's what they say. I wouldn't know, since I'm fortunate enough to have both parents still. But I'm the oldest in the family, so they're only in their fifties. I hope to have you meet them someday."

"Why?"

"Mary."

She broke a pretzel half, then in fourths. She inspected the boards on the porch floor, took the toe of her shoe and shoved a stray leaf, then leaned over and undid the laces of her shoes, removed them, and set them aside.

"I miss sandals," she said quietly.

"You don't wear them here?"

"No. Of course not."

"But there's no future in Lancaster for you?"

"I don't know if there's a future for me anywhere."

"Don't say that."

She shrugged, said the casserole was done, likely. He followed her inside, where he found the kitchen stifling, in spite of the mountain breeze. She said nothing as she opened the oven door, lifted the lid of a glass dish, and stirred the contents. A delicious aroma rose from the dish, and he realized how hungry he was, having done without lunch. She set two plates and the iced tea, then went to open a cabinet drawer. They sat together and bowed their heads in silent prayer. When they lifted their faces, their eyes met, but hers slid away before he could say anything.

The chicken and rice was hot, filling, and delicious. She served a slice of apple pie with ice cream for dessert, but conversation was stilted, starting in self-conscious fits and coming to immediate halts. The sheer togetherness of sharing space at a kitchen table, the unspoken world of feelings between them, rendered them both helpless.

"I have to go to work tomorrow," she said stiffly.

"You can't cancel? I was hoping to go hiking."

"Hiking? In this heat?"

"Why not? It would be cooler in the mountains. I know you said you wanted to take a solo hiking trip, but I thought maybe we could do a test run together. See how you like it."

"I can't cancel."

As the late afternoon turned into evening, they retired to the back porch where the best breeze from the open backyard was available. They had just settled themselves when the sound of steel rims on wooden buggy wheels alerted them to someone's arrival. Mary was out of her chair in one frightened move, her hands cupped beside her face as she stared through the screen door and out the front window.

"Quick, Steve. You have to hide."

Irritation rose in his chest. Here was a grown woman, an adult in her own right, terrified of introducing him to a family member, likely. None of this was right, and he told her so, without a care for consequences. He needed for her to see how unfair this really was.

"Who is it?"

"My sister Mattie and her husband."

"I want to meet them. I refuse to hide."

"You can't. Please, Steve. There will be talk. You have to listen to me."

"I'd love to visit with them."

So he stayed, was introduced, shook hands with the stalwart Reuben, and found the brilliant green eyes on his face were welcoming, curious. Mattie was a thin little woman, surrounded by three children of various ages, all toddlers hiding behind her skirts, completely covered in chicken pox, the lesions red and sore.

"Mary, I figured you'd have had chicken pox as a child, right?" Without waiting for an answer, she plowed on. "Well, but this is something. I didn't know you had company. And who did you say he is?" She lifted her apron, fished out a gray, crumpled handkerchief and blew loudly, then bent to wipe the noses of all her children.

"It's Steve Riehl, from Lancaster County. A friend."

"Where's his wife? Oh, you don't have a beard. You don't have one." She laughed, then asked how a single man could come visit a girl like Mary, living here by herself. She looked around, but Mary had vanished.

The sight of those lesions, the remembered misery, had dislodged an unwanted emotion, the specter of an instance in her childhood she had forgotten. Her father had wanted to visit someone, but she'd come down with chicken pox, so he was unable to go. He told her only disobedient children got chicken pox, and they were a sign of God's punishment.

She heard her name called, so she went back to the porch, effectively subduing the swift breaths, the pounding heart.

She met Mattie in the kitchen.

"Mary, where were you? Listen, you can't have this chappie staying here. Dat would have a fit."

"He's not my chappie, and I've already told him he can't stay." This was true. She absolutely had told him that, whether or not she changed her mind before evening.

This seemed to calm Mattie somewhat. Looking around, she observed the fact that Mary's house was fancy, and what was she thinking with those blinds?

"I haven't gotten around to changing them yet," Mary answered patiently.

They found Steve immersed in a lively conversation with Reuben, his wide-brimmed straw hat pushed back on his head, his green eyes alight with interest. It didn't seem as if it mattered at all to have Steve sitting hatless, in a polo shirt, his suspenders store-bought with black and white stripes. One of the little boys stood at his knee, waiting to be held, and with a smile, the child was lifted, cuddled. There was no evidence of impatience, only a caring thought for his son's welfare. The little girl, Sarah, whined for a drink, but Mattie told her to hush, she was listening to Steve. When Sarah began to cry, she reached out with thin lips and pinched the little arm, hard. The child cried even harder.

Reuben bent down and spoke to the small boy, then placed him on the chair he vacated, smiled at Sarah, and gathered her up in his arms.

"Are you thirsty, Sarah?"

She nodded, a smile breaking through her tears.

Mattie told Mary he spoiled the children, but she tried to make up for it when he wasn't around. Mary's chest fell as if an elephant stepped on it and squeezed the life out of it, the raw pity for Mattie's children almost more than she could bear. Was this, then, the legacy her father left behind at his passing?

The time passed reasonably, with Mattie convinced there was no romance between Steve and Mary.

When the buggy crunched its way down the gravel drive, Mary fell into her chair, arms extended, and breathed deeply of the cooling night air.

"Mattie looks like you," Steve observed.

"Huh. She's half my size."

"I'd pick you any day."

Mary frowned. "Now what am I supposed to say?"

"Thank you."

Far away, a screech owl began its high, undulating call, a sound always putting her teeth on edge.

"Do you have whippoorwills here?" Steve asked.

"I never heard any."

"Tell me, Mary, why were you afraid? Why did you think I should hide? They seemed fine with my being here."

Mary shook her head. "Mattie wasn't."

"What is she going to do about it?"

"I have no idea. Something, no doubt."

JULIA GLADSTONE PICKED Mary up the following morning, with Steve at home doing the breakfast dishes. He said he'd clear the stable till she returned.

She had never exactly told him he could stay, but at some point, it became so late that it would be ridiculous to ask him to leave. And in the morning, she reasoned it would be inhospitable to kick him out. Far into the night, they'd shared thoughts, hopes, and dreams, made coffee, and shared half a shoofly pie. Steve told her she was the only girl he'd ever met who enjoyed a sizable slice of pie, which he found very attractive. It was nice to see her really enjoy her food.

Mary told him that honestly, food had always been a comfort, and did he think there was something wrong with that? They were standing in the kitchen, by the stove, waiting for the coffee to finish dripping, and he'd never wanted to take her in his arms quite as much as he did then. When she opened her heart like that, saying nothing but the truth, she revealed a rare glimpse of her real self. He expertly chose to stay away from all religious or spiritual subjects, knowing they would only make her defensive and mistrusting.

At Julia's Mary hummed and pushed the vacuum cleaner, dusted and sang snatches of songs, did loads of laundry and folded them fresh and warm from the dryer. Julia noticed the change in her and wondered, but it was only when she dropped her off that the reason presented itself, in the form of a young man sweeping the cement floor of the barn.

"You have company?" she questioned.

Mary's face flamed, but she only nodded, exited the vehicle, and hurried away, which seemed a bit suspicious. She didn't think these Amish people lived together without getting married, but then, you never could tell.

THEY HATCHED A plan to take a short hiking trip. Mary found the idea exciting, and somehow it felt less improper than having Steve in her home. She didn't want to send him away, but she was nervous that another sibling would swing by and discover him still there.

Art took them to town, where Steve purchased two pup tents, two Coleman sleeping bags, backpacks, and dried food. He would not allow Mary to pay for anything, saying it was a gift that she was willing to accompany him on this adventure. He had no idea where they would start, but had a map of the Adirondacks and the many trails through state game lands. He loved the wilderness, loved to hike, and would be thrilled if she shared his enthusiasm.

They'd go for three days. They pored over maps, stuffed their backpacks, and tried them on. Mary said there was no way she could take one single step forward with this buffalo-sized thing on her back, and no, she wasn't going. And another thing, she wasn't wearing hiking boots lacing up over her ankles, either, so he might as well forget that.

She did not wear a covering but instead tied a navy blue triangle of cloth on her head and pinned it securely. With Steve, she was beginning to forget everything about guilt and sin and frightening admonitions coming from nowhere. She fished out an old stack of black bib aprons, the comfortable tie aprons she missed so much.

They were off to Three Springs armed with a map, a compass, bug repellent, food, water, tents, and sleeping bags.

Finally, they stood alone in the deserted trailhead parking area as their driver pulled away onto the highway.

Mary took a few steps closer to Steve, a shiver going up her spine. They were really doing this. Everywhere, there was thick green forest, droning insects, a hazy blue sky overhead with a white-hot sun spreading its heat over their shoulders. The shadows beneath the trees seemed hazardous, filled with dark spirits having the power to instill panic. When Steve spread his arms, breathed deeply, and shouted to the sky, she jumped, then lowered her eyebrows and glared at him.

"This is scary," she muttered, stepping even closer.

"What? This is great, Mary. There's something so freeing, so exhilarating, about the wilderness."

"Steve, are you sure about this?" she asked quietly.

"Of course. Mary, hiking is when I find myself closer to God than anywhere else. Completely surrounded by nature. There's nothing like it."

"Good for you," she muttered.

"Mary, don't you want to go?" he asked, peering into her face.

"I do, but it's so, well . . . wild."

He hefted her backpack onto her shoulders, secured it around her waist, then looked at her as she fussed with the straps.

"You okay?"

"This is crazy heavy."

"You'll get used to it."

He led the way, entering the forest by following the signs. They both stopped to read the signpost with an inscription of the trail rules, their location, and the projected time to reach certain points.

Mary was having serious doubts. The trees. It was these towering dark trees with heavy leaf cover that shook and shuddered and called out accusing names. All these green little ghosts dancing and swaying to their own wailing musical notes.

Steve walked ahead, his black trouser legs like scissors, his steps long and sure and, yes, covering ground. Too much ground. After ten minutes, she was breathing hard, then irregularly, as she tried filling her screaming lungs with a reserve of precious air.

Every single step was uphill. She hadn't imagined any of this. A trail went uphill and down, twisted around, and doubled back on itself, didn't it? The backs of her legs ached, then burned. The straps on her backpack dug into her soft flesh, with only her dress and apron to cushion the steady pressure.

She kept the figure of Steve as a goal, putting one foot in front of the other, and decided she was not going to yell uncle. She would not disappoint him. After what she thought was at least an hour, he stopped, turned, and asked how she was doing.

"Okay," she puffed, stopping to lean an elbow against rough tree bark, which she decided was the scratchiest thing she'd ever encountered. She took her elbow away and rubbed it with the palm of her hand, perspiration trickling down her face, soaking her dress and causing her feet to slide around in her sneakers, creating painful burns. This was, hands down, the most miserable thing she had ever done.

Why had she agreed to go?

"Thirsty?"

"Not yet."

She wiped her streaming face with her shoulder, wishing she'd brought a handkerchief. As if he read her thoughts, he shook out a clean men's handkerchief, wiped her face like a child, then put one hand on each side of her face and looked into her eyes.

"You're a real good sport," he announced, then let go abruptly and swung back on the trail.

It was the only thing that kept her moving, those words. By mid-morning, she wasn't sure which would happen first, whether she'd be cut in half by the backpack straps, die of strangulation by the shoulder straps, or simply be mummified by the lack of fluid in her body.

"Steve?" she squeaked.

He didn't hear, so she clenched her teeth and tried walking faster. Why didn't he show an ounce of mercy? Well, if she didn't take care of herself, she'd die like an animal, simply crawl beneath an old rotten log and take her last breath. She stopped, her chest heaving. She loosened the plastic clasp around her waist, shrugged off the cumbersome pack she'd dubbed "The Buffalo," and watched as it hit the ground with a dull thud.

Greedily, she drank the cold water. Insanely thirsty, she almost cried at the beauty of cold liquid sliding down her parched throat. She didn't care if Steve never found her, didn't care if he was five miles ahead, she was done. She sat down hard, her back against her backpack, heaved a deep breath, then reached down, grabbed the corner of her apron, and swabbed her face. She relaxed. Blissfully tired, every muscle throbbing, she felt sleep creeping up on her, like a soft blanket ensuring comfort.

He found her like that, fast asleep, sitting upright under the shade of a spreading pin oak, her face smudged with dirt, her eyes closed, two dark sets of lashes on her freckled cheeks. His first thought was to wake her, but he decided against it, and instead reached out and laid a palm very gently on her cheek. She slept on. He smiled, lowering his own backpack; he sat down lightly, took a few swallows of precious water, and leaned back, closing his own eyes.

He awoke, finding her awake, watching him. She looked away, quickly.

"Why didn't you tell me you needed a break?" he asked gently.

"I tried, but you were too far ahead to hear me. So I took matters into my own hands."

"I'm sorry."

She shrugged. "When do we eat?"

"Soon."

She stifled a groan as he helped her adjust her pack. Two and a half more days of this. She'd never survive. She was a fool for thinking she could ever do a solo hiking trip in the wilderness. Gritting her teeth, she moved one foot, then the other, plodding steadily behind the black scissor legs ahead of her. She felt like a pack mule, then an overloaded burro, a pitiful creature with aching legs and heavy ears. Even her ears hurt. It was sheer willpower that enabled her to reach the projected rest stop.

When he stopped, she stopped.

She came to a standstill, surveying the patchwork of green spreading below them, ravines and cliffs, undulating hills folded like a half-open accordion, in every shade of green and blue imaginable. Above, the patterned blue and white of the sky was like a marbled bowl, an immense expanse turned upside down on the assortment of greens.

The whole scene was breathtaking, the word coming to mind a bit late, the way her breath had been taken by the grueling climb.

"Beautiful. Absolutely," Steve said softly.

He spread an arm, his fingers splayed. She wondered how he could manage to lift it, or move his fingers, but she nodded, a silent acknowledgment of his words.

He looked down at her. "Pretty, isn't it?"

"It is. But some food would look even better."

As they shared protein bars and chocolate, her irritation dissipated, her spirits lifted as they pored over the map. Six miles. They'd walked not quite six miles.

She looked straight into his eyes and told him she'd never walked that far in her life. He said they had to go another eight, at least, if they wanted to reach their destination.

"I can't walk eight more," she said quietly.

"I'm sorry, but you have to. I think we may have overextended ourselves, but we don't have much choice now."

"Too bad. If I have to walk eight more miles today, you may as well leave me here for the buzzards."

He laughed, genuinely enjoying her sense of humor.

"It's no longer all uphill. See here?"

His finger traced a dotted line, where another rest stop was supposedly by a pond or a lake.

"I guess I don't have a choice."

"You can do this, Mary."

No, I actually can't, she thought. *And you're stupid if you think I can. I wish I never would have agreed to this craziness.*

But she shouldered her pack and followed him.

Bluejays screamed as they passed. The trail leveled, then began a slight descent, which lifted her spirits immensely. She felt invigorated by the lack of effort, covering an amazing distance as the sun slanted toward the west in late afternoon. There were short distances of walking uphill, but the trail always headed to a lower level until Steve announced an opening in the trees.

Sure enough, they came through a line of trees, a grassy area like an oasis, the sun slanting through trees on the opposite side, the breeze creating ripples on the brackish pond water. It smelled. The whole area smelled. She imagined dead fish.

Her nose wrinkled, but it was the only thing that could move on her entire body. He helped her with her pack, spread her sleeping bag, and told her to rest, that he'd get dinner going.

She almost laughed, thinking of her dream of hiking alone. She would never have made it. Would never make it. She simply was not a hiker, and if you saw one tree, you'd seen them all.

CHAPTER 19

BUT WHEN A FIRE CRACKLED IN A RING MADE OF STONES, THE SUN sank in a glorious blaze of red, orange, yellow, and lavender, there was plenty of boiled, filtered water to drink, and the smell of ramen noodles made her mouth water, she decided she could survive these three days.

Steve caught three fair-sized bass, fileted them, and fried them on his camp pan, and with salt, they were hot, flaky, and delicious with the noodles. A chocolate bar and a cup of coffee was pure decadence. Afterward, she got up stiffly to wash dishes with pond water and help set up the pup tents.

"I'll set them up close together, in case a marauding bear sniffs us out," he said, between whistling and humming.

"Are there bears?"

"I doubt it."

"I wish I could have a shower."

"It's dark out. You can bathe in the pond."

"You have got to be kidding me." Her voice faded into horrified stillness.

"Well, if you're not going to, I think I will." With that, he grabbed a few things from his pack and headed to the pond, coming back some time later in clean clothes and with wet hair.

"Warm as bath water," he said, grinning.

She simply couldn't make herself do it. She thought of turtles and snakes, lizards and other weird living microbes and bacteria, then sat in misery, slapping at mosquitos so bloodthirsty she found twelve on one arm. She felt filthy and itchy. Her spirits fell. They watched the full moon rise in a perfect white orb above a black layer of pine trees. Night sounds were an orchestra of rasps and shrill calls, an occasional yip of a fox or the call of an owl, wide awake and preparing to hunt.

"This is why I love the wilderness so much," Steve said softly. "You can't even begin to compare this to anything else on earth. I'm afraid I'll have to admit it's most of the reason I never married."

"You saying if we got married, you'd spend all your time off in the woods?" Mary asked unexpectedly.

"Boy, that's a shock, you saying those words."

"Just saying."

"Look at that. Just check out that sky."

"It is amazing, it really is."

The fire crackled. Steve put on another log, creating a shower of sparks. The night was damp, the temperature dropping, so he suggested they retire, each to their own tents.

She climbed into her sleeping bag, punched and rolled the flat pillow, sighed, and could not remember being more uncomfortable, ever. But within moments she fell into a sleep so deep she didn't hear a thing until Steve began cracking dead branches for the morning fire.

She groaned when she sat up, muttered as she crawled out of the tent, and howled with pain when she stood on her feet.

"I can't do this," she wailed. "Call a helicopter to come get me."

"Good morning to you, too!"

"Stop being so chipper."

"I love it out here in the morning. All cool and fresh."

"I'm filthy."

"Go for a swim."

"Of course not."

But she did wash and brush her teeth, combed out her thick red hair, and put it up in a bun again. She tied the navy triangle around it and felt a bit better. He smiled and whistled low as he cooked some powdered eggs and heated water for coffee and instant oatmeal.

"Sun's red in the east. Red in the morning, sailor take warning," Steve chortled.

"You seem happy to announce the prospect of rain," she observed drily, as he scattered the ashes of the campfire.

"I am. There's something comforting about walking in the elements. It tests your endurance, which is good for the human spirit, you know?" He glanced at her, noticing her blank expression. "I can't really explain what I mean."

"Don't try."

He laughed. She thought how much he smiled and laughed and whistled and sang out here in the mountains, which meant he must be happy, pleased to find himself enduring obstacles. Good for him. Her shoulders hurt, the straps pinched into her waist, there was a blister forming on her little toe and one on her heel. She had no idea how she would survive the second day.

They packed up and were on their way again. They hiked side by side, the trail widening as it wound through low clearings, beside creeks and small rounded hollows. They talked of family hardships, their views on church and politics, the differences in the ways they were raised, and more. Mary forgot her pain as she listened to his voice, and wondered how she would go through life without hearing it after this hike was over.

When the trail turned uphill again, her will floundered, her spirit recoiled. She simply could not imagine trudging another six miles, but that was precisely what she did, placing one foot in front of the other, her heel and at least six of her toes on fire, the skin rubbed off and the pink, shiny dermis underneath rubbed raw.

At one point, the trail was merely dabs of orange paint on old trees, where they stepped across fallen logs, skirted rocks, and crumbling trees felled halfway by winter storms. Steve walked on, finding the orange spots, and she followed blindly, drawing up on reserves she had no idea existed inside of her.

She felt almost exhilarated now. The pain was so intense it ceased to bother her. She was a warrior. Miles? What were they? Mere distance, a length to be conquered by placing your feet one ahead of the other, gobbling up the ground.

She heard the falling of water, thought she might be imagining things, the way people dying of thirst saw an oasis, a mirage. But Steve stopped, held up a hand, then unrolled the map. She peered around his elbow. He lifted an arm and placed it around her shoulder.

"Here. Look. Right here. Shelter Falls. We're here!" he shouted.

He tightened his grip on her shoulder, and she leaned in. They laughed, then set off toward the sound of falling water.

In the light of early evening, the sight was astounding. A small bowl containing no trees, only an outcrop of rocks with a stream of clear sparkling water tumbling into a still pool, grass growing abundantly on every side. Ferns as if a landscaper had designed it. Twittering birds in a myriad of colors and shapes.

"It's like a bit of paradise dropped out of Heaven," Steve said softly.

Mary said nothing, trying to understand the deep well of emotion straining at her throat. Cold chills crept up and down her arms. Her feet felt as if they were rooted to the edge of the woods, as if she was a tree and was created to stay there and worship with them.

She might be losing her mind, she reasoned.

Steve watched her face, saw the containing of something. She turned to him. Tears filled her eyes. She blinked rapidly. He reached out an arm and drew her in. She yielded, her head on his chest.

"Do you feel it, Mary?"

"Yes. But what is it?"

"It's the presence of God. We are on holy ground."

Mary wept softly, the tears cleansing and healing. She felt as if she should lift her arms and worship. She wanted to say thank you to the sparkling water and the waving ferns, bow down and say another thank you to the birds for their song.

She did not understand this, but with Steve beside her, it was all right. She believed he had the Spirit within him, even if she didn't, so maybe if she stayed here, she'd soak up a bit.

"See?" he said softly.

He pointed an index finger in the waterfall's direction, then to the ferns, circled a hand to include the sky, the birds.

"This, Mary, is God. Here, He is visible, through Creation. His Spirit floated above the water in Genesis, and it is still with us today. The reason we weep is because His Spirit is working in our hearts."

She held very still, afraid to let go of this broken, nameless goodness, afraid to leave the warmth of another person's chest.

"What did you feel, Mary?"

"I don't know."

She stepped out of his arms, away from the safety and the warm beating heart that contained the Spirit he was talking about. She looked up at him, found his eyes alive with a glowing light.

"I just, I don't know why I'm crying. I'm not, really. I'm shaking inside, and I had chills on such a hot day."

"You felt the presence of God. He touched you."

She drew back. "He wouldn't do that. You don't understand. I mean, I've come a long way, but I'm not wearing a covering or my belt apron. I am not a complete sacrifice yet."

Steve was gently shaking his head. "That has nothing to do with it."

"You don't understand. It does."

They were interrupted by the sound of voices behind them. They turned to greet two men, long haired and unkempt, bandanas tied around their foreheads, grizzled, lean, their legs beneath their shorts browned and sinewy with muscles. Packs protruded far above their heads, so Mary assumed they were serious hikers.

They stood, surveying Mary mostly, then extended a hand, wide smiles revealing clean white teeth.

"Hey, guys. Good to see two human beings. Haven't seen anyone all week."

Steve shook hands, then Mary introduced herself.

"You guys Mennonite?"

"No, Amish."

"Oh, great. Yeah."

"So, where you headed?" the quiet one asked.

"Only another day. To the Point, then we're getting off," Steve answered.

"Up to the Canadian border. We own ground there. Started in Maryland."

Mary felt her mouth drop open in disbelief. How far had they come? How many miles did they still need to go?

They surveyed the scene before them.

"Wow. Just goes to show you, the Man Upstairs outdid Himself right here."

"Amen, brother," Steve said, lifting a hand for a high five.

A sound slap, a wide grin, and Mary received the sight of joy from the face of one she suspected did not know God. What was this "brother" thing? She had been taught all her life, and taught well. The Amish had nothing to do with the world. You couldn't serve God and the world, and if she ever saw the world in human form, it was right here. That long hair. Shorts. And two men . . .

Steve had better watch it, or he'd be misled. Perhaps he was already, and taking her down the broad way, thinking feelings were of God, when very likely it was from the devil himself. Her breathing increased, the wonder of a few moments ago replaced by lowered brows, a great and justified suspicion.

She sat by the edge of the forest, staying away from the men who had walked down to the water, smashing ferns, upending rocks without any respect for the natural beauty around them. They talked, waved their hands, laughed, while Mary eyed them with distrust.

Her feet and toes were red with blisters peeling, the skin completely gone. She really wanted to walk down to the water and feel it close over them, but she was afraid of the men. She should not allow herself to have a conversation with them at all. She recalled that the devil could appear like an angel of light, which was what this was, and Steve was too blinded to see, walking with the world.

My goodness, she thought. He was fortunate she was here to set him on the right way.

She lay back in the moss, thinking all this through, and eventually drifted off to sleep. She woke to find every blister stinging, flies on her skirt, the men gone. She sat up and looked for Steve, bewildered. She sat very still, the sound of the birds twittering now fully penetrating her senses. They were calling their babies to come to bed.

She'd always listened to the robins when they chirped repeatedly at twilight, calling home the summer fledgling birds for the night. She had found this fascinating, how mother birds chirped and worried at bedtime, just like her own mother, calling them in to sit in the *kesslehaus* (wash room) where she'd drawn hot water to wash their feet before they went to bed.

Moving to Lancaster had been a real eye-opener, the way she'd been able to shower every night, shampooing hair three times a week. The memories that came back with the twilight—running with her sisters, racing to get her feet in first, the call of the robins in the background—felt sweet. Sometimes she still longed for those childhood moments, the fluid way life rippled along easily, knowing the rules, the punishment that followed if you didn't obey. It was very simple. Do this, don't do that, and if you did that, there were painful consequences.

She'd opened another dimension the day she moved to Lancaster. She'd left her old life behind and discovered a different way, one she'd thought better. Most of the time, she still thought it was better, if she was being honest with herself. She had loved her life in Lancaster, had discovered so much about herself and those around her. She'd experienced a diversity of people, ways, and ideas. The conservatives lived peacefully with the more liberal-minded, which was surely a glowing testament to the power of love.

Why had she moved back to New York?

She'd been shoved there by the sheer magnitude of her fear, the consuming power of the awful panic attacks, the slipping away of her mind.

She shuddered, remembering the liquid door knob, the cracks in the sidewalks. Even now, she felt the pounding of her heart as her breathing shifted gears.

She would have to have a talk with Steve.

Where had he gone? Night was approaching.

Her feet felt as if they were on fire, the blisters throbbing, her legs aching. She had to summon the will to help herself, so she pushed her bare toes into the grass, twisted her body, and got to her feet, swaying slightly, the pain in her heels like knife blades. Gritting her teeth, she hobbled to the water. Finding a rock to sit on simply wasn't possible, so she put in one foot, gasped as the cold water stung the open sores, then tentatively put in the other. Her skirts were gathered in one hand, another held out for balance. The bottom of the pool was full of pebbles, sharper, bigger stones, and a slippery layer of moss and decaying leaves and twigs. She hated the feel of slime, the yucky gunk in the bottom of any farm pond, but this seemed slightly cleaner with the flow of the water falling over rock, forming this pool and spilling over into a small creek winding its way over a course through the woods.

The absence of pain was blissful, so she stayed still, allowing the cool water to stop the burning. All around her, the call of birds held her spellbound, the warbling, trilling, piercing whistles, with the chirping and varied calls of colors flashing from tree to tree. The water tumbled from a cliff, splashing its own harmony with the birds. The colorful sky was now darkening with the gray light of evening.

The ferns nodded their heads, waved their arms, ushered in thoughts of how heavenly it would feel to grab a bar of soap and a washcloth, but she stifled that immediately, thinking of Steve.

Where was he?

She let her skirts go, bent to wash her face and hands, her arms, anything she could wash discreetly, then stood, dripping, watching the water tumble over the cliffside. A thin stream, but it made a resounding splash, a sight that held her in its power.

Yes, God had created this, like Steve said. Of course he had. But she wasn't sure about actually feeling God. How could that have been possible?

No, you couldn't go by feelings, the way they changed so easily. They'd both been tired, at the end of their tether, so they were in a weakened state, allowing the devil to arrive in the form of an angel of light. The worst deception.

Slowly, with caution, she made her way out of the pool, determined to stay calm, to have a talk with Steve when he returned. She would help him back onto the straight and narrow road, to make him see how God required perfect obedience to His Word. How could His Spirit touch them here, dressed as they were, doing something they both knew was questionable by church standards?

After this hike, she would work harder to attain perfection, perhaps even change the color of the blinds in her house. She'd throw away the sneakers she wore to work, those Nikes leftover from her days at the bakery. They were far too flashy with the white soles and the large swoosh symbol.

She lifted the small tent from her pack, untied the strings attaching it, then set to work preparing a site. She was bent over, removing pebbles and loose branches from the ground, when she sensed his approach. Instantly, relief washed over her, though she didn't let on.

"Sorry, Mary. We got wrapped up in a longer conversation than I was expecting. Interesting guys."

Mary gave no indication of having heard.

He stepped closer, asking if he could help. She shook her head, so he retreated and went to work on his own tent. Resentment bloomed in her heart like a gigantic hothouse flower, red and much too prominent. Did he really have to disappear for their long conversation without telling her where he was going? What kind of sinful thinking were those men leading him into? And now, there he was, humming and whistling again, acting as if he couldn't care less.

After their tents were up, he set to work building a fire ring, gathering twigs, leaves, and dead undergrowth. Mary sat sullenly, her wet skirts covered in grime, thinking of burgers and chicken corn soup with saltines and applesauce. Chocolate cake with buttercream icing. The lemon doughnuts they'd made at the bakery.

"Well, I'll get the rice going," he said cheerfully.

"I am not fond of rice. We never ate it growing up."

Steve's hands were propped on his hips when he faced her, his pleasant countenance smudged by his lowered eyebrows.

"You might have mentioned that when we were shopping and packing. It's heavier than the oatmeal, so I'm making it. Less to carry tomorrow."

His words were level, a bit stern, which surprised Mary. All around them, the sounds were changing from the bird's symphony to an array of insects creating an implosion of shrill calls, coupled with the deep bass of a bullfrog outdoing the voice of another.

A mosquito's high whine rang in her ears, and she swatted viciously. She got to her feet and unzipped the flaps of her tent, then lay down on the thin sleeping bag, trying one position, then another.

She heard the fire popping as well as the sound of the thin metal camp pot on stones, his steps, the unwrapping of food. She swallowed. Her stomach growled, but she chose to ignore it, wanting to hurt him for deserting her, going off with the heathen men. Her breathing stopped when she heard the zipper of her tent being drawn upward, her name called in soft tones.

"Mary, come on out. The rice is good. It's flavored and has dried vegetables and spices. You need to eat."

She considered staying, but hunger won over. She crawled out, disheveled, her face averted, her dress rumpled and filthy. Without speaking, he handed her a tin bowl of rice, a folding spoon inserted thoughtfully. She ate and it was surprisingly good, though she didn't admit it. She started back to her tent, leaving him to do the cleanup. She felt like that was the least he could do, though her reasons for feeling that way were getting murkier.

"Okay. Tell me what's bothering you," he said resignedly.

She stopped, turned, glared, but would not speak.

"Come on, Mary. I'm trying here, but you're acting like a child."

"Excuse me? A child? You're the one who left me by myself while you slunk away with those heathen. You were afraid I'd call you out on your sinful behavior, so you hid, leaving me wondering if you'd ever be back," she barked.

Instantly, he was on his feet. She could feel the anger like waves surrounding her, snapping into the night sky like sparks.

"They are believers, Mary. You should be careful who you call a heathen."

Her breath came in hard spurts.

"You're lost and don't even know you're on the wrong track!" She was almost shouting now. "You're pathetic. Don't you know the outward appearance is a sign of the inward heart? How can you even think they believe in God?"

A few firm steps and her shoulders were clenched in a hard grip, his face lowered much too close.

"Don't, Mary. Don't you ever let me hear you say such a thing. We cannot judge, ever. We are only imperfect human beings who have no idea what God sees. I don't care how you were raised; this is the truth."

"Oh, so you know the truth?" she said mockingly.

His hands dropped to his sides and he turned away. He took up a long stick and poked the fire. A shower of sparks went up and disappeared. After a few breaths, his body noticeably relaxed.

"Come on, Mary. Let's discuss this like the two adults we are."

She found that her shoulders loosened up too, almost as if in response to his. She sat down opposite him, but her knees ached too much to sit cross-legged, so she thrust her feet to the fire, leaned back on the palms of her hands, and stared into the flames.

"Tell me why you're upset."

She watched the fire display light and shadow across his face, the strong set of his jaw, the smudge of ash across his cheek, the way his hair was stiff and disheveled from the perspiration of the day. He was crouched by the fire, adding a few sticks of wood, then reached for the tin pot to boil water for coffee.

"It's those men. You shouldn't have talked to them. They are of the world, and . . . and how could you say 'amen, brother' as if Christianity was one big free-for-all? Don't you know we are a chosen people, set apart? We hear this over and over in our church services, don't we?"

It was the statement ending in a question that softened his heart. He had felt his anger provoked, prodded by her mockery, but he had to remember she was raised in an extreme environment, where the outward appearance was a visible testimony to anyone's soul. He had never accepted or understood this ideal of all plain people being elevated, living in their own bubble of righteousness, untouched by the trials and conflicts of every other human being that walked the earth. In kind words, with much patience, he tried to explain his views, and she listened. He reminded her of the verse about our own righteousness being like a filthy rag to God, that all goodness is a gift from Him alone.

She simply could not grasp his view on spiritual matters, and as the night wore on, her eyelids became heavy and she found herself skeptical and annoyed. She was sure he was wrong, but she couldn't pinpoint why, and that in itself was frustrating.

Finally, she told him that one thing was sure and that was that her earthly father was a picture of her heavenly father. If you did what was right, you were okay; if you did wrong, you were punished. The only difference was that God punished with an everlasting lake of fire.

"But, Mary, what about Jesus?"

"What about Him?"

"He died for you. He opened everything for you."

"But you still have to be good enough. And so far, I'm not."

"You'll never be good enough."

He searched her eyes, tried earnestly to convey the truth, but her mind was closed.

"Yeah, well, you can say what you want. If it's as you say, then anyone, any old filthy sinner can believe, and he'll be just fine. You know that's not how it works."

"Of course we have to come to the end of ourselves, repent, and run the course, but . . ."

"You don't even know."

"Well, it's time to turn in. We're both tired, a bit sore, and still hungry, so maybe it's a good time to say goodnight. We have to be up at daylight and probably shouldn't take time to start a fire in the morning. We have plenty of protein bars."

Suddenly, she made a whimpering sound.

"My feet, Steve. I don't know if I can do it."

He looked at her, then got up and knelt, taking her feet in his hands, peering at the red blisters, the torn heel.

"You should have said something. I have stuff to put on this."

He got up and returned with a tin of salve and heavy cloth Band-Aids. She reached for them, but he shook his head, knelt, and cleaned the blisters, administered the salve, and bandaged each toe with great patience and precision. Sitting back, she observed his hands, the long, tapered fingers with the short nails, the muscled arms with a dusting of fine hairs. His touch was gentle, the salve like a blessing.

"There you go. By morning they will be so much better."

"Thank you for bandaging my feet," she said softly.

"You're welcome."

Their gaze met and held. Something passed between them, a truce, the beginning of patience, a small amount of trust buoyed by understanding. But was it enough to build a relationship, or would it be made of sand and clay and gravel, like a foundation not built on the solid rock of Jesus Christ?

Steve realized the enormity of this question, knew this small incident with the two through hikers was only the tip of a troubled marriage to come. He had offended her in his innocence, had no idea she thought along those lines, and how far apart in faith they actually were. He rolled into his sleeping bag that night, and for the first time since he had met Mary—this confused, oppressed girl, bound to the rigors of wrestling with the impossibility of attaining eternal life through her own merits—he tasted the bitterness of defeat.

How long, Lord? Or should I let her go?

He lay awake far into the night, his eyes trained on the cheap plastic frame of his tent, thinking how much his strength was ebbing, how skinny and hollow his own faith really was. She was obstinate, maddening beyond anything he'd ever seen. Steve saw what Mary was capable of, the amount of hurt she could inflict, the same hurt she received from a tyrannical parent, and a mother too weak, too cowed by the same outsized authority to stand up for herself.

Thy will be done, Lord, and only thy will.

He knew he wanted her, but was a one-sided love enough? He honestly did not know if Mary was capable of loving anyone.

CHAPTER 20

SHE STUMBLED THROUGH THE EARLY MORNING DARKNESS, BARELY awake, her filthy skirts stiff with dirt and creek water. The Band-Aids on her toes made a difference the first hour, but by the time the first rays of the sun hit the long line of mountains ahead of them, they had rolled into uncomfortable ridges of pain. Ahead of her, he strode on, his long muscular legs propelling him forward. She pushed back the rising irritation and vowed she would keep up if it killed her.

The trail was bringing out the worst in her, the hatred bubbling up like a concoction of every vile feeling she hadn't known she'd been capable of. It was alarming, in a way, wanting to throw a stone at the back of his head, kick him in the shins, yell at him, or merely sit down and allow him to disappear. She had not slept well. Her toes had swelled, the Band-Aids tightening miserably, plus her mind was spinning with all of Steve's liberal ideas.

For the first hour, they had walked gradually uphill, then the trail became steeper, and the reality of ascending and descending the mountain ahead hit her. She groaned within herself.

She shifted her pack, eased a shoulder away from the painful burn, hiked the strap around her waist away from the offending pinch, before realizing she'd drawn the back of her skirt up over her knees. She stopped and yanked at her skirt, watched the receding figure ahead of her, and howled for him to stop.

He came back, his eyebrows lifted, and she raised swollen eyes and a streaming red face and told him he'd gotten her into this and now he could just figure out how to get her out. She was done. She was going to sit right here by the trail and the rest was up to him.

He laughed.

She watched in disbelief when he lifted his face and howled. He told her of course she was going to make it.

"You're capable of more than you think."

And then he was off, saying there was no time to waste, that the driver would be waiting at Gate 19 of the State Game Lands. If they made good time, he planned on finding a diner, and how would she like a burger and fries?

She itched to throw something at him. Anything. A stick, a rock, her shoe. Her whole backpack. Clobber him over his head. How dare he propel her with visions of a burger, like shaking a can of grain to get a horse to move.

But she walked. Angry as a hornet, she marched up the trail, the backs of her thighs burning in protest. Her breathing increased. Sweat dripped from her forehead into her eyes. She was hungry and thirsty. She thought of the Diet Pepsis she used to enjoy at the bakery, the tall glass filled to the top with ice, the carbonated beverage a perfect accompaniment to the club sandwich, her favorite. The thought made her head spin with longing. She imagined sitting at the table by the window in air-conditioned comfort, watching the heat simmer above the street.

Her chest felt as if it would tear apart with the effort of her breathing, but she pushed on, around rocks, occasionally slipping on loose gravel. Her tongue was so dry she felt as if there was a corncob in her mouth, so she tried to call out, ask for a rest, but she could barely make a squeak.

She kept plodding on. She thought if she could reach the top of this mountain, she could likely make it down the other side, but right now she was in grave danger of keeling over, dead as a doornail. She wondered if Steve would be held accountable if she passed away, or if God would forgive him for it.

The sun rose higher, the only mercy the dappled shade they passed through. Her toes felt as if each one had its own little bonfire built on top, her heels like rings of fire all their own. She didn't realize pain could be endured for so long, or the fact you could get used to it, in a way.

Mind over matter, just keep marching. One foot then the other.

She imagined she'd turned into an enormous stink bug, as ugly and as cumbersome, but still she walked on. The idea of ice-cold Pepsi taunted her, made her weak. She'd had it often at the bakery, but now she never bought it. She'd been taught that soda was bad for you, was a frivolous use of money, and had absolutely no nutritional value, so that was that. They drank meadow tea, a delicious blend of tea her mother dried and placed in the attic for the winter. Mima made tea concentrate and froze it, but it all tasted much the same.

She missed Mima, who had turned out to be a real friend. Had her marriage to her father been worth the years she'd spent with him? Was any marriage worth the effort? Was love sufficient to keep you happy?

She gazed through bleary eyes, surprised to see Steve standing still, facing to her left, having reached the top of the trail. He watched her struggle to catch up.

"You okay?" he called back.

She didn't bother answering, merely placed one foot in front of the other, unbuckled her pack, slid it off, and sank by the side of the trail, stretched out with her pack as a pillow. She sipped water in small amounts, then took huge gulps, realizing how thirsty she was.

"You did it!" Steve shouted.

Mary closed her eyes, ignoring the palm he extended for a high five.

She closed her eyes, wanting to drift into a long sleep, but it was only a few minutes before Steve interrupted.

"Mary, I'm sorry, but we have to keep going."

He crouched beside her, smoothing the map. She watched as his finger traced the blue dotted line.

"This is where we're headed. See the downward shift, then right? It's a good distance, but it doesn't seem as if there's another mountain, barely a ridge. Ready?"

She had no choice, so she got up. She had not realized how hard going downhill could be, her toes pushing into the top of her shoes, her knees aching. She had to do this. It was the only way to the finish line—the driver in his blue mini-van, the soft seats, the cool air pouring out of vents. A cold drink. Food.

Steve stopped, waited till she caught up.

"How are the toes?"

She nodded grimly.

"Once we only have a few miles left, we'll take a proper rest."

Vultures circled overhead, their monstrous wings outstretched, their beady eyes searching for carrion. Mary wanted to make some witty joke about them, but found she had no humor anywhere. She felt like a dry cornstalk in winter, dead and hollow, battered by the elements.

After a lunch of two protein bars, she felt a bit better and took notice of her surroundings, catching sight of a chickadee emerging from his nest, an oblong opening in an old pine tree.

They came to a small clearing, overtaken by briars and wild grasses, rife with ticks waiting to leap on a warm-blooded host. Steve found three on his arms, and one on his trouser leg, while Mary had none, no matter how they both searched.

"Well, I'm the one getting bitten by mosquitoes, so you can have a few ticks," she commented.

"Don't need Lyme disease."

"Me either."

They walked side by side now, the trail widening through level ground. A couple from Arizona, who resided in a village for seniors, approached from the opposite direction, and stopped to chat and wish them well.

Mary's strength was flagging after five o'clock in the evening, and she asked to sit for a while, but Steve said they had another five or six miles, and in order to reach their goal, they had to keep moving.

"I don't know, Steve. Can't you just borrow a four-wheeler and come get me later? I feel so weak."

"Here. Eat this." He handed her some jerky.

She obeyed wordlessly and hobbled on. She found if she curled her toes a certain way, she felt momentary relief, and it gave her something to think about, like a mini goal, a bit of a distraction.

The sun slid lower, and Mary began to think they would actually make it. She felt revived, as if the best of her energy was reserved for the final sprint. The forest was thinning, the trail only turning upward for short distances before going downhill, then following level ground.

The temperature dropped as evening fell, a stiff breeze bending tops of pine trees, scattering leaves in shimmering waves.

On the horizon, the sky darkened above the mountain. Steve pointed, said there would be a thunderstorm.

"I think we can beat it if we hurry."

Amazingly, she found she could move even faster.

And finally, he announced they were on the final mile, if his calculations were correct. Mary's spirits rose like campfire sparks, with a fresh burst of adrenaline propelling her over stone, through mud and gravel, the burn in her feet only an irritation now. She glanced down at her sneakers, knew the folly of having worn them, and regretted the quick decision she'd made against hiking boots and wool socks. At the time, in the stifling heat, it had been unimaginable, but now, well, she'd learned a lesson.

No matter. There would never be another time. As long as she lived, she would never attempt a hike. Nope. Never again.

He spied the van first, pointed and yelled. She looked up, found the blue vehicle parked just beyond the gate, and started to run, catching up to Steve, catching his hand, lifting her grimy sweat-stained face crowned by filthy perspiration-soaked hair, and shouted, "Yes!"

"Yes!" was his resounding answer.

Hand in hand, they made it to the gate, swerved around it, laughing, Mary half crying, hysterical with the great relief of having finished.

They faced each other, high-fived, then did it again, before Steve caught her in a triumphant hug of victory.

The driver opened his car door and extended his own congratulations, his smile wide and welcoming. Mary had not imagined the sheer luxury of sliding off her heavy backpack for the last time, or stowing it in the back, hearing the door click shut behind it, then sitting on a soft seat, her legs bent at a comfortable angle, the sliding door closing, a resounding click.

Jagged ropes of lightning were sighted above the mountain, and the wind picked up simultaneously. Steve exulted in this, saying it was a grand send-off, a signal of having been successful. Mary was close to tears, so she said nothing, only watched the streaks of lightning and sat back in her seat, overwhelmed with gratitude in its purest form.

Thank you, she whispered, then stayed in quiet solitude as Steve relayed their days on the trail to the driver.

The vehicle wound its way along dirt roads, then onto a macadam one as the first drops hit the windshield. Steve raised a fist, pumped. The driver grinned, then they both burst out laughing.

Mary was quiet, immersed in her own thoughts. She had finished, had walked those miles in rough terrain, steep unforgiving hills, painful descents, uncomfortable nights lying on the ground. Yes, she had done it, but now that it was over, would she lose Steve?

She'd been deeply disappointed over their failure to connect, to feel united in their goals, their faith, their dreams. As if that wasn't enough, there was the episode at the falls, which would take the rest of her life to untangle. She was a disappointment to him, and he to her.

When Steve announced an open diner ahead, Mary tried to smooth her hair, but realized the futility soon enough. She followed him eagerly and sailed happily ahead of him as he held the door for her.

The first sip of a Diet Pepsi was everything she'd imagined, and the mashed potatoes and hot beef melted in her mouth. Steve ate chicken and stuffing, and they both had pie and ice cream as the rain was driven against the window of the diner, the neon red sign shining through in spite of it.

"Can you imagine, Steve?" Mary asked wide-eyed.

"Sure can. I've been caught in worse than this. You just accept the fact you'll be cold, drenched, and miserable."

"I cannot wait to get home, take a shower, and sleep in my bed," she said quickly.

He sighed, his eyes going to the lashing rain, the red sign swinging in the wind, the hissing tires of moving vehicles on the highway.

"Yeah, I'll head home in the morning."

"Yes. Guess you will."

He ordered coffee and another slice of apple pie, told Mary he was considering chocolate cake. Really, he was just trying to extend the time.

He started in tentatively asking if she'd do it again, but was not surprised when she shook her head no. Absolutely not. It was grueling, a genuine hardship.

"But think about it, Mary. What if I'd ask you again? Like to go to the west coast or go to Georgia and walk the Appalachian Trail?"

She looked at him, said nothing, then lowered her eyes and toyed with her pie crust.

"You wouldn't ask me."

"I would."

"I was a grouch."

"No, no. We just had a misunderstanding."

Hope sprang up as they exited the diner. Real hope of perhaps having seen her at her worst. And he thought about the presence of God, how pure and unblemished, but how with people, nothing stayed pure and sweet and simple, everyone ruined by the warring nature within us all. The anger and disappointment had taken place at almost the same spot as the uplifting presence of God, but that was the way of living in an earthly body.

After they arrived home, the summer storm had blown itself out, and Mary busied herself opening windows, pushing doors open to let the night air in. They cleaned up with showers and clean clothes, then talked far into the night, till Mary could not keep her eyes open.

He asked her to come to Lancaster to meet his family, but she shook her head, saying they still weren't dating. And besides, she looked much too plain for his family.

No. She would not go.

"I wish you would. You need to visit your aunt and cousins."

"Looking like this?"

"If you're doing it for God, Mary, then why are you ashamed?"

For a long moment, she was completely still, then became agitated, one hand wringing the skirt of her dress, another hand going to her throat as if to quell the pounding of her heart.

"Am I doing it for God?" she whispered.

A raw vulnerability passed over her features, as if she'd peered into her own soul and saw the unlikely portrayal of her own motive.

"You must know," he answered.

"I don't know. It could be God isn't even really involved. It's my father. The voice of my father. Perhaps the two are inseparable."

And Steve realized she was cautiously picking her way across a frightening chasm, placing one foot, then another, on a swinging bridge, with no one to tell her to keep her eyes on her Savior.

"Steve, before you go home, I have to be honest. This thing about Jesus. Well, it's complicated. I'm scared of Jesus, the way He's absolutely perfect, so far above me in every way. And I'm afraid of those verses in the Bible printed in red. Why are they printed in red? And how can you ever understand the way He talks? He doesn't know me, and I have no idea who He is. Not really. So when you say he died on the cross for *me*, I don't really get it. I mean, it's always spoken in German in church, and I understand it very well—the words, you know—but somehow, I just can't grasp it."

She stopped, then faced him with honesty, her face softened with defenselessness. There was only the raw truth, spoken from the turmoil in her soul.

At that moment, an understanding awakened within him. Her anger and rebellion were the shield she used to protect herself from revealing the frightened places, the unguarded hurts and betrayals.

"You are being open and so refreshingly honest, Mary. For real. And it makes me love you more than ever."

"But you can't say that, Steve. You have no right. I don't love you."

"I know. But I can say what's on my heart, honestly, just like you have, and hopefully our friendship will be based on that."

"But . . ."

"Mary, I'm going home, but I won't let you go. You can talk to me about your deepest fears, and I will never make fun of you. I'll listen, and not judge you, okay?"

"But you can't come here again."

"Why can't I?"

"The church. My father."

"Your father is dead."

She began to weep softly, her face hidden from him.

"But his teaching, his disapproval of you, of us. That still stands, and it still condemns me in our sinful actions."

"How are we sinning? Just tell me what it is that you call sin."

She blinked, wiped her eyes, then her nose.

"I don't know. Being together? You being seen here. It would not be allowed."

"Mary, this is an endless circle with no common sense to be found. Do you, for yourself, before God and in your conscience, feel it is a sin for me to visit once in a while?"

She shrugged. "What do you think?"

"You know what I think."

She nodded, then asked when he was coming back, and he told her it was whenever he would be welcome. He said that if she was willing, he'd like to meet more of her siblings. She took a deep breath, squared her shoulders, and said he could come for a visit in two weeks, when there were no church services, if he promised he would not plan another hike. He laughed, then lifted her chin and looked deeply into her eyes, allowing his own to shine with the pure and tender love he felt for her.

CHAPTER 21

After he left on that Monday, she felt a new gratitude for her home and the comforts she enjoyed every day without thinking. A glass of water, a chair to sit in, clean clothes, and a variety of food. The comfort of the back porch on a warm evening, the sound sleep after tumbling onto her mattress covered in clean sheets.

But there was something else that dogged her thoughts. She had done it. She had accomplished the impossible. Somewhere inside of her, she'd found the strength to walk those miles in three days. She relived the feeling of being strong, of being a warrior, which was embarrassing now, even causing her to cringe, but she had felt that way.

Perhaps there was a lesson somewhere, one she could not yet decipher on the blueprint of her life. And now there was Steve. He was in her life, and he was not going away. It was so scary.

But she mowed grass and worked in her garden, canned red beets and green beans, tomatoes, and zucchini relish. She went to work for Mrs. Bates and Mrs. Hatch, collected her cash, and drove Honey to the local bulk food store for groceries, humming and whistling like Steve.

He sang a song called "It Is Finished," which was a beautiful song, one that made tears come to her eyes, the same way the Mennonite songs had done. She found herself humming the same tune, but certainly didn't understand those complicated words. What was finished?

She greeted the proprietor, Annie Stoltzfus, a single girl who made a good living selling groceries to the local folk. Annie was a tall girl of considerable build, the traditional wide hips of the German ancestry, a pleasing smile coupled with confidence.

"*Vell, hiya* Mary."

"Hello, Annie."

She drew a card from the line, turned to go back, and was stopped with a resounding, "I heard you went on a hike with your chappie from Lancaster."

Mary went cold, then felt the heat rush to her face. Stalling for time, she dug in her purse for a Kleenex, her grocery list, anything.

"Who is he?" she asked, chortling in that way she used when she had latched on to an entertaining morsel of gossip.

"Oh, here it is. Whew. Thought I'd lost my list."

Annie waited.

"Come on, Mary. You're stalling." Annie said, smiling broadly.

"Steve. His name is Steve Riehl."

"So you're *schtick* (dating)? "

"Uh, no. He's a . . . a cousin. A cousin on my mother's side."

She felt the palms of her hands slick with perspiration.

"A cousin? Your mother wasn't a Riehl."

"No he's . . . his mother is a sister. Well, not a full sister, but, *ach*, Annie. I'm not good with this type of thing."

Annie pursed her lips, drew her eyes into sharp focus, brought a laser beam straight into Mary's evasive, bewildered eyes.

"I'll have to get out my Fisher book. What's his dad's name?"

Before she could think of a proper reply, she blurted out, "I don't know."

"*Ach* Mary, now come on. A cousin and you don't know his parents?"

Almost, Mary grinned and admitted her lie, but the fear of being caught by members of the ministry, those who were in authority and looked out for the well-being of her soul, kept her frozen. To be caught in a sin, to push the boundaries of the church, was humiliating and shameful, the following formal confession the worst thing she could imagine.

She followed up with some stumbling nonsense, pushed her cart away from Annie, and blindly searched for unknown items. She was only digging her hole deeper, with a cold fear gripping her, the fear of being caught in a lie. She was caught by God. He had his ears open, had heard every word.

Her heartbeat drummed in her chest as her ears roared with pressure.

She imagined a fearful God, cloaked in pure white, his eyes blazing with the wrath of his displeasure. A lie. She had spoken a lie outright. She had to fix this somehow, but her spirit flagged within. Her courage hid behind her pride, the pride coupled with fear and dogged by humiliation.

She inhaled deeply, exhaled, brought her watery eyes into focus, desperate to still the panic that was steadily rising. Oatmeal. Brown sugar. Flour.

Only by repeating the simple names of food items could she finish her shopping as she stilled the storm in her mind.

"Hiya, Rachie," she heard Annie sing out.

"*Schöena myat*," was the thin reply.

Mary tried to avoid Rachie, but then faced her as she approached the register.

"*Vell*, Mary. *Vee bischt?*" Rachel said quietly, her kind face without guile.

"*Goot.*"

Her voice sounded strange to her own ears, as if she was choking on the large chunk of sin contained in her body. She kept her eyes averted, afraid that if one as pure as Rachel penetrated her gaze, she could see the startling depth of her turmoil. The lie sat on her nose like a hideous tumor, in plain view of these two women who were obedient, who carried their cross daily, and would inherit eternal life. She swallowed, turned away, the set of her shoulders giving away the tension in her body.

Luckily, Rachel turned away, pushed her cart into an aisle, and began to load items into it. Mary reached the register, keeping her eyes hidden from Annie. How had she found out? The question burned in her mind, creating an even bigger confusion. She had not told anyone, had she?

"You work for Erma Hatch, don't you?" Annie asked in hushed tones.

"Yes," Mary answered in a stifled voice.

"She said you canceled, then went on to tell me why. She said you went hiking with your boyfriend. She was so glad to tell me you had a friend."

Almost, Mary confessed the lie, but her fear of being less than perfect kept her from it. She mumbled a denial of having a friend, said she wasn't dating anyone, that Erma Hatch was mistaken.

Wisely, Annie kept her peace, smiled, and totaled the line of grocery items, but bent toward her and whispered, "Come visit me sometime, and we'll talk."

Mary couldn't answer, only shot her a frightened look, before digging in her purse for her wallet. She found the amount she needed and began to throw items in plastic bags, her heart racing. Thoughts of losing her mind terrified her, the times she'd barely managed to hold it together, and now her sin was compounded, one piled on top of the other. The things she'd done! The unspeakable ways in which she had indulged the flesh. God's displeasure rode on her shoulders as never before.

She remembered nothing of her ride home, the specter of accusing demons bringing down the reins on Honey's back, the horse startled into a fast trot, then faster as Mary applied taps of the buggy whip. It was only when she was putting her groceries away, opening cabinet doors, wiping pantry shelves before emptying flour and sugar into Tupperware containers, that her rapid breathing slowed, and tears of frustration rose to the surface.

Oh, pathetic mortal she was. Vile, filled with sin rotting her from the inside out.

A thought broke through the shame and misery. Yes. She would change the color of her blinds, the last admonition from her sainted father. She would bring all the lust of the eyes into subjection, would obey his words to the letter, carry her cross gladly, willingly, if only it would allow her to rise above this.

She measured the windows, adrenaline flowing through her veins now as she worked, measuring from tip to tip. Then she wrote a letter to the store, promising a check in the mail as soon as the blinds arrived.

Dark green blinds were the required decor for many years, a signal for passersby that a plain family dwelt within. The only other acceptable curtains were homemade, stretched on a rod halfway up the window frame, necessary for privacy only. Over the years, the rule for curtains had been pushed to the limit, plain housewives who were hungry for beauty or fashion lifting the curtain rods higher and higher until they were on top of the window frame, with tie backs, creating a thing of beauty like they saw in magazine pictures.

Eventually, there were many other forms of window coverings, until there was no difference in one house from the neighbor's, whether they were English, Mennonite, or whatever.

Here in conservative New York, however, the rule of green roll-down shades was observed, mostly. Complying with the rules assuaged her guilt over lying to Annie. What a relief flowed through her veins as she told herself the final victory was within reach, the last bit of the flesh and earthly desires conquered, in spite of her misdeed at the store.

WHEN THE BLINDS arrived, she eagerly took down the almond-colored ones and replaced them with forest green. She stood back with her arms crossed and surveyed her domain. Very Amish. She pursed her lips, squared her shoulders, exulted in the sight of her own obedience.

She took a deep breath and waited. She cleared her throat, sat on the reclining chair, and waited again. The clock ticked, the muted sound coupled with the sound of chirping sparrows on the porch.

Honestly, she felt nothing at all. But then, a blessing was invisible, which meant no one could actually see or feel it, so she would go about her day's work and believe she had attained it.

Oh, it was good and precious, this giving up your own desires. Nothing more would be required of her now. She had reached the pinnacle of self-denial.

She fixed a salad for her supper, with fresh tomato and cucumbers from the garden, sat on the back porch in her lovely chair, and surveyed the backyard garden with appreciation. Yes, she was grateful, more than grateful, for the comforts of her home, and the health to work and make the small mortgage payment.

There really was nothing more she would need in life. Her mind wandered back over the days of hiking with Steve, and the discomfort of a few days of hard walking. Always, her thoughts returned to the episode at the falls, and the need to stand fast to her truth. But now, since she had come under full obedience of the *ordnung* by changing the color of her blinds, she should be able to help Steve even more, having chosen the way of truth. Yes, her father had often warned her of these *fer-fearish* times, and now she'd encountered one and remained steadfast.

A sense of peace washed over her, and she sat back, relaxed. But that evening, when the twilight was erased by nightfall, the crickets set up their grating clamor and nighthawks screeched from tree limbs, the peace was replaced by remembering the outright lie she'd told Annie, together with the fact she'd paid four hundred dollars for a porch chair that was far too worldly, and she'd pleased the lust of the eyes when she bought it. The knowledge of wrongdoing kept her awake, her breath coming in short hard puffs until her bed tilted at wrong angles, and she felt as if she might faint.

Despair gripped her. She climbed out of bed, drew on a light housecoat, and groped her way to the kitchen. She found the battery lamp and clicked the button, flooding the room with light.

She knew she had to make the lie right at all costs. She had to tell Annie. Humiliation must be borne. It was good for the soul. The desperation for a clean conscience, for lasting peace, became a driving force as she picked up the battery lamp and carried it into the living room to view the forest green blinds.

She had done it, denied all her earthly desire for beauty. Why was she consumed by more thoughts of sin? The lie. It was the lie.

As she struggled to quiet her racing heartbeats, she was consumed by the inner conviction that she must hitch up Honey and go to see Annie.

Yes, that was all it would take.

Calmed now, she made a cup of chamomile tea, carried it to the back porch, and sat in the dim, starry light, the fir trees surrounding her etched against the night sky. She could sense the cool moisture of fallen dew, the scent of wet grass and dew-covered vegetation in the garden.

She would tell Annie, then write a stern letter to Steve, which would multiply the blessing she deserved. A vehicle passed on the road below, and somewhere, a cat screeched hideously, then another. She shivered, thought of her father's warning, how the devil took on the form of a lion, prowling around and seeking whom he may devour. She should look that up in the Bible, but had no idea where it would be found. Besides, her father's words were true and good, but you could take anything out of the Bible and twist it around to your own way of thinking. That's what he always said.

HER FACE WAS pale, the freckles darkened by the sun, her breathing in short, hard puffs, her covering drawn forward over her red hair and most of her ears, the plain fabric of her navy blue dress faded by many washings as she stepped through the door of the store, the bell tinkling, like the knell of perdition announcing her sin.

Annie looked up from writing at her cash register, her small eyes alight with interest.

"Why Mary. Hiya. *Guta marya*."

"*Guta marya*."

"Did you forget something?" Annie inquired.

Mary's eyes darted furtively, searching the small store for customers, then came to rest somewhere between Annie's eyes and mouth.

"Uh, no. I didn't forget anything. I mean, yes, I guess I did. I have to make something right. I . . . uh . . . you know, I told you I went hiking with a cousin. He isn't my cousin. He . . . I mean, I said a *schnittza*."

Annie's eyes narrowed. "Why did you do that?"

"I don't know. I suppose I didn't want to have to confess in church?"

Annie's eyebrows lowered, and she made a grunting sound in her throat.

"Why would you do that?"

"It would be found out, and someone would disapprove and tell the ministers."

"*Ach*, Mary. Just for hiking together?"

"At any rate, can you forgive me for lying?"

"Of course. I'm just sorry you felt you had to lie about such a trivial matter. I'm sure Jesus forgave you the moment you asked Him to, but thank you for coming to tell me. I do appreciate it."

Almost, Mary nodded, but she caught herself. She had not thought to ask Jesus for forgiveness. She had a hard time with the thought of Jesus, let alone asking Him for something He wouldn't supply without making it right first. She'd ask God tonight. Not really Jesus. She felt more comfortable approaching the *Gott* she had always heard about, the one who sat on His throne and scowled down on wrongdoers, giving them what they deserved. The thought of talking to Him wasn't pleasant, but at least she could understand that God. Jesus, not so much.

"Mary."

Mary looked up, startled to find the small eyes filled with a tender light.

"You seem to be anxious. Is there something else you wanted to say?"

Instantly, Mary was defensive. "No, of course not."

Mistrust clouded her vision. Nosy old thing, digging around with more information to spread through the community. She spun on her heel and walked out, her head held high. Annie watched after her, then shrugged her shoulders and went back to her writing.

Driving home, Mary was filled with indignation and embarrassment. Well, Annie didn't have to know she hadn't even thought of asking Jesus for forgiveness. Anyway, she had to make it right with Annie first. It was complicated, this forgiveness thing.

You had to repent first, then go to the person you sinned against, then begin to pray, and often, it took repeated applications. And even then, the sin was to be kept as a reminder that you were nothing but a worthless person with a wretched heart. In her father's words, "no one knows how often we sin, nor how much we sin against God. Even King David cried out in despair for God to search his heart."

Yes, the road was very narrow, and few would be chosen. That was the truth, the real and awful fact. She would have to write to Steve this very evening to save him from the broad way filled with worldly views and attitudes.

She concocted a letter, which started with the danger his soul was in and ended with rejoicing that she herself had finally attained the elusive blessing through replacing her blinds. She only needed to sell the four-hundred-dollar chair now. She hoped he would see his error, realize he'd been misled by those men at the waterfall, turn from his ways, and find the same peace that she was now experiencing.

When he received the letter, the smile on his face turned to a scowl, then a slight shaking of his head. He crumpled the letter and threw it on his bed.

He was outraged, then patient, then filled with pity, after which he was consumed with the need to help her see. The obstacle to his path was her stubborn will and the voice of her father banging around in her head, blocking the light she so badly needed.

He trembled, he prayed, but in the end, he unwrinkled the letter and showed it to his parents, asking their opinion. He waited till the clamoring sisters had taken themselves off to bed, the only time of the day when a measure of peace existed in the farmhouse. His father read the letter aloud, his mother's facial expression one of disbelief, then pity, then a shaking of her own head.

"Steve, Steve," she said sadly, as his father's voice faded away.

His father nodded in agreement.

"You sure you want to get involved?" he asked.

"I did. I mean, I do. But . . ."

"What happened on that hike, at the waterfall? What is she talking about?"

He told them in detail, including the two men who were through hikers, two men who would not appear to the Amish as being believers, but who felt the presence of God, and had shared their Christian faith. Mary had taken offense, saying he was misled and they were wolves in sheep's clothing.

His father laughed, then shook his head soberly. "I don't know the girl. I only know she seems to be misled herself and is completely unaware. She'll never find salvation in the rules of the church, the poor thing. Is this how she was brought up?"

"Oh my, yes. Her father's voice is her conscience."

"And he died?"

"Yes."

His father sighed. "Well, he did what he knew. We have no right to judge, and I'm so glad of that. We're all at different places in our walks with God, so we leave all the judgment up to Him."

His mother nodded. "Absolutely."

She gave Steve a piercing look. "I would rather you forget about this girl, Steve, really. She is so embroiled in her own doctrine, and now, living in New York, she seems to be worse than she was here. She seems a bit . . . unhinged."

For a long moment, Steve was quiet, his eyes downcast.

"You're probably right, Mam. But I need to talk to her a couple more times, see if I can get through to her. I have never felt this way about anyone and was convinced this way was my future. But this letter is a tough one, for sure. She's just so afraid. She's afraid of her own confusion, afraid of what others think . . . she's even afraid of Jesus, I think."

"Well, there's one thing for sure," his father said, clearing his throat and running a hand through his hair. "She's sincere, and I believe she feels she's doing the right thing. But let me tell you one thing. Right now, she is not capable of love. Not the real kind. If you do decide to include her in your future, I assure you, you will have your work cut out for you. A long, bumpy road. She will mistrust you, criticize you, be jealous of you—the list goes on and on. I wish she could find a good counselor."

"Not happening, Dat," Steve said sadly. "They are the worst of the false prophets."

"Then we suggest you let her go. Save yourself a life of heartache."

"But I was so sure."

"Give it time, Steve. Be patient and see what God has for you."

His mother knew what she hoped God had for him, in the form of the girls' new teacher, a Miss Sylvia King from Drumore, coming to board with her sister and her husband about half a mile down the road. Tall and willowy, graceful, with dark hair and a shy smile, well known in her area as the best teacher to put a problem school back on track, in her late twenties, it was a match made in Heaven, she was convinced. As so many mothers will do, she saw only the good in her son, expected the best in a potential wife, and would rail at the throne of grace for exactly this.

To saddle beloved Steve with this hive of bees was too much to contemplate, so she trusted God to steer him gently away, and hopefully straight into the long, graceful arms of Sylvia King.

But his father watched the struggle on Steve's face and thought perhaps he was meant to pursue this troubled girl. If so, God would need to supply the love and wisdom to deal with the future. But to his way of thinking, it was like walking through a war zone, rife with land mines, or swimming an Amazonian river filled with ravenous crocodiles.

When Steve rose from his chair, he seemed aged, his movement slow as he thanked his parents. But once in the safety of his room, he fell on his knees and put his face in his hands, finding no words, only the groaning of a deeply troubled soul.

He saw her walking along, her face red from the heat, her feet cross-hatched with blisters, the heavy pack chafing her shoulders, scowling in misery, but moving on, determined to keep up. She was honest, flopping at the base of that tree when she was exhausted, and he loved her for that rare glimpse of vulnerability. He loved her when she yelled at him, the pack hiking up her skirt, and he loved her when she sucked up ramen noodles, the juice running down her chin.

And when she walked ahead of him, and he saw the width of her, he found her attractive, a strong, well-built young lady who seemed to hold a place in his heart he didn't understand himself.

She had so much going for her, but so much against her. If he carried out his own desire, he'd hop on a bus and leave for New York tomorrow morning. But he needed to be careful, to seek advice, knowing she wasn't the ideal companion at all. But his feelings mattered, too. The hardest thing to do was to exercise patience, and often the answer lay in the path of most resistance.

He found himself smiling, thinking of her refusal to accept the thought of the through hikers as Christians. Well, for her, it was a tall order, but what a thrill it had been for him, to find the spirit of God swirling like beautiful, invisible banners above humanity, to touch down here, then there, in all manner of folk, in all manner of dress, each and every one a believer in Jesus, called to His service in all walks of life. In all honesty, nothing disgusted him quite like the spirit of the Scribes and Pharisees, the ones who elevated a person's thinking of himself far above others. But Mary. *Ach*, but she'd been steeped in it, raised by the instruction to be above others, in word, in deed, in dress, in every aspect of life.

Would he need to understand that somehow?

CHAPTER 22

MARY STOOD ON THE BACK PORCH, HER HANDS ON HER HIPS, SIZing up the chair, taking note of the woven brown resin, the beige cushions with a button in the center, the sheer beauty and elegance of the design. She weighed the love of the chair against the good works she would be able to accomplish with the money she could still get for it. The price of self-denial. This chair was a test, and she was determined to pass with flying colors.

She would advertise it in next week's paper. Jessie told her she'd put it on Facebook, but Mary said absolutely not, she wanted nothing to do with the internet. She felt completely justified in her scorn of that brain child of the devil, and closed her mouth in a tight line when Jessie told her she was weird. Weird and old-fashioned, plus, she was getting sick of answering the door every time she needed to use the phone, so she may as well get her own.

Mary said fine, she would, and didn't talk to her for weeks, feeling huffy every time she looked up the hill toward her house.

She looked at the green roll-down blinds and waited to feel the peace she'd written to Steve about, realizing these things took time, and then sent the ad to the local paper. When Steve didn't show up the evening she expected him, didn't answer her letter or anything at all, she went into a tailspin of anxiety, resulting in debilitating nausea, canceling a few days of cleaning and lying on the couch with the worst migraine headache of her life.

The paper would not print her ad without a phone number, and since she was too miffed at Jessie to ask about hers, she let the chair sit where it was, telling herself she'd use it till summer's end, then get rid of it. As long as she intended to do what was right, it was the same as actually doing it.

Wasn't it?

Her brother Ezra and his wife Becky came for a visit, their six children seated on the couch, dressed in their Sunday best, until Becky told them they could go play. Mary told them there was a croquet game in the barn, and they walked quietly out the door without a word.

Her own childhood came to mind, the way they dressed, the expectation of quiet behavior, the fear of wrongdoing going undetected until they were home, where the voice of their father explained their sins, after which they went meekly to the woodshed for the administering of the stick, a punishment fully deserved.

How well she still remembered the Thanksgiving dinner at Uncle Henry's. She must have been ten or twelve years old and looked up to find her father's frown directed at her as she reached for the second slice of chocolate layer cake. She had a hand extended in midair, couldn't pull it back with the others noticing, so she went ahead and forked it onto her plate and ate it with the cornstarch pudding.

He explained to her, later, the sin of gluttony, and whipped her with the buggy whip, the lashes biting through the thin fabric of her dress. She cried, brokenhearted, and was shoved out of the woodshed by a hand on her shoulder. She went crying into the house to her mother, who told her to hush, go sit down, but sitting was far too painful. No one seemed to notice, or hear her strangled sobs, and she felt then that she was truly alone.

Her brother was saying something about going to the singing, but she had barely heard a word of his quiet monologue.

"What?" she asked, embarrassed.

"I was just saying, you don't seem to be present at the singings on Sunday evenings anymore."

"No, I have no way of going, and besides, don't you think I've set-tled into the role of 'single woman' at this point?" she asked lightly.

"That's up to you, of course."

The silence was a bit awkward, then, until Mary offered to make supper, which was eagerly accepted, especially by Becky.

When Ezra was out of earshot, she said she was *hesslich* glad to be here for supper, getting so tired of her own cooking. Mary smiled, set yeast to rise in warm water, mixed flour and oil for homemade pizza crust, and asked Becky to peel potatoes for french fries.

"What a treat, Mary!" Becky beamed.

They kept up a lively conversation as they prepared supper, with Ezra and the children praising her pizza-making ability, dipping the fries in ketchup with delight. There was ice cream and the leftover peach cobbler for dessert, and the children went outside to finish the game, as Ezra and Becky's mood expanded, good food warming their outlook.

"My, Mary, it does seem like a shame for you to be single," Becky commented.

Ezra harrumphed agreement, sounding so much like her father.

"Why is it everyone's goal to have everyone married off?" she asked, thinking how an older unmarried girl was treated like a wart, or a two-headed calf.

"I don't know the answer to that," Ezra said, in a truly humble tone.

"Well, I don't either. I have no plans of getting married, so you'll just have to get used to the idea of an old maid in the family."

Becky laughed softly.

"I love the old maids. They are the spice of life. I have two maiden aunts named Ruth and Bertha, and they enjoy life to the fullest. They work in their gardens and clean houses. They travel in the fall, go to Missouri and Indiana. Free as birds."

And Mary saw herself sitting in a bus, or a train, stout, matronly, alone in the world, still working, providing for herself, childless. And the crippling thought entered her mind: *Without Steve.*

She might never see him again.

She felt a sadness as thick as ink, followed by the realization of this being her destiny.

Would it really be so?

But when they left, she felt a kinship, a certain warmth toward Ezra, the quiet one, aware of his lack of self-righteousness. He lived a life of peaceful days, farming like his father before him, milking cows and doing what he felt was right and good. She had never heard him or his wife say a bad word about anyone, which was as refreshing as a cool drink of water.

She swept the floor, put away the dishes, then set about getting ready for a shower. She was ready to close the bathroom door when she found a horse and buggy coming up the drive.

Hoping it wasn't another load of visitors at this late hour, she slowly drew the door shut and stepped into the living room to watch as the buggy passed the sidewalk and went to the barn. A tall form climbed out, a man wearing a navy blue shirt, black vest and trousers, a wide brimmed hat, but she did not recognize him at all. A minister come to see her about hiking? Her heart beat crazily. She steadied herself, then saw he came to the back porch, instead of the front. She thought of the sinful chair, hoped he wouldn't notice.

She was at the screen door when he tapped on it.

"Hello."

"Good evening."

"Are you Mary Glick?"

"I am."

A deep, pleasant voice, kind hazel eyes, dark hair. A long, thin beard, silver at the sides.

She stepped aside. "Come in."

"No, it's pleasant here on the porch. Do you mind joining me?"

"Not at all."

He extended a hand. She took it. His hands were dry and hard with callouses, but it was a pleasant handshake, not the hard pumping kind or the limp, lifeless one, either.

"Good to meet you, Mary. My name is Bennie Lapp from way down the line. Have you heard of me?"

She shook her head.

"You may sit down if you want." She motioned to a chair.

The chair.

"Nice chair," he said in an offhand manner.

She said nothing.

"Well, this visit would be easier if you had heard of me."

Mary raised her eyebrows.

"You see, my wife passed away about a year ago. I have eight children, ages from fifteen to two. I had no address and thought I would see if I can find your house. I know about where it is."

Eight. Eight motherless children. Eight of them.

"I'm sorry, Mary. I can see this is unexpected, and I don't mean to be bold. I simply wanted to see you, talk to you, and had no intention of telling you all that so soon, but as you can see, I need someone."

All manner of answers shot through her head.

Eight is a lot. You don't even know me. There's another man. No, no, and no.

"I wish you'd say something," he said quietly.

"I . . ."

She swallowed, gripped one hand with the other until the knuckles whitened.

"I hardly know what to say."

"Of course you don't, and I understand that. I realize this must come as a shock to you. Eight children is a load to consider."

"No, no. I mean, it's not a fault of the children. This is just so unexpected."

"I imagine so. Let me introduce myself further. My wife's name was Anna. She died of heart failure before we knew there was anything wrong. She just fell over in the living room. A terrible blow. She meant the world to me."

Mary nodded assent, fastened pitying eyes on his face as the shadow of remembered pain passed over it. He had truly loved her.

"I'm so sorry," she managed.

"I'm not a farmer—I own a cabinet shop. We built a new home about five years ago. So you wouldn't have to worry about milking cows or anything like that."

He gave a short, embarrassed laugh.

"Guess I shouldn't say these things, so soon, but I'm in desperate need, with Sarah only fifteen and too much on her shoulders."

"I can imagine."

"Would you like to come for a visit next Saturday evening? Meet the children? See the place?"

His eyes were kind, pleading. He had nice hands. His shoes were clean black lace-ups. Plain Sunday shoes. No doubt he was well respected in the church, garnering sympathy everywhere he went, half the single ladies wondering if they'd be the chosen one.

His face was not unpleasant, a certain handsomeness to it, actually. What should she say? To send this kind man on his way was too cruel, so there was no harm in going to see where he lived, meeting the eight children.

"Well, I suppose I could take a tour. Although it will be that. Only a tour. It's far too soon to make decisions, isn't it?"

"Of course. I don't expect you to."

"I appreciate it."

Then, when the air between them was thick with unanswered questions, the conversation stalled.

"Would you like a glass of meadow tea?" she asked, when it seemed as if she would choke on the awkward silence.

"I would appreciate it."

She felt terribly self-conscious getting out of her chair, knowing he'd watch her, his eyes taking stock of what he was hoping to obtain. She saw herself hanging out a mile of socks and trousers and dresses and underwear. She hoped he had a wheel line. Did stepmothers ever truly love children who weren't birthed by them? What if they were rude and talked about her behind her back? She'd done it to Jemima.

By the time she returned with two glasses of meadow tea, her mind was overwrought with anxiety, overthinking the smallest detail. Her hand shook as she gave him the tea.

"It's a lonely life," he began. "In spite of the children, there's a void that was occupied by Fannie. She was the best wife any man could hope for, and sometimes it's still hard to understand why she was taken, and I'm left alone. But God makes no mistakes, so it's up to us to give in to His will."

"Yes."

"So, you're not seeing anyone?"

"No. Well, yes, in a way, but we're not dating. He's a friend from Lancaster."

"I don't want to make trouble."

"You're not."

"Alright then. I'll send a driver for six o'clock on Saturday evening. I'm looking forward to it."

"Yes. Me, too."

He stood up, looked into her eyes with the kindness in his heart.

"Goodbye till then," he said softly.

"I'll go with you to water your horse."

He smiled. "I feel like Isaac, when Rebecca watered his camels."

"Is that in the Bible?"

They walked together, and she did draw cold water for his tired horse, as they made small talk about the weather, the distance, what she did for a living. And then he was off, the sturdy Standardbred horse seemingly eager to draw the buggy back the sixteen miles they had come.

She walked slowly through the dark, her head bent, her thoughts cavorting like drunken sailors. There was no rhyme or reason for this.

It seemed as if God had played a cruel trick on her, taking Steve and supplying Bennie Lapp and his load of eight children.

She couldn't stand the name Bennie. Why not straight-up Ben? *I'm not going to marry a man named Bennie. Neither will I like his load of eight children.* Why in the world would God give them eight children and then cause her to die? Maybe it wasn't right to think like that. Where was Steve when she needed him?

At one thirty-one, she still had not slept a wink, but had wailed aloud, begging for help, although she figured God wouldn't supply it, the way He always had it in for her.

There were a thousand reasons to say no. One reason to say yes: They needed her. But she was not a sweet or unselfish person, neither was she cut out to be a mother of someone else's children. She would never love them the way they should be loved. She remembered Tiger then, and realized that perhaps she had loved him, though it wasn't quite what she'd imagined being a mother would feel like.

Did a single girl ever refuse a widower in need and truly receive a blessing? Well, what did it matter? She was still waiting for her blessing after changing the green blinds, and now her path had become a series of difficult decisions, again.

She clapped her hands over her eyes and wailed again.

Saturday night arrived, in spite of Mary thinking the end of the world might come first. Wearing her dark green Sunday dress, she was whisked the sixteen miles by a competent driver named Bill Dander, at her service, who kept glancing slightly sideways, no doubt assessing her to see if she was worthy of his friend Bennie Lapp.

The home itself was attractive enough, if plain, the white siding a testimony to his conservative thinking. A two story, with porches, trimmed hedges, and a neatly mowed lawn. A maple tree in the front yard. A fair-sized barn. Gravel drive. A barking dog.

He met her on the porch, flanked by eight pairs of curious eyes. Sarah was as tall as she was, and pretty, followed by Jessie, John, Amos, Betty, Annie, Reuben, and the baby, Leah. Clean children, well mannered, the house presentable, if not as clean as some.

Bennie held Leah, spoke kindly to the little ones, took her on a tour of the woodworking facility. "Beautiful cabinets," she said.

Jessie and John beamed approval.

Sarah showed her through the house, her quiet voice directing her to the *kesslehaus*, a fairly new wringer washer powered by air, a pleasant well-lit place to do laundry, a sink and more cabinets.

Bennie watched with kind, pleading eyes.

The oilcloth-covered tablecloth was smudged. Their mother's obituary was placed on the hutch, with a copy of poetry someone had written about her death, and a dried white rose behind glass.

She stood in the kitchen and gazed through the double windows, the view containing the opposite ridge covered in green trees with leaves showing occasional color, and imagined herself here with these children, twenty-four hours a day, seven days a week, never a moment to herself.

Bennie was affable, eager to please, but most of all, kind and softspoken to the children. It was, indeed, one of the most pleasant places she could ever hope to inhabit, and she thought about it quite rationally, the longer she stayed.

She could do much worse.

She took a long look at Bennie himself, and decided she liked what she saw, and yes, in time, she could learn to love him. Wasn't that more than she could reasonably hope for?

Sarah had baked cupcakes for the occasion, and there was storebought iced tea. They sat around the table, all the children watching as she helped herself to a cupcake, took a bite, and complimented Sarah, who blushed attractively. Bennie smiled and smiled.

He walked her to the car when the driver showed up, and presented her with a timeline. He'd give her a month to think it over, after which they'd start seeing each other on the weekends if she agreed.

She looked into his kind eyes and did not look away, but absorbed the kindness, the goodness of him. No, he did not repulse her, and when he stepped close and touched her opposite shoulder as they shook hands, she wanted to be closer still.

Back home, her own little house greeted her warmly, and she opened the door, thanked Mr. Bill Dander, and walked slowly up the stone walkway, darkness enveloping her softly. The harried thoughts and tough decisions would come later. For just this evening, she'd love her little house, be thankful, find patience, and stay calm.

When a dark figure rose from the porch rocker, she jumped, both hands flying to her mouth, a stifled shriek escaping through her fingers.

"Mary, I'm so sorry. I was afraid I'd scare you."

Limp with relief, she whispered hoarsely, "Steve. Oh, Steve."

After which she burst into heaving sobs, and he gathered her tenderly into his arms and simply held her quietly as she wept.

He'd find out the cause later, but for now, it was enough, standing here in front of her little house on the stone walkway, surrounded by the scent of a late summer night, complete with the katydids' symphony and the fading green leaves turning into the glorious colors of the Artist's palette.

THE END

ABOUT THE AUTHOR

LINDA BYLER WAS RAISED IN AN AMISH FAMILY AND IS AN ACTIVE member of the Amish church today. Growing up, Linda loved to read and write. In fact, she still does. Linda is well known within the Amish community as a columnist for a weekly Amish newspaper. She writes all her novels by hand in notebooks.

Linda is the author of several series of novels, all set among the Amish communities of North America: Lizzie Searches for Love, Sadie's Montana, Lancaster Burning, Hester's Hunt for Home, the Dakota Series, The Long Road Home, New Directions, Stepping Stones, and the Buggy Spoke series for younger readers. Linda has also written several Christmas romances set among the Amish: *Mary's Christmas Goodbye*, *The Christmas Visitor*, *The Little Amish Matchmaker*, *Becky Meets Her Match*, *A Dog for Christmas*, *A Horse for Elsie*, *The More the Merrier*, *A Christmas Engagement*, and *Love Conquers All*. Linda has coauthored *Lizzie's Amish Cookbook: Favorite Recipes from Three Generations of Amish Cooks!*, *Amish Christmas Cookbook*, and *Amish Soups & Casseroles*.

OTHER BOOKS BY
LINDA BYLER

LIZZIE SEARCHES FOR LOVE SERIES

BOOK ONE   BOOK TWO   BOOK THREE

TRILOGY   COOKBOOK

Sadie's Montana Series

BOOK ONE

BOOK TWO

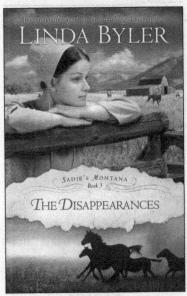

BOOK THREE

TRILOGY

LANCASTER BURNING SERIES

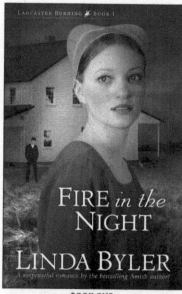

BOOK ONE

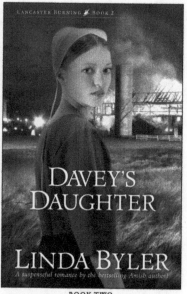

BOOK TWO

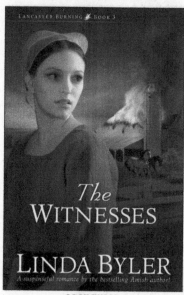

BOOK THREE

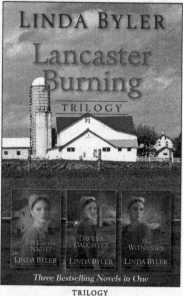

TRILOGY

HESTER'S HUNT FOR HOME SERIES

BOOK ONE

BOOK TWO

BOOK THREE

TRILOGY

THE DAKOTA SERIES

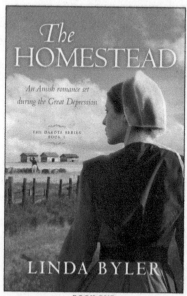

BOOK ONE

BOOK TWO

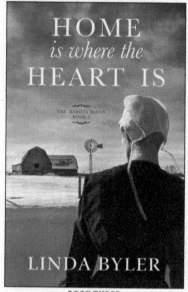

BOOK THREE

TRILOGY

LONG ROAD HOME SERIES

BOOK ONE

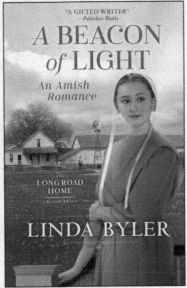

BOOK TWO

BOOK THREE

NEW DIRECTIONS SERIES

BOOK ONE

BOOK TWO

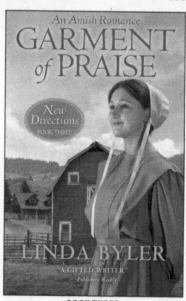

BOOK THREE

LONG ROAD HOME SERIES

BOOK ONE

BOOK TWO

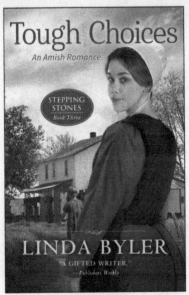

BOOK THREE

BUGGY SPOKE SERIES FOR YOUNG READERS

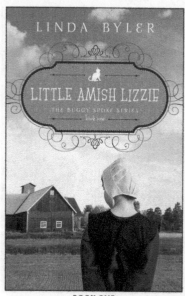

BOOK ONE

BOOK TWO

BOOK THREE

CHRISTMAS NOVELLAS

THE CHRISTMAS VISITOR

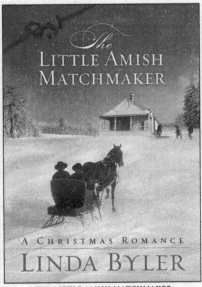

THE LITTLE AMISH MATCHMAKER

MARY'S CHRISTMAS GOODBYE

BECKY MEETS HER MATCH

A DOG FOR CHRISTMAS

A HORSE FOR ELSIE

THE MORE THE MERRIER

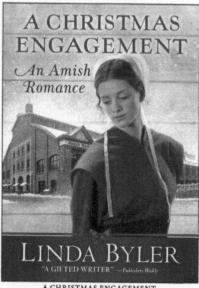

A CHRISTMAS ENGAGEMENT

LOVE CONQUERS ALL

CHRISTMAS COLLECTIONS

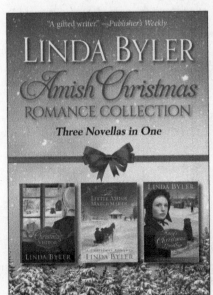

AMISH CHRISTMAS ROMANCE COLLECTION

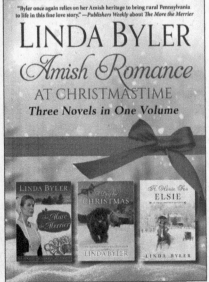

AMISH ROMANCE AT CHRISTMASTIME

STANDALONE NOVELS

THE HEALING

A SECOND CHANCE

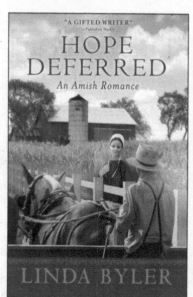

HOPE DEFERRED

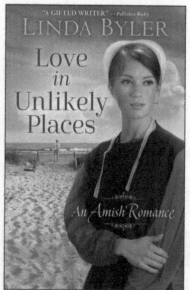

LOVE IN UNLIKELY PLACES